Tutti Frutti

Second Edition

Tutti Frutti

Second Edition

Mike Faricy

This is a work of fiction. All of the characters, organizations, and events portrayed in this novel are either products of the author's imagination or are used fictitiously.

Library of Congress Control Number: 2023913905
Paperback ISBN: 979-8-988684-79-4
e-Book ISBN: 978-1-962080-00-2

MJF Publishing books may be purchased for education, Business, or promotional use. For information on bulk purchases, please contact the author directly at mikefaricyauthor@gmail.com

Published by

MJF Publishing
https://www.mikefaricybooks.com

To Teresa

"It was the simple things; her smile, her hand,
or just the sound of her voice
that offered protection from the world."

Acknowledgments

I would like to thank the following people for their help and support:

Special thanks to my editors, Kitty, Donna and Rhonda for their hard work, cheerful patience and positive feedback.

I would like to thank Ann and Julie for their creative talent and not slitting their wrists or jumping off the high bridge when dealing with my Neanderthal computer capabilities.

Special thanks to Ann for her patience.

Last, I would like to thank family and friends for their encouragement and unqualified support. Special thanks to Maggie, Jed, Schatz, Pat, Av, Emily and Pat for not rolling their eyes, at least when I was there, and most of all, to my wife Teresa whose belief, support and inspiration has from day one, never waned.

One

She rolled on top of me, then whispered, "Dev, wake up."

"What? God, my head's killing me."

We'd met at a concert earlier that night. I smacked my lips then blinked in an attempt to come awake. I couldn't believe she wanted to go at it again. Oh well, I was game.

"Shush! Did you hear that?" she whispered, then sat up in bed and turned her head toward the bedroom door. She was naked, and the moonlight shining through the window made her white skin glow almost iridescent.

"Hear what?" I said as I tried to recall her name then clearly heard a door close downstairs.

"That. Jesus, I think it may be my husband."

"Husband?"

"Shush! Quiet."

I heard a noise that sounded like a floor creaking or worse, the tread on the stairs. She suddenly pushed me out of the king-sized bed with her feet. I went over the side, landed on the rug, and rolled under the bed just a moment before the bedroom door swung open.

"Gary," she cooed. "What time is it? I didn't expect you home until tonight."

"Drove all the way up from Saint Louis. Was outside Madison when I read your text that said you couldn't wait, and I figured, well, why the hell should we?" The voice was deep and had the slightest hint of a twang, maybe Missouri or southern Illinois.

I slithered farther under the bed and cautiously pulled my clothes on top of me just as one of his cowboy boots was kicked off in my general direction. I was still holding my breath when his jeans dropped to the floor, and he crawled into the bed where I'd been less than a minute ago.

"You've got it all warmed up for me."

"I've been dreaming about you, Baby. You were about to be a very naughty boy. Let's see if we can still make that happen."

"Oh, it's happening…"

I heard the rhythmic squeak of the box spring and her by-now familiar moaning. Then I laid there for what felt like hours, listening to his snoring. Eventually, I got the courage to quietly slink out the bedroom door, all the while afraid the pounding from my heart would wake him. I cautiously crept down the stairs and quickly made my way to the backdoor, where I pulled on my jeans, then slipped outside. I finished dressing in their driveway when I remembered my car was still parked at Charlie's, a bar about a mile away. I started walking.

I was almost to my car, in fact I could see the parking lot when it hit me, her name, Bunny. It was close to five by the time I pulled into my driveway. The sky was gray and just beginning to lighten on the horizon as the sun came up. At least it was Sunday, and I could sleep in.

TWO

I was on my second cup of coffee and staring out our office window, watching co-eds waiting for the bus. I had it down to a system. The working girls would board a bus and head east into downtown. Eight minutes later, the co-eds boarded a bus and headed west toward St. Catherine's College. In between buses, I could see who was going into The Spot bar for a liquid breakfast.

I was leering at a particularly breathtaking brunette waiting for the downtown bus when Louie opened the door. Louie Laufen is my attorney, officemate, and pal. He is also certifiable and was about an hour and a half late. He threw his laptop case on his desk, actually a picnic table, and made his way toward the coffee pot.

"You get tied up in all the trouble after that concert Saturday night? God, the riot is still on the news this morning. They had to call out the damn SWAT Team. All that looting and damage downtown, I don't get it."

"You mean the cars set on fire and battling the cops?" I asked, then set my binoculars on the window sill.

"Yeah, you didn't have any trouble, did you?"

"Yes and no. I met someone."

"Spare me the details. Hey, I got a guy coming in around eleven. Joey Cazzo, ring any bells?

"No, not really, but I'm guessing you're going to tell me."

"How about the Tutti Frutti Club?"

"Yeah, I've heard of it. One of the few bars I've never been in," I said. I was back on the binoculars, checking out a young mommy pushing a stroller down the street. She was blonde, wearing tight white shorts and a powder blue top with spaghetti straps. I was searching for tan lines.

"Hey, pervert," Louie said.

"I think she's someone I know." I was appraising her rear as she turned the corner.

"Sure she is, not that she'd ever admit knowing you. Anyway, the Tutti Frutti Club, I think the joint is owned by the D'Angelo brothers."

"Those gangster guys?" I lowered the binoculars and turned to face him.

"Allegedly," Louie said. He sat down behind his picnic table desk, put his feet up, and sipped his coffee.

"Allegedly? Sounds like you're representing them. That's heavy-duty, man. You're really scraping the bottom with those creeps."

"Alleged creeps. Actually, Cazzo represents them, or at least he thinks he does. He was disbarred awhile back, so he does the work and just needs someone with a license to file motions and shit. I'll do it strictly for cash."

"File motions and shit, is that more of your legal talk? How'd he find you?"

"We were in law school together. I think I'm one of the few people who answered his phone call. Come to think of it. I may have been the only one."

"And he's coming in here this morning?" There was no way we were going to get the place looking professional in that short time frame. Maybe we could ditch the dartboard and the empty beer case. I couldn't come up with much else we could do to spruce up the dump.

"How about if you take a hike for an hour? You know, get some fresh air. All in the interest of client confidentiality and that kind of bullshit."

"More legal talk? Yeah, sure, I suppose I can do that. We wouldn't want your client to get the wrong impression when he sees your picnic table. When do you want me out of here?"

"How about now?" Louie slurped some coffee.

"Now?"

"Yeah, now. Why? Are you working on something important?" He ran his eyes up and down, studying me. I was dressed in sandals, shorts, a St. Paul Saint's T-shirt, Summit Beer baseball cap, and still holding my binoculars.

"I suppose I could take a break from all this. Call me when you're finished. I'll be over at The Spot," I said and placed the binoculars in my open desk drawer.

"I appreciate it, Dev. We shouldn't be more than an hour or so," Louie said.

It turned out to be closer to two and a half hours. Jimmy was bartending. I'd read the newspaper, made a couple of phone calls and was nursing a beer when the bar phone rang.

"The Spot," Jimmy answered. He glanced over at me while he listened to the caller. "Yeah, he's sitting on his usual stool. I'll send him over. It's bad for business to have him in here for any length of time," he said, then hung up.

"Louie?" I asked.

"Yeah, he said it's safe for you to go back to your office. Besides, you're chasing away all our business."

I looked around the place. It was apparently a light traffic day for The Spot. There were two other guys at the bar, sitting three stools apart. Neither one had said a word during the two hours I'd been here. A regular named Rita occupied the far back booth. She was either passed out or asleep, not that there was much difference. Everyone knew that leaving her alone was the lesser of many evils.

"Yeah, I can just imagine the line forming to get in this place as soon as I leave."

"It could happen," Jimmy said, sounding hopeful.

Three

When I entered the office, Louie was seated behind my desk, counting out a large stack of twenty-dollar bills. He didn't bother to glance up. He remained focused on his task, moving his lips silently, counting each bill he peeled off. When he finished, he looked up at me with a big smile.

"You feel like grabbing dinner somewhere tonight? My treat."

"Can we get out of the car, or do we have to order at the drive-up window again?"

"I'm serious, man. I mean it, a restaurant with table cloths, fine wine, and all that shit."

"Yeah? Why, what do you want?" I asked, immediately suspicious.

"What, I can't ask a pal, the guy I share an office with, to dinner?"

"No, it's just that I have this feeling you got something up your sleeve. You know, like you're going to expect some favor."

"Dev, all I want to do is have a nice dinner with you. If it's going to be a problem, you don't have to go. That's fine. I've just come into a little bit of good luck." He glanced down at the pile of cash he'd just counted out and now neatly stacked in front of him. "I just thought it might be fun to share a bit of my good luck with you. No problem if you don't want to go."

"As long as you put it that way, okay. How 'bout the Five-Ten?" I asked.

"The joint over on Hennepin Avenue? Umm, I'm not sure they want me back there just yet. Have you ever been to Café Biaggio?"

"Yeah, and not a good idea. That's the place I took that Terry chick when we broke up. She made a scene, threw her pasta at me, and then ran out the door with the wine bottle."

Louie nodded, remembering my tale. "The Saigon?"

"Probably not. I dated one of the daughters. If she's working, she'd probably do something to our food."

We went back and forth like this for a few minutes. Wherever one suggested, the other wasn't all that welcome. I guessed it was one of the things that happened when you were an actively-dating individual, some not-so-great memories, and the occasional repercussion. Anyway, we ended up at Shamrock's because we both liked the burgers, knew most of the bartenders, and the waitresses were nice.

* * *

I was on my third or fourth Summit, enjoying the scenery strolling past us when Louie finally got around to why he was plying me with beer and burgers.

"So, what's your work schedule like?"

"I'm pretty busy from eight-thirty to about nine-fifteen every morning and maybe four-thirty until close to five-thirty every night, watching chicks get on and off the bus. Other than that, I could probably fit something in. Why?"

"Remember I mentioned the Tutti Frutti Club?"

I nodded and let my eyes follow a woman walking past our table.

"I might need you to do a little bit of checking for me on the D'Angelo brothers."

"Define checking," I said, returning my gaze to Louie.

"I'm not sure to tell you the truth. I told you Joey Cazzo was in this morning. There's just something fishy whenever he's involved. I have to file some motions for him. Everything looks okay, but I just want to be sure. I dodged that disbarment a while back, and I just don't need the state board folks taking a closer look at me."

"So, I'm still not clear what you want me to do. What am I supposed to look for?"

"Just get a feel for the place is all, the clientele, any sense of the gambling deal they're always rumored to be running."

"You mean, if I see a room with a sign that says, 'Illegal Gambling Here' I'll know something's up? Look, if they're involved, they've been somewhat subtle about the operation for a while. Years, now that I think of it. It's always been rumored, but they've never been charged, have they?"

Louie shook his head.

"Besides, isn't one of those guys locked up? I thought he got sent away a couple of years ago."

"Yeah, that's Tommy, or is it Gino? I always get them mixed up. Anyway, the one who's not quite right, he's out on an appeal right now."

"Not quite right?"

"The guy played football as a high school kid. I think he forgot to wear his helmet. Did some boxing, I'm guessing as a middleweight. He was wounded in the service. Had a stroke a few years back that left him with some short term memory loss."

"He sounds like a medical case. He got sent to prison?"

"That's part of what Cazzo wanted to talk about. I'm gonna file an appeal on medical grounds."

"I don't know, it seems like those guys have gotten away with murder, literally, for years."

"Maybe, but we're supposed to have a little tougher burden of proof than "seems like" in our system."

"When it works," I said.

"Anyway, they got this appeal going to court."

"So, what's the worry?"

"Just a feeling I've got. If Joey Cazzo's involved, there's a good chance it ain't quite right. And then, of course, there's his clients, the D'Angelos."

"Okay, so why take the work in the first place?"

"Thirty-five hundred cash upfront," Louie said and patted the wallet in his pocket.

"Something ain't right," I said.

"Most likely. I just want to find out what it is before it hits me over the head, that's all."

Our waitress was suddenly there with our order. "Bourbon bacon chicken sandwich?"

I nodded, and she placed the basket in front of me.

"And the Nook burger with a double order of fries," she said, sliding a larger basket in front of Louie. "Anything else, gentlemen?"

"We better have two more beers," Louie said.

Four

I didn't think Linh would take my phone call but decided to try her anyway. That turned out to be a waste of time. Macey's phone transferred the call to an official recording that informed me my number had been blocked. I phoned Heidi. She was still talking to me.

"Heidi, Dev."

"Long time no talk. No offense, Dev, honey, but I meant what I said before. If you need bail money, I'm not in the mood to help out."

"Gee, sorry to disappoint, but I was just calling to ask you out for a fun-filled evening."

"What's the catch?"

"Come on, Miss Cynical, why does there have to be a catch? I just heard of a club I wanted to go to, and you were the first name that popped into my head," I lied. "Thought it might be a fun date. You don't want to go, that's okay. I can just—"

"I was just kidding about the catch," she said. "What's the name of this club?"

"The Tutti Frutti Club. It's . . ."

“Oh, God, I love that place. Didn’t know you were into that stuff. Wow, you learn something new every day. Yes, yes, when were you thinking of going?”

“Thursday night?”

“Tomorrow? Great that gives me time to get a new outfit. Okay, let me make a call and rearrange something. This will be a lot more fun. Pick me up at eight-thirty. You mind if I call and reserve a table?”

“Reserve a table?”

“Of course, that figures, clueless. Okay, I’ll set it up, don’t worry. See you tomorrow at eight-thirty.”

I hung up the phone and began to worry.

* * *

I arrived at Heidi’s stylishly late. She tore open the front door just before I rang the doorbell.

“You were supposed to be here twenty-five minutes ago. God, I’ll have to call them from your car and make sure they hold the table. Come on,” she said and rushed passed me.

I stood on the steps and stared for a moment, then regained my composure. “What the hell are you wearing? And what in God’s name did you do to your hair?”

“Like it? It’s just a wig I got this morning,” she said, standing at the curb, waiting for me to open the car door.

The wig was fire-engine-red with a purple stripe running down the center of her skull. She looked like a freaked-out skunk. She had on a revealing top. At least I thought it was on. It had two large swirls of black sequins illuminating her chest. She had squeezed into a tight, black skirt that didn't cover. A garter belt extended three inches below what served as a hem and was clipped to black stockings. The stockings had a seam that ran up the back of her leg. She had some silver-studded thing wrapped three or four times around her waist.

"Is that the new outfit you were going to get? You look like Betty Page on an acid trip. Planning to pole dance in that?"

"Shut up."

"What's with the costume? Is that nose ring real?"

"No stupid, just open the door, okay? God, we're late. By the way, what happened to the side of your car? It looks like someone sprayed graffiti on it. "

I could have stood there and explained how Rose went ballistic after a slight misunderstanding a few weeks back and sprayed painted "asshole" along the passenger side, but why get into it? Instead, I said, "Just some kids being jerks. I had a pal buff it out."

"You might want to have him give it a second shot. I can still read it."

By the time I got behind the wheel, she was on her phone. She glanced over at me as I turned the ignition. "I'm just going to . . . Oh, hi, let me talk to Biker. Just tell him Heidi, with the licorice ropes, yeah, right."

"Who are you calling?"

"Just drive, will you, Dev? God, we're late as it is."

"What's with the—"

"Hello, Biker? Woof, woof, woof, grrrr. Yeah, it is, thanks for remembering. Oh, yeah, right. Bad puppy. Hey, listen, we're running late. What? No, I wish. But get this, I'm bringing a virgin."

"Virgin?" I said and glanced over at her.

She frantically waved her hand to indicate I should start driving. "Yeah, I thought you'd like that. Hey, I reserved the table up front in the firebase for the first show, but like I said, we're running late." She shot me a glance as I pulled from the curb.

"What? No, don't worry, he'll make it worth your while. Yeah, right, I might just hold you to that. See you in fifteen. Bye, bye, bye," she said, then stuffed the phone back into her purse, a little black leather thing with studs that matched whatever was wrapped around her waist.

"What in the hell is going on?" I asked. Ten minutes later, we were on the exit ramp off I-94, heading into downtown St. Paul. I turned to look at her again just as we blew through the yellow traffic light. I couldn't help but stare at her barely covered chest. "Heidi, did you pierce your boobs?"

"You like?" She giggled and pushed her chest out.

"You've gone off the deep end. When did you get so, so, I don't know . . ."

"Oh, will you relax? They're clip-ons. Where's your sense of adventure, Mr. Dull and Boring?"

"Clip-ons? What's with you? I didn't know there was a Halloween party at this place tonight."

She turned in the seat to face me. “Dev, are you dense? The Tutti Frutti Club, don’t you know?”

“Know?”

“It’s a bondage Dom club.”

“Bondage? You mean like tying you up and spanking?”

“Well, among other things. Turn here. We can park in the back and go in the employee entrance. It’s faster.”

“How often do you come here?”

“Just pull in here. Yeah, great . . . see, there’s a spot right there. No, there next to the dumpster.”

“I don’t want to park next to the dumpster.”

“Oh, yeah, right, I forgot you wouldn’t want to ruin that special flat black spray paint on this side of your car. Classy, Dev, really classy. Now pull in. We’re late, and Biker isn’t going to hold that table forever.”

The noise assaulted me about three feet from the back door. I thought someone might be screaming. “What the hell is that?”

“Don’t be silly. That just sets the mood,” Heidi said and pushed open the door marked, “Employees Only.”

Five

We entered a dark hallway and walked down toward a light hanging above a jail cell door. A big guy with a shaved head, wearing a prison guard uniform and combat boots, sat on a stool just in front of the door. He had a woven, black leather belt strapped around his waist with a nightstick and a pair of handcuffs. Strobe lights were flashing from inside the place.

"Hey, Heidi, how's it going, Nasty Cat?" he said.

Heidi smiled, and half turned to point her rear at the guy, exposing a bit more than the back of her upper thigh in the process. She squealed as he spanked her somewhat forcefully. Then he looked over at me. "I'll need to see your ID, sir. We check everyone."

I pulled out my wallet and flipped it open to my driver's license.

"Could you remove your license, please?"

I was going to say something, but thought better of it and just pulled my license out. I was already getting a headache from the strobe lights, and we weren't even officially in the place. He looked up at me, back down to my photo, back up at me and studied my face. Eventually, he handed my license back to me and then opened the jail cell door that led into the Tutti Frutti Club. "I guess you're okay. Ten dollars cover."

I hated cover charges. I don't like to pay money so I can then pay for a drink. I pulled out a five, counted another five ones, and handed it to him.

"That's apiece, twenty total," he said deadpan. He wasn't joking.

"He's a virgin," Heidi yelled by way of explanation. As we stepped into the club, there was a pulsating bass beat coming from the sound system in the cavernous room. The beat assaulted my body with vibrations, boom-boom, boom-boom, boom-boom.

"I don't think I'm going to like this joint," I yelled to Heidi. But she was already making her way toward the front of the room and a little stage. I stood there watching her weave her way through a crowd of turning heads up toward an area with a half-dozen tables slightly elevated and surrounded by what looked like sandbags and concertina wire. I definitely wasn't going to like this place.

By the time I caught up to her, Heidi was talking to a large, furry-looking guy. Biker. I knew it was him, not from the hairy bare chest, not from the black leather gang vest emblazoned 'Bad Boys,' nor from his black leather motorcycle chaps. No, it was his name that gave him away. 'Biker' was tattooed across the top of his chest, which I guessed complemented the rest of his artwork. He had some crucifixion scene covering his entire right arm and goldfish or trout covering the entire left arm. I thought it might have been a holdover from the days when Catholics were supposed to just eat fish on Friday, but kept that thought to myself.

He had just finished giving Heidi the gratuitous spanking, which apparently served as a greeting in this place when I caught up. She was leaning against a hand-painted sign that read "Firebase", standing on one of the three steps leading up to the tables surrounded by concertina wire. She leaned down and yelled in my ear, "Give Biker twenty bucks," she shouted.

"What?"

"Biker, give him twenty bucks. He held our table."

I was about to say something in protest, but her glare had me reaching into my wallet for one of Louie's twenties. Not bad. Forty bucks and I hadn't even sat down. I handed Biker the twenty, then turned like Heidi had done so he could spank me. He did, the flake, and then raised his eyebrows two or three times before walking away. He glanced over his shoulder a few steps later and blew me a kiss.

"He really likes you. See, I told you this place was fun," Heidi yelled in my ear.

"Thanks for the warning," I said, but she was already up the steps and settling into a table marked reserved.

About three minutes after sitting down, I was ready to admit there weren't any bets being made in the place, and we could leave. The noise was so loud I couldn't think, and the damn vibrations from the thumping bass beat were so strong I was about to go into shell shock. I was afraid my PTSD might kick in.

"Anytime you're ready, we can go," I shouted into Heidi's ear.

She leaned back, smiled, and shook her head no. A waitress made her way up the steps. At least I thought she was a waitress. She was in a skin-tight latex outfit, looking like a crazed Cat Woman, except the thing was unzipped to reveal about twelve inches of deep cleavage. I pegged her a good decade older than me and maybe a little over the weight limit for her latex. She wore the same belt with a nightstick and handcuffs that the prison guard guy at the door had on. Plus, she had two bandoliers crisscrossed over her chest. Instead of cartridges, the bandoliers held test tubes with a thick, golden liquid. She made a fluttery motion toward Heidi with her hands and then turned for the requisite spank.

Heidi gave her two spanks, then shrugged her shoulders and gave a little "aren't we cute" smirk.

The waitress pulled one of the test tubes out and handed it to Heidi, then held one out to me. I shook my head no and waved her off. Heidi handed her empty back, then grabbed the one I refused and quickly downed it. Then she pointed at me and mouthed the word "virgin." The waitress nodded and leered down at me.

I waved her down to my level and yelled into her ear, "What kind of beer do you have?"

I thought she listed off a couple, but I couldn't hear what she was saying, so I just nodded. She turned to

Heidi, who grabbed another test tube out of her bandolier and downed the thing. The waitress waggled a disapproving index finger at her and giggled. Heidi placed a drink order that apparently required a lot of gesturing with her hands.

"Are you ready to go?" I asked a few minutes later.

Heidi shook her head and said something. Not that it made any difference. I couldn't hear a damn thing. Ten minutes later, our drinks arrived, my warm, flat beer and Heidi's birdbath martini. I liked the Tutti Frutti Club even less if that were possible.

The noise stopped for a moment as an elevated stage off to our left was illuminated. There was a fat, almost-naked, bald guy handcuffed to what looked like a medical examination table. I thought it was our waitress who was waving what looked like a riding crop as she strutted around him. Occasionally, she would stop and slap him on the rear with the thing, causing the crowd to cheer as he jumped. Heidi leaped to her feet and gave a shrill two-fingered whistle, which prompted more whistling and shouts from the crowd. I looked at my watch.

"You're no fun," she yelled into my ear a few minutes later. "Just order me another drinky, party pooper. I'm almost finished with this one."

Since our waitress was taking a riding crop to the fat, bald guy up on stage, it took a while to get someone's attention. Eventually, another waitress struggled up the three steps to our table. As she turned so Heidi could spank her, she faced me and smiled. Her teeth extended fang-like over her blood-red lower lip, and she half snarled then glared at me. Heidi ordered her drink, complete with all the gestures. I declined another warm beer and sent her on her way.

Once Heidi finished her second giant drink, she leaned over toward me, glassy-eyed, and slurred, "You're such a Dev, drag, you gotta loosen up."

Actually, that sounded like a pretty good idea.

"Okay, let's go back to your place and get really nasty," I said.

She stared at me through her glazed eyes. "You mean it? I get to do whatever I want?"

"Yeah, I'd really like that. Come on, let's go." I said, and a moment later, I carefully guided Heidi down the steps.

On the way out, I saw two guys at the bar who seemed more out of place than me. They looked to be twins, older, maybe mid-fifties, and both balding. One wore a neon red Hawaiian print shirt and the other a white golf shirt. No wonder I had to wait twenty minutes for a waitress, these two clowns were chatting up four of them. The guy with the Hawaiian print shirt had his arms wrapped around a slutty blonde and a brunette.

His golf shirt pal kept bobbing and weaving his head, all the while dancing around the group. As we got closer, I could see the guy weaving and bobbing seemed to blink a lot, or maybe it was just a slight facial twitch from the dreadful base beat thumping in the place. I couldn't be sure.

"Hey, look, two guys who are more out of place than me," I said.

"That's Mr. D'Angelo and his brother, Mr. D'Angelo. They're twins." Heidi slurred and then staggered back and forth a step or two to maintain her balance before she turned to face them.

"The D'Angelo brothers…you mean the ones who own this joint?"

Heidi nodded clumsily. I grabbed her arm to help her stay on her feet.

"Yeah, Tommy and Tommy. I think. They own the place. Real, real nice guys," she said, then staggered another half step or two before I reeled her back in.

"You know them?" I asked.

"Who doesn't?" She gave an overly dramatic wave in their general direction, almost falling over in the process.

The blonde with the guy's arm wrapped around her laughed then gave me a wink before running her tongue suggestively over her lips. She held her stare longer than necessary with a look that advertised availability. Even from this distance, she appeared pretty intoxicated.

Not that I could take her up on the suggestion. I held onto Heidi and guided her out the back door. I helped her into the car, then buckled her seat belt while she sat there, giggling.

"Dev, Dev, you're tickling me. Stop, I'm going to wet my pants. Oh my God, ha-ha-ha, stop it, stop it."

Past experience told me she wasn't kidding.

I suddenly had a lot of questions, but I'd been here before, knew where this was going, and it wasn't going to go my way. Once I was buckled in and started the car, she looked over in my general direction.

"I'm just gonna close my eyes for a teeny, tiny little minute."

Three minutes later, her wig had shifted sideways to cover half her face, and she had begun to snore. Somewhere between the Tutti Frutti Club and my car, her fake nose ring had fallen off.

* * *

She must have gotten up in the middle of the night because I found her asleep on the bathroom floor half curled around the base of the toilet. She'd pulled the fuzzy white bathroom rug over her in an attempt to stay warm.

"Come on, back to bed, party animal," I said and gently shook her shoulder.

"Oh, please, just let me die in peace."

"I will, but you're going to have to die in bed. It's only proper. Come on, up, up."

"Don't touch me," she growled once I helped her to her feet and pointed her in the right direction.

"Pretty tough talk from the girl with clip-on piercings," I said.

"Oh, God, I know, I know."

“Look, you crawl into bed for an hour. I’m going to shower, get dressed, get us some breakfast, and then I have some questions for you.”

“Oh, God, please don’t make a federal case out of whatever I did or didn’t do last night.” She didn’t bother to wait for my response, but just crawled into bed and pulled the covers over her head.

Six

Louie had his feet up on the picnic table with an open file face down on his chest. I had the distinct impression I woke him when I entered our tiny office. "So, how'd things go last night?"

"At the Tutti Frutti Club?"

"No, that church meeting you were planning to attend. Yes, the Tutti Frutti Club."

"First of all, I lost what's left of my hearing. Jesus, that place is loud. I'm apparently out of the demographic that really likes pounding bass music."

"Yeah, tell me about it." He sat upright in his chair, then stretched and rolled his shoulders.

"I can't believe anyone is gambling there. At least, the area I was in. The whole damn building has to vibrate with that horse shit music. I don't think you could find a room in the place where you'd even be able to think straight. I did see your clients, the D'Angelos."

"Tommy and Gino?"

"Is there more than one set of D'Angelo twins? Yeah, your clients. They looked more out of place than I did. Did you know that joint was a bondage Dom place? They had a woman spanking a handcuffed, bald, fat guy.

She was using a riding crop, and everyone was cheering."

"The fat guy?"

"No, the woman with the riding crop. She was our waitress for a while, until she got into spanking this guy. They were up on this…"

"Oh, so you caught that act. It's pretty erotic. Were they up on that illuminated stage?"

I looked at Louie for a long moment before I shook my head. "Look, I don't know what I was supposed to learn there that I couldn't find out online. Like I said, I saw the D'Angelos, and they didn't seem to fit in any better than I did. Well, except that they had the undivided attention of three or four waitresses. I had to wait forever just to order another overpriced drink."

"Sounds like them. Tommy likes the ladies, and Gino probably just watches and then can't remember what he saw."

"Louie, if they're running illegal games, I can't believe it's happening in that joint. The place might be filled with some pretty strange dudes, but no one who looked like any high-priced game players I've ever seen."

"What about the D'Angelos?"

"What about them? I don't know. Like I said, they looked more out of place than me. Your guy Tommy had his arms around a couple of women who didn't seem to be in any hurry to leave. Two other girls flirted around, and the other guy, Gino, was bobbing and weaving in his own little world. Doesn't sound like any gambling set up that I know of."

"Yeah, along with the stroke and the short-term memory loss. Gino lost a leg when he was in the service."

"Huh?"

"Yeah, he's got a fake leg, a prosthesis. Course, between that and who knows what kind of brain damage there is from football, boxing, and a stroke, he's a bit of a mess."

"That why he twitches or whatever the hell he was doing?"

"Gino bobs and weaves back and forth, never really stays still, just moves his fists like he's shadowboxing or something."

"Did the leg loss cause his stroke?" I asked.

"No, I think the stroke was probably a result of his boxing. Given the years and the time, it would be a pretty safe bet he was probably on steroids, not to mention a lot of hard hits to the head. He might be able to tell you his fighting weight, but he wouldn't know who was president or probably what his address is."

"Sounds like my date last night."

"A night of babysitting?"

"Let's just say she deliberately over-served herself."

"Maybe you should go back and check the place out on your own. It might be different on the weekend."

"I think once was probably more than enough. Besides, isn't Thursday supposed to be the new Friday or something like that?"

Seven

I placed a few calls to Heidi throughout the course of the day. I ended up on her answering machine each and every time. Vintage Heidi, I knew she wasn't out running errands or working at her office. More likely than not, she was still in bed and under the covers. She did this once or twice a year. The drinks just hit her wrong, or the sheer volume of consumption became a recipe for disaster. Then she invariably paid a heavy price over the following forty-eight hours.

Against my better judgment, I let Louie hire me for the night at a discount rate plus expenses. I returned to the scene of the crime, the Tutti Frutti Club. This time I went in the front door with the "normal" folks.

"Ten bucks," the guy at the door said. Once he checked my I.D., and I paid, he slapped a rubber stamp across the back of my hand in the shape of a set of purple handcuffs.

"Does that come off?" I asked.

"Yeah, usually takes just a couple of days to a week," he said, then stared at the leather-clad couple behind me, and said, "Ten bucks, each."

I wandered toward the bar. It ran along the length of one wall and then made a half-hearted L shape at the far end. That was where we saw the D'Angelo brothers last night, but as I glanced around, I couldn't see them anywhere. Mercifully there wasn't any music playing. One could only hope the speakers had all blown out.

The firebase looked crowded with a group of Goth-looking couples, or was that just the bad lighting in the place? I could just make out the spanking stage, although it wasn't illuminated. If you didn't know it was there, you could miss the thing completely.

I'd been waving a twenty-dollar bill back and forth for ten minutes in an attempt to get the attention of a bartender. None of them seemed interested in me. Not that I was all that eager for another warm, flat beer.

"Get you something, stud?" a woman in latex stopped alongside me and asked. I recognized her as our first waitress and the chief spanker from the night before.

"Actually, I'm just ordering a beer."

"Did you place your order?"

"No, I've been trying to get someone's attention and I—"

"Well, you got mine. You want a beer, or do you want to wait some more?"

She had frosted hair, brown eyes, high cheekbones, and that massive cleavage now stuffed with a wad of currency. She seemed heavier than the usual woman I was attracted to, and the Cat Woman outfit accentuating her curves and love handles did nothing to help. She was clearly older than me. Still, there was something there that was extremely intriguing, plus she'd offered to get me a beer.

"You got Summit EPA, a cold one?" I added just in case.

"Oh, God, now you want the thing cold? You're a pain in the ass."

"Gee, that's what everybody says, and you don't even know me." I moved my hip to the side like Heidi had done the night before so she could spank me.

"Not bad," she said in a way that suggested I needed practice. Then she gave me the requisite courtesy spank. "I'll be right back."

I continued to look around the place and came up with the distinct impression I was the only normal person there, which was a frightening thought since I'm not that normal.

"Here you go, sweetheart." She was back with my beer setting it down on the bar in front of me. The glass was frosted, and the creamy head looked perfect. I took a sip. "Mmm-mmm, great. Man, the beer I had in here last night was luke-warm and flat."

"That the beer or the bartender?"

"No, the beer," I said before I caught the joke.

"Candi Slaughter," she said, extended her hand and didn't blink.

"Dev Haskell," I replied.

She looked into my eyes, smiled, and held on to my hand for a moment or two longer than necessary. I didn't mind.

"Enjoy your beer, Sunshine. Give me a yell if you need anything."

"You want to get paid?" I asked.

"This one's on me. What'd you say your name was, Dan?"

"Dev, kind of like Devil."

"One can only hope. Just give me the high sign if you need anything else, Dev."

I sipped, watched, looked around, and learned absolutely nothing. I didn't see anything or anyone that might suggest gambling, betting or even so much as a game of solitaire. I didn't see the D'Angelo brothers either.

If I thought the place had been busy last night, it was jammed packed tonight. At nine o'clock on the dot, I was disappointed to learn the speaker system hadn't been blown out. Thumping bass music vibrated and sent shock waves through my body. Occasionally, there was a scream coming across the sound system, which I could only guess was a paying customer who simply couldn't stand the place anymore.

"Ready for another, Dev?" Candi had come around behind me, brushing up against my back. She had to almost yell in my ear to be heard. Once she finished her question, she remained in place, pressing her breasts against me. I decided to give her thirty minutes to knock it off.

I had about an inch left at the bottom of my glass. I checked my watch and figured I could probably stay for just one more. Who knew? Maybe the D'Angelo brothers would show.

"Yeah, I guess maybe just one more."

She was back in a minute or two with my beer. Another frosted mug, perfect head. She centered the pint glass on a coaster and pushed it my way.

"Thanks, Candi, here," I said, handing her a twenty.

"That's okay, my treat."

"Thanks, but you've been great. I insist and keep the change," I said. Besides, what did I care? It was going on my expense report to Louie.

"Oh, thanks, you're so sweet," she said, then stuffed the bill deep down in her cleavage with a practiced tuck.

"Wow, from pain in the ass to sweet in one beer. That beats my old record."

"You're still a pain in the ass, but a sweet pain in the ass." She smiled then patted me on my thigh before walking off.

I never did see Tommy or Gino D'Angelo. Before I knew it, the lights flicked on, and the bouncers were shuffling everyone out the door. Gazing around at the inebriated crowd and the tawdry decoration, I suddenly understood why they kept the place dark. I looked at my watch. It was almost two.

"I'm sorry, sir, but it's time to leave."

"Yeah, okay, I'll just finish my beer and—"

"Actually, Sir, we need you to leave now. It's the law, you know."

He wasn't huge, but he was bigger than me. My eyes rested on his chin. There was a zigzag kind of scar running across his cheekbone, almost back to where his hairline might be if his head wasn't shaved. The curves along the bridge of his nose suggested he may not be the discussion and contemplation type. Sill, I had a good half-pint remaining in my glass.

"Okay, I'll finish up in just a minute and—"

"Now," he exclaimed loudly then attempted to herd me in the general direction of the door. Someone else came up behind him. It may have been Biker, but I wasn't sure.

"Problem, Bruno?"

"No, he's just leaving. No problem, right, pal?"

I was about to make it a problem. I know, stupid. There were two of them, double dumb.

"It's okay, guys, he's here with me. I got him." It was Candi suddenly alongside me. She linked her arm around mine and moved me back in the general direction of my beer.

"You sure, Candi?"

"Yeah, very. Dev and I go way back. Go flush out the rest of this place so we can talk in private. Okay?"

They nodded, gave me a quick second appraisal, and moved on to some poor slob three stools down, wearing a thinning Mohawk.

"Thanks. You didn't have to do that. I was about to—"

“You looked like you were about to try and punch Bruno. Bad idea, given your condition right now and his black belt. That other idiot, Curtis, just likes to hurt people. You’d find yourself sitting in the ER until about noon tomorrow.”

“Actually, I can handle myself pretty well.” I took a sip of my beer, then went to rest my elbow on the bar. I missed and lurched for half a beat.

“God, tell me that wasn’t faked, you goofball.”

“It wasn’t faked, Candi. Okay? But thanks, I appreciate your help.”

“If I ask you nice, you got time for breakfast?”

I nodded.

“Come on, I better drive,” she said.

Eight

Candi lived in a two-and-a-half story stucco house, beige with brown trim and a peaked roof near St. Thomas University, I think. I wasn't completely sure because I dozed off during the short drive, but I could tell we were still in St. Paul. The place just has a feel to it, and if you're a local, you seem to know it, even if you'd been asleep in the passenger seat.

"Wakey, wakey," Candi called as she pulled into her driveway and parked. I followed her up to the heavy oak front door sporting a small leaded window. A yellow porch light illuminated the front stoop. We stepped into an oak-floored entryway. Directly in front of us was a fairly substantial carpeted staircase leading to a darkened second floor. To the left was a long living room with a fireplace centered on the wall and off to the right, a dining room with a polished wooden table and silver candlesticks. Cabinets with glass doors were built-in at forty-five-degree angles in the far corners of the room.

"Come on into the kitchen," she said, walking through the dining room. She slid her purse across the dining room table, then pushed through a swinging door that led into her kitchen. The lights came on automatically with the motion of the door. She pointed toward a stool and said, "Grab a seat." Then she moved to the range and began clanging pans.

It seemed like in no time we were seated at her granite-topped kitchen counter. She'd cooked us omelets, bacon, toast, decaf coffee, and I grew more sober than not. I finished slathering about a half-inch of orange marmalade on my final slice of toast and then took a bite.

"So that's pretty much it. I got laid off as a third-grade teacher. With the district's seniority policy, I'd be about one hundred before I ever got rehired. It may sound crazy, but I make about four times as much hustling drinks and stuffing cash between my boobs. Besides, all my tips are tax-free."

"I understand, but the Tutti Frutti Club? I mean, why there of all places? I don't know, maybe I'm just so far out of the demographic that I don't get it."

"Well, like I said, the money. I make more in tips than any teachers I know. You saw how crowded it gets, right?"

"Actually, I've only been there twice. Last night and tonight." I glanced at my watch. It was really late.

"Well, there you go. You saw how busy it was on Thursday and Friday. Saturday is even busier. There'll be a line to get in the place from about nine o'clock on. We always end up turning people away."

"Lots of heavy tippers?"

"You'd be surprised. I know the crowd looks a little squirrelly—"

“Squirrelly? They’re downright strange. And who wants to pay to watch some fat guy getting spanked?”

“Fat guy?”

“Yeah. Thursday night, there was this fat guy up there. Wasn’t that you on the delivery end? Who wants to watch that? He’s got a nice job, by the way.”

“Job? Dev, those aren’t employees. Those are customers who buy that option. They have to pay for it.”

“What?”

“Oh, yeah, they pay for the privilege.”

“Privilege? You mean they pay to get spanked by someone with a riding crop while a barroom full of drunken folks watch and scream?”

“Yeah, sure, it runs about one fifty during the week, and two twenty-five Fridays and Saturdays. Of course, they get to choose who spanks them.”

“You’re kidding me?”

“Nope, staff gets half, fifty percent of the one fifty, so seventy-five bucks goes to the house, and we get seventy-five to spank ‘em.”

“They pay for it, the privilege?”

“Yeah, well, and the bragging rights, of course.”

“I knew I was out of the demographic, but I had no idea.”

“See, you learn something every day.” She smiled, then slid off her stool and began clearing dishes.

“Oh, here, let me help,” I said.

“No, you just sit there. This’ll only take me a minute.”

"Well, I suppose I should call a cab, get back to—"

"Are you kidding? I saved you from getting your fat head kicked in by Bruno. I just cooked you breakfast, and you think you're going to call a cab? You've got some work to do, Mr."

Her bedroom was at the top of the stairs, first room to the right. It housed a large queen-sized four-poster with an attached bathroom advertised by subtle, dim lighting.

"I've got a Jacuzzi in there. I like to grab one after being on my feet all night. Join me?" she asked.

She was standing alongside her bed, holding onto one of the carved bedposts for a bit of balance as she kicked off her heels. When I turned to look at her, she unzipped her outfit, slowly lowering the zipper from the end of her cleavage down to below her waist.

"How old do you think I am?" she asked, looking up at me.

"Oh no, that's right up there with, *'Is this gun loaded?'* I'm not touching that line."

"I probably babysat you when I was in high school," she said, then twisted her arms out of the tight sleeves and pulled the upper half of her outfit down around her waist.

"No, believe me, I would have remembered," I said, staring.

"Oh, much better, much better. I always forget how good it feels to get out of these things until I start to pull them off. What?" she said, looking at me, staring back at her.

"Wow!"

"Yeah, right. Really, how old do you think I am?"

"Oh, no, you don't. Like I said before, I never go near that line."

Nine

Louie shook his head. "Let me get this straight. You're telling me this woman you never met buys you beers all night, saves you from getting the shit kicked out of you, brings you home, cooks you breakfast, shares a Jacuzzi bubble bath with you, and then forces you to have fantastic, wild sex with her until after sunrise?"

"Yeah, that about sums it up. Except you left out the part where she gave me a backrub until I fell asleep. No wonder I'm dragging. It's all part of my ongoing investigation."

"And I'm paying you for this? You should be paying me. You learn anything other than she had a great body?" Louie asked.

"Actually, she doesn't."

"Huh?"

"She's maybe got a few extra pounds. I guess you'd say she has a little flab. She's older than me. I don't know. I'm guessing ten years, maybe more. Tell you the truth, I don't really care. Definitely not the sort of woman I'm usually attracted to, but there's something there, Louie. I mean, in her own way she is hot. Scalding. I couldn't keep up."

"You're nuts."

"No, I'm serious. All this time, I've been chasing after the perfect 10's. You know what? She beats them hands down. And God, the sex drive in that woman! I barely made it out of her place alive."

"She didn't want to beat you with a riding crop or a baseball bat?"

"Louie, I'm telling you she is the sexiest woman I've ever been with."

"Hotter than that woman who sold cars?"

"No contest."

"How about that attorney, the one from Chicago?"

"Much better."

"What about that lounge singer, the churchwoman, or that kinky one that worked for the state?"

"Like I said, she beats 'em all hands down."

"You better watch it, man. I've never seen you like this. You're scaring me. You're not falling in love, are you?"

"Jesus, I honestly don't know?"

"What's her name?"

"Candi, Candi Slaughter."

"Candi . . . God, are you kidding?"

"Hey, look, Louie, I only just met her last night."

Louie picked up a pen and scribbled something on a legal pad. I guessed it was Candi's name. He stared for a moment, shook his head then snorted, "You got more action last night than I've seen in years."

I let that last remark slide. I loved Louie, but at best, he was mildly drunk by four o'clock on just about any afternoon. At worst, he was totally hammered. He was grossly overweight. His personal hygiene left a lot to be desired. He usually wore one of three suits, all wrinkled from sleeping in them. A remnant of whatever he last ate was always dribbled across his untucked shirt. His idea of a balanced meal was beer and bourbon. And those were his good points. None of which seemed to be a ringing endorsement in a woman's quest for a life partner.

"Candi," Louie said, gazing up at the bare light bulb in the ceiling, lost in his thoughts.

"Just lucky, I guess."

"You didn't happen to see your friends the D'Angelo brothers or anyone doing something suspicious like rolling a roulette wheel out a side-door did you?"

"No, far as I could tell Gino and Tommy never showed."

"Gino and Tommy, you're on a first-name basis now?"

I shrugged.

"This Candi Slaughter does she know anything?"

"Actually, the subject never came up. I'm working on it, Louie, relax. If there's something there, I'll find it."

"Sounds to me like you already have."

Ten

Ten-thirty on a sunny Sunday morning, and I was sipping coffee at Nina's. The place was filled with people. All of them looked like they were in no hurry to be anywhere. I was waiting for Aaron LaZelle to show up. He was my pal from the police department, currently a Lieutenant in Vice, although it was rumored he was on the move up the ladder again.

He came in through the back door and was behind me with a hand on my shoulder before I knew he was in the place.

"Need a refill?"

I half jumped out of my chair. "Damn it, Aaron, don't do that. God, I'll drop over from a heart attack."

"Sorry, Mr. Touchy, I thought you private investigator types were supposed to have eyes in the back of your head."

"I do, but they were closed."

"Need a refill?" he asked again.

"Yeah, black."

"I'm gonna get some pastry. You want something?"

I was going to tell him I'd already had a caramel roll, but the last one was so good I said, "Yeah, sure. I think maybe I'll try one of those caramel rolls."

"Good, give me ten bucks, will you?"

"What?"

"Hey, look, you called me. I'm here. I know you plan to pump me for some information. The least you can do is buy me coffee and a pastry. What's the problem? I'm the guy bringing it all to the table."

I gave him a twenty and made a mental note to list it on my expense report to Louie. I went back to checking the crowd while Aaron worked his way forward in line. I was studying two women who I would have rated 9's or 10's before I'd met Candi. Now I was thinking they probably had pain-in-the-ass personalities.

Aaron set the coffees down and slid a hubcap-sized caramel roll toward me. "See anything worthwhile?" he asked.

"Actually, no, I'm guessing they're probably a pain-in-the-ass."

"The blonde and the Asian woman?"

"Yeah, you checked them out?"

"Hello."

"God, they're doing the little piece thing. You know, where they pull a crumb off, so it doesn't look like they're really eating a lot. I've had dates eat their meal and half of mine, like that."

"Yeah, it's the kiss of death when they just want a little bite of your dessert."

We chatted on for a few minutes until Aaron got tired of me wasting his time.

"So, what do you want?"

"Want? Why do I have to want anything? Can't I just want to see you, hang with my pal? Apparently, buy him breakfast."

"Possibly, but that's not the way you usually work. You want something, so what is it?"

"What can you tell me about the D'Angelo brothers?"

"Hmm-mmm, moving up from cheating spouses to major bastards, are we? How can I put it? I guess if they were eliminated by their competition, it would only make the city a little better place to live."

"Just background for a client. I know the one brother, Gino, has a hearing coming up in the next week or so. My client doesn't want to get blindsided. All I'm after is strictly background information."

"Okay," he said, then took a large bite of his caramel roll. "Well, they're your typical idiot criminals, only maybe a little smarter. Have they murdered people? Possibly. Other than Gino getting nailed on a frankly questionable gambling thing, I don't think they've ever been prosecuted. At least not successfully. And, by the way, word is Gino's going to win his appeal."

"He'll get off?"

"He's got the perfect alibi, short term memory loss, and it seems legit. The guy can't honestly remember anything. He certainly can't take care of himself. Frankly, there isn't a jury in town that'll convict the guy. And if for some reason we were able to catch him red-handed, the worse that would happen is he'd get sent to a state hospital and take it easy for a few months. Talk about a waste of taxpayer money. With all the austerity measures coming down, I think we'd all just as soon see his brother Tommy picking up the tab for the guy's maintenance."

"So, he's getting off?"

"I'd say there's about a ninety percent certainty. Look, he served six months of a six-year sentence, and the state taxpayers picked up the tab. Nice if it would make a difference, he learned his lesson, but I'm not sure he even knows he was locked up."

"And the gambling?"

"If it's going on, it's nothing we've been able to substantiate. To tell the truth, with all the cutbacks and the crime lab problems, we got a lot bigger fish to fry than those two clowns taking bets on the Super Bowl or whatever. You know who you should try? Manning in homicide."

"Manning? Detective Norris Manning, that by-the-book whack job?"

"He calls them, like he sees them."

"That guy is nuts and has never really been a fan of mine."

"He's a straight shooter. I'll give you that, but he has his hand on a lot of different pulses out on the street."

"Yeah, well, the only place he'd like his hands is around my neck. Maybe you could touch base with him for me and—"

"No."

"You want to think about it? I mean. I did just buy you coffee and enough calories to last both of us until Wednesday."

"Yeah, thanks for that, but my answer is still no," Aaron said, then stuffed some more caramel roll into his mouth.

"I'll figure something else out. On a more pleasant note, I'm picking up some rumors you may once again be anointed."

"How's that?" Aaron asked.

"Moving over to head up the homicide unit."

"Where'd you hear that?"

"Maybe, like your pal Manning, I just have my hand on the pulse of the street."

"I don't know what you're talking about."

"Thanks, Aaron, you just confirmed it."

He sat back and looked at me for a moment, then smiled and changed the subject. "How's the love life? Whoever she is, has she dumped you yet? "

"Very funny. For your information, I've met a very nice woman that I find myself smitten with."

"Umm-hmm, and let me guess, she's drop-dead gorgeous, you've had wild sex with her, and this will be great for about three weeks until she all of a sudden comes to her senses. At which point, you'll call her by the wrong name in bed, smash up her car, or do something equally stupid, and she'll probably file a restraining order. Sound familiar?"

“That may have been the old me, I grant you. But, no kidding, this one seems to be different.”

“Has anyone told her?”

“She’s got a good head on her shoulders.”

“Really? You suddenly recognize women can think beyond choosing a different position? This is new. In that case, I wish you all the luck in the world. How long have you been seeing her?”

“Oh, well, actually, we’ve only been going out a short while. I—”

“Oh, don’t tell me, let me guess. She was drunk in a bar, you picked her up some night and brought her home, right?”

“No, she wasn’t drunk at all. In fact, she wasn’t even drinking. We just met one night and started chatting. That turned into an opportunity for some further conversation, and anyway, it’s been going pretty well.”

“Humpf, conversation, what do you know? Maybe you can change. Hope it works out, Dev.”

“Thanks, me too.”

Eleven

I didn't have Candi's phone number, so I called and left a message for her at the Tutti Frutti Club. She phoned me back later that night.

"Dev, hi. I was wondering if I was ever going to hear from you again, or did you just want to grope me for that one night?"

"Sorry. I didn't have your phone number, and I couldn't find you in the phone book."

"You actually have one, a phone book?"

"Just for old times' sake. You interested in getting together sometime?" The background noise sounded like she might be working.

"Actually, I'm just finishing up here."

"You got time for dinner?"

"Tonight? Yeah, as matter of fact, that sounds great. I need maybe an hour to get home, hose the club off me, and get dolled up. How 'bout I meet you somewhere?"

"You know Charlie's, about Larpenteur and Lexington, a low key burgers and jeans kind of place?"

"See you there in an hour, and I'm known to not be on time," she said.

"I'll be waiting."

Apparently, forty minutes late was still considered to be in the realm of acceptability. Who knew? There were maybe a half dozen people in the place. I was seated in a booth just beneath the plastic, faux-stain-glass lamp shade advertising Old Style Beer. When she entered, Candi was the only woman in the place. She quickly looked around, and I waved. A couple of heads turned, but no one stared as she made her way around the pool table to the booth where I was seated.

"Hey, how's it going? Sorry, I was running a little behind," she said. She planted a kiss on the top of my head, waved me into the corner of the booth, then slid in next to me.

"Actually, I was going to go to the bar and get us a drink. There's no waitress here, not classy like the Tutti Frutti Club. What can I get you?"

"Relax, I'll get it. You want another beer?" She nodded at my half-empty glass.

"No, I'm okay for now. Put it on my tab. That's Charlie behind the bar."

She nodded and went to the bar. At first, I thought she was chatting with one of the patrons at the bar, but then it looked like she might be exchanging words with him. I was going to go up and make sure everything was all right when she returned smiling, and carrying a frosted martini glass with two large olives.

"Everything okay?" I looked over toward the bar.

"Just some jerk that has a problem with sexy women. Don't worry about it. I deal with a dozen guys a night like that. I think I may have seen that idiot at the club a couple of times. Come on, this looks good." She smiled and grabbed her glass.

"That your drink of choice?"

"Yep, double vodka martini, two olives. I found gin changes my personality."

"Well, here's to you," I said and raised my glass.

"No, to us." She smiled, and we clinked glasses. As she gulped, she stared at me over the frosted rim of her glass with those gorgeous brown eyes.

"Any trouble finding this place?"

"No, I've been past it a million times, just never made it inside. Didn't it use to have a different name?"

"Yeah, really clever, Ted's. I think Charlie was in here so much he decided to just buy the place and here we are."

We talked for a while. Candi finished her martini, ate the two olives in one bite then looked longingly at her empty glass.

"Want another?"

"You mind?" she asked.

"God, no, except that we're going to switch places so I can run to the bar and fetch the drinks. You're supposed to be off work and relaxing. The menu is posted behind us, on that chalkboard on the wall," I said, then followed her out of the booth.

She took a step or two toward the chalkboard to read it. Not that there was much to read; a half dozen versions of cheeseburgers, and for an additional buck and a half, you could substitute onion rings for fries.

"I think I'll have that bleu cheeseburger. You feel like splitting some onion rings?"

"Instead of the fries? Charlie has great fries?"

"No, as a side. I like fries, too," she said.

"Back in a minute." I smiled.

I gave our order to Charlie. He poured my beer and was getting a frosted glass for Candi's martini when the guy Candi had words with glanced over at me. I could tell he was drunk, not falling down drunk, but definitely not sober. Probably the resident barfly. He gave me a stupid grin and wobbled his head.

"You must like 'em big," he said. There was a familiar sounding twang to his voice, but I couldn't place it.

"Excuse me?"

"Your gal there looks like she knows her way around the dinner table, and probably ain't seen her feet in twenty-five years." He chuckled and looked at the two guys within earshot. The one closest half turned his back.

I looked at him for a moment, trying to place the voice, thinking maybe he knew me and was just making a really bad joke. He was big, out of shape, in a purple Vikings jersey with a baseball cap pushed back on his head. The cap was embroidered *Local 120*, St. Paul's teamsters union. I considered dropping him right there, knocking him off his stool. I thought about slamming his forehead against the bar, maybe breaking a glass over that baseball cap perched on his fat head. The old Dev would have done it in a heartbeat.

Charlie placed Candi's martini on the bar. "Everything okay here, Dev?" he asked, then stared at the barfly.

"Yeah, Charlie, no problem. Enjoy your night, pal," I said, then picked up our drinks and walked back to the booth.

"You okay?" Candi asked.

"Hmmm-mmm, yeah, sure," I said and raised my glass.

"You sure? Your face looks kind of red," she said, then glanced over my shoulder toward the bar.

"No, I'm fine. To us," I said, and we clinked glasses.

"It was that drunk with the baseball cap, right?"

"You're right. He's a drunk and an idiot."

"Bastard called me fat."

"What?"

"Relax, I'll deal with it."

"I'll have Charlie toss him out."

"No, don't, please, let's just enjoy the night."

Our burgers came, along with a heaping basket of onion rings. Charlie told me the onion rings were on the house. We devoured the entire basket in just a few minutes.

"I'm running to the can. You want another while I'm up?" I asked.

"I better not if I'm gonna drive. You got vodka at your place?"

“I do, along with chilled glasses and olives. Can I make you a nightcap?”

“Thought you’d never ask.” She smiled. “Go on now, out, out. Get going so I can get my hands wrapped around that martini you promised.”

I came out of the men’s room and went to the bar to pay my tab. I handed the cash to Charlie. “Give yourself five out of that for the tip, Charlie.”

“Hey, sorry, man, I was out of line. Just the beer talking. I’m really sorry.” It was the barfly, and he looked like he was ready to cry.

“No harm, no foul. Thanks,” I said, taking my change from Charlie.

“Buy you and the lady a drink? What’s she like?”

“Naw, thanks, we gotta get going. Have a nice night,” I said and headed back to our booth.

Candi had her back to the bar and was talking into her cellphone.

“…with a Viking’s jersey. I want you to deal with it.”

I waited quietly at the edge of the booth. Candy seemed somehow to sense my presence, turned, and looked surprised I was standing there.

“I said I expect you to handle it,” she said, then hung up and smiled at me. “That didn’t take long,” she said.

“Everything okay?”

“Just one of the girls at work, no big deal. Ready?”

“She like doing shots?” barfly called.

“Give it a rest, Gary.” I heard Charlie say.

I was still trying to place the voice as we headed out the door.

"You want to follow me?" I asked her out in the parking lot.

"I think I better since I don't know where you live," she said, then clicked a button on her key ring. The lights flashed, and an alarm chirped on a dark blue BMW 750. I was pretty sure it was the same car Candi had driven me home in the night we met, although my memory was a bit fuzzy. I did know the car retailed for close to a hundred grand and was way out of my price league. In fact, if you combined the other five or six cars in the lot, mine included, Candi's car was worth about ten times the total amount.

"Nice wheels."

"What are you driving?"

I pointed across the lot to the red '95 Fleetwood. I knew it was mine because the rear door on the driver's side was blue. There was an oil slick about the size of a dinner plate glistening underneath from the light of a distant street lamp, and you could still read the word "asshole" spray-painted along the passenger side.

"That's your car? God, you could land fighter jets on the hood of that thing."

"Yeah, I'm in the process of restoring it," I lied. "I'll be easy to follow. My passenger side tail light is out."

"Did someone spray paint your car?"

"Just evaluating some retouching techniques," I said.

"Oh. Well, I'll just look for the single tail light. Shouldn't be much of a problem. That'll be me right behind you," she said.

It took all of fifteen minutes to cruise through Como Park, down Lexington to Selby, and, a mile and a half later, into my driveway. Candi and her BMW remained right behind me the entire route.

"Any problem finding the place?" I joked after she'd pulled into my driveway and climbed out of her car.

"No. Hey, did you know both your tail lights are out?"

"They are?"

"Yeah, surprised you haven't been ticketed yet. You better move that up to the top of your restore list."

"One more thing to do."

She comfortably settled into the far end of my couch, kicked off her shoes, and looked completely at home by the time I came out of the kitchen with her martini.

"You know, if I drink this, I'll probably be unable to drive home tonight," she said, then smiled wickedly and took a very big sip.

"Counting on it." I smiled back.

Twelve

I waved good-bye to her as she backed out of my driveway. She'd just finished mauling me for fifteen minutes inside my front door. It was a little before noon, and I debated about going back to bed. I'd cooked her a breakfast of French toast and whatever syrup I'd found in the back of the cupboard. Fortunately, I was able to scrape up a couple of eggs and some Wonder Bread I'd had in the refrigerator for a few weeks.

Amazingly, even with her hangover, Candi still had an appetite. Then again, if last night was any indication, she had an awful lot of energy that seemed to build up quickly and needed to be released.

I made it into the office, feeling like I'd been ridden hard and put away wet. Louie looked like he'd arrived all of ten minutes before me.

"Hey, Dev, want some coffee? It's just about ready."

"No, thanks, I'm all coffee'd out, just coming from a breakfast meeting."

"Really? Pardon me for being cynical, but you smell like someone's perfume, unless you've started wearing the stuff yourself."

"Really?"

"Yeah, it floated in here with you. Actually, it seems a lot more pleasant than what this place usually smells like."

My cell rang at that moment. "Haskell Investigations."

"Hi, Dev? Aaron. Where are you?"

"In my office." Aaron might have been a good friend, but when a cop asks me where I am, I immediately get defensive.

"Hold on a minute, someone here wants to speak with you."

"Who—"

"Haskell? Detective Norris Manning. Thanks for taking my call."

"Actually, Detective Manning, I didn't. I was talking to Lieutenant LaZelle and all of a sudden . . ."

"Say, I've a couple of questions I'd like to ask you. Just routine stuff. Wonder if I could swing by, oh, say in the next ten minutes?"

"The next ten minutes? What's this about?"

"Just some routine questions so we can clear up a couple of things."

I was racking my brain, trying to remember if I'd done something I should be worried about. Oddly, I couldn't come up with anything.

"Yeah, I suppose that would work. I've got a two-fifteen appointment so it would have to be quick. Course, I'll have my attorney present." I glanced over at Louie in the process of dribbling coffee down the front of his shirt.

"Your attorney. Would that be Mr. Louis Laufen?"

"It would."

"I look forward to chatting with the both of you. I'll see you in about ten minutes," he said and hung up.

"Great, God damn it."

"Who the hell was that?"

"St. Paul's finest, Detective Norris Manning."

"That red-headed, bald guy who always looks like he's ready to explode?"

"Yeah, I'd say that's a pretty accurate description."

"What's he want?"

"I got no idea. I'm wracking my brain, trying to come up with something I've done, but I can't."

"There's a surprise. Hey, this new Candi chick you're seeing, she's over eighteen, isn't she?"

"Yes, she's over eighteen."

"You're sure?"

"Believe me, I've examined her very closely. Don't worry, she's over eighteen."

Vintage Detective Manning, he was there in eight minutes. They must have driven over with the flashing lights on. He was accompanied by a uniformed baby-faced officer named Richardson, who looked to be all of about sixteen.

"Your license must still be suspended, Manning. I see they gave you a driver."

Richardson didn't smile, but I could see a twinkle in his eye.

Manning gave his ever-present wad of gum a couple of audible cracks. His bald head shone pink against the fringe of red hair that ran around his skull. He flashed a smile for all of a half second, but his blue eyes seemed to grow decidedly icy. He glanced at Louie, standing behind the picnic table.

"Mr. Laufen, glad to hear you came out a winner on that disbarment hearing a few months back, never enough lawyers in town."

"Appreciate the thought, Detective," Louie said and then took up a relaxed seat on the corner of the picnic table.

"I hear you're providing your services to Joey Cazzo. That should keep you busy for the foreseeable future."

"Client privilege," Louie replied.

"Mmm-mmm. Long time no see, Haskell. You must have turned over a new leaf. What have you been up to lately?"

"Tell you the truth, Detective I'm probably the dullest guy in town."

"I'll bet. I might be looking for a place we could grab a burger for lunch. Anywhere you can think of to recommend?" Manning asked.

By this time, Richardson had stationed himself next to the door and was leaning against the wall. He tried to be casual about it, but his position wasn't lost on me.

"Hey, look, Manning, I don't know what this is all about, but I'm pretty sure you didn't drive over here just to get a lunch recommendation from me."

He stared at me for a moment and then said, "True. You weren't cruising around town last night, were you, Haskell?"

"It sounds like you're fishing, Manning. To tell you the truth, I was in a bar named Charlie's last night. I'd say I was in there from about nine o'clock until maybe ten-thirty or so. Charlie, the owner, can attest to that and maybe a half dozen guys that were in there. I had dinner with a woman, paid in cash, tipped Charlie. I left with the woman once we finished our dinner. She had two martinis, and I had a half glass of beer. We drove from there directly to my house."

"Gee, a dinner date at Charlie's bar. You're a real high class, big spender."

"We needed a quiet night. Then, like I said, we ended up at my place."

"Drove her car?"

"No, actually, I drove mine. She followed me in her car."

"You talk to anyone there?"

"At Charlie's? No. Except to place my order. It was just me and this woman. I was waiting for maybe a half-hour before she showed. We sat alone in a booth. Of course, she was obviously enthralled with my company."

"Yeah, who wouldn't be? You didn't talk to anyone at the bar then?"

"Not really. Some drunk made a comment, but I let it go. I think I said something like no hassle or see ya. He apologized later and offered to buy us a drink. I had other things on my mind to tell you the truth. Why, what's this all about, anyway?"

"You know anyone named Gary Ruggles?"

"No, not that I can recall at this time." This was taking a turn I didn't like, and I began to hedge my answers like one of those creeps in Washington.

"Is your vehicle here, Mr. Haskell?"

"Yeah, it's right out on the street."

"Mind if we take a look?"

"At my car?"

"Yeah, your car."

"No, I guess not. What's going on here, Manning?"

"Just want to check license and registration is all. That okay with you?"

"Is my client suspected of something, Detective? I'm guessing sooner or later you'll arrive at the real purpose of this harassment."

God, it took Louie long enough, but I didn't have anything to lose with Manning checking my car unless Candi had called him to report my tail lights. "Car's out on the street. You want to follow me. I'll show you the license and registration."

Manning nodded, and the four of us went down the steps and outside to my car.

"I should have known this beast would be yours when we first pulled up," Manning said, looking back and forth along the length of my car. "Why the blue door?"

"A work in progress," I said. I had climbed behind the wheel to reach over into the glove compartment. I handed Manning my registration and insurance card. "Sorry, didn't realize you'd been promoted to traffic division."

"A note from one of your fans?" Manning asked, indicating Rose's spray paint along the passenger side.

"Just a slight misunderstanding."

While we talked, Richardson walked around, studying the car, then looked over at Manning and shook his head.

"You're leaking a good bit of oil there. You might want to get that checked," he said.

"Thanks, I'll be sure to do that."

"Surprisingly, this all seems to be legitimate and up to date," Manning said, sounding just a little disappointed as he handed my insurance card back to me.

"Gee, thanks," I replied.

"What kind of mileage do you get with this beast?"

"It's improving, somewhere between eight and ten miles to the gallon. To tell you the truth, with gas only about four bucks a gallon, a high roller like me doesn't have to really worry about fuel costs."

He shook his head in disgust then said, "Enjoy your day, gentlemen." They crossed the street, climbed in the front seat of a squad car, and drove off.

"You seem to have a strange effect on certain people," Louie said. We watched as the squad car slowly disappeared down Randolph Avenue.

"I have no idea what any of that was about. What was that guy's name, he mentioned?"

Thirteen

Louie had a four-sentence article displayed on his laptop. "Yeah, here it is, right here. Jesus, a hit and run victim last night." Once Manning left, he'd done a search on the name Gary Ruggles. It hadn't rung a bell until he began reading out loud.

I guessed Ruggles was walking home when he was struck by a car and killed. The accident happened in a residential neighborhood. The street was about two blocks from Charlie's bar.

"Oh, shit, I get it," I said. I'd been standing behind Louie, reading the screen over his shoulder. I'd walked back to my desk chair when it dawned on me. The story had read more like a notice. It was probably just a summation of a police report coming across the wire rather than an actual story.

"You knew this guy?" Louie asked, looking over at me.

"Not really, but we maybe had words last night."

"Define '*Maybe*.'"

"He was a little drunk, maybe a lot, made some dumb ass comment to Candi. Then when I was at the bar, he said something stupid. I let it go. In fact, when we were leaving, he apologized and offered to buy us a drink. Like I said, the guy was drunk."

"Did you threaten him, tell him to apologize? Touch him? Anything like that?"

"No, nothing like that. I think I told him to have a nice night, and when he offered to buy us a drink, I probably said no thanks we had to get home or something. At least if it's the same guy, I'm thinking of. I remember Charlie called him Gary. The guy was wearing a teamster's baseball cap."

"Be a strange coincidence if it wasn't him. I'd say the police talked to patrons at the bar, probably Charlie, and your name came up."

"Yeah, and that prick Manning jumped on it," I scoffed.

"Just doing his job. That's what the license and registration deal was about, just an excuse to look for any damage to your car. Which was why that cop was walking around your bomb, he was checking it out."

"That was plain old harassment. They don't need an excuse to check my car. Certainly Manning doesn't. He just hoped my insurance had expired or there was some obscure violation he could nail me on."

"You might want to give your love buddy Candi a call, let her know she might have visitors. Make sure she has her timeline correct."

"That article doesn't actually give a time. I'm guessing it was probably a little after closing. By then she was at my place, wearing a smile and putting me through a workout routine."

"Too much information, Dev. That's a pretty quiet, residential neighborhood, a strange time and place for some idiot to be speeding."

"Who knows, maybe that Gary guy staggered into the street, someone bumped him, and he hit his head on the curb. Or hell, it could be a million and one things. Too bad, he might have been a drunk with a big mouth, but he didn't deserve to die."

"Manning doesn't seem to be your biggest fan."

"You think?"

"I'd say he's a major coronary just waiting to happen."

"You pick up on his Joey Cazzo comment?" I asked.

"You mean about keeping me busy? Well, it's no secret I filed the motions. You said your cop pal LaZelle figures Gino D'Angelo is going to win his appeal. Maybe that was the whole purpose of his visit."

"What, to let us know he's going to get off and they're watching? Why would we care? And why would they care if we knew? That doesn't make any sense."

I phoned Candi, but she didn't answer. Maybe she'd gone back to bed. I sure could have used the rest. I left her a brief message with the details about Manning's visit. It suddenly dawned on me he never asked Candi's name.

I listened to a short news report on the radio while driving home. Nothing really enlightening other than

Gary Ruggles was thirty-seven years of age, lifelong resident of St. Paul, over-the-road trucker, and the city's third hit and run victim this year. Anyone with information was asked to contact the police.

God, didn't that just figure? The guy drove day after day, hauling freight, and he gets run over walking home from a bar. You gotta wonder.

When I got home, I opened a beer and put a call into Candi. I had to leave another message.

* * *

My phone rang later that night. I was halfway through my fourth beer, maybe fifteen minutes into a nap. The Twins were down by four runs.

"Hey, baby," I answered, still half asleep and dreaming of wild sex with Candi.

"Dev, you okay? Am I interrupting something?" Louie asked.

"No, no, not a problem. Just reviewing some notes here. What's up?"

"Joey Cazzo just called and wants to meet tomorrow at ten."

"You want me out of the office? I can come in after . . ."

"No, he wants you to be there."

"Me? What did I do?"

"Nothing, as far as I know, he just said he wanted to meet with you. I got the feeling he may have an investigation project he wants you to work on."

"What'd you tell him?"

"Said I'd try and get hold of you, that you were working on something, and I hadn't seen you for a few days."

"Huh, you're almost as good a liar as me. I got nothing going other than watching women board the bus. What time?"

"Ten tomorrow morning."

"I'll be there."

Fourteen

I thought I'd go in early just to play it safe. I opened the office door at nine-thirty. Louie was already seated at my desk behind stacks of files.

"What are you doing?"

"Good morning. Oh, sorry, I left Cazzo with the impression that this was my desk, and I just set these files out to make me look busy.

I picked up a manila file folder from the nearest stack. It was relatively thick and labeled with some nine-digit numeric code written in black marker. The thing held maybe thirty sheets of paper, all blank. I glanced from the file to Louie.

"Are all the files like this?"

He was inserting a grocery store circular into a file and cramming the thing back into the middle of a tall stack.

"No, some are thicker, some are thinner."

"I meant blank."

"Look, just a little window dressing. I don't want Cazzo to get the wrong idea about us."

"And you're at my desk."

"Yeah, you mind sitting at mine?"

"The picnic table?"

"Just while Cazzo is here."

I noticed Louie was wearing a reasonably clean white shirt. At least it was clean before he managed to get a half dozen black marker stains across the front.

"You actually think this will work?"

"Why wouldn't it?" Louie said, then Googled the Thompson-Reuters website on his laptop.

"Want me to ditch the dartboard?" I asked.

"Just pull those darts out of the wall and stick them in the board. Better not make them a bull's eye. Stick them in a little off to the right."

"You're really taking this serious."

"Joey Cazzo is a big deal, Dev. He could get us out of hock."

"I really don't owe anyone."

"Yeah, and you're about a hundred bucks ahead of the game if things break your way every month. I'm talking some serious dough here. If all goes right with the motions I filed, it could lead to lots of work. The D'Angelos own a lot of property. Of course, the Tutti Frutti Club, along with a number of apartments. This could mean our train has finally come into the station. They even have land way up north."

"Where they probably bury bodies."

"Allegedly bury. Come on, last night you said you were going to be in on this."

"I did, Louie. It's just that you forgot to mention you'd have a hundred fake files stacked across my desk. That fake phone there next to you with multiple lines that will never ring because we don't have a landline in here. Then again, why would we need multiple lines? Our office consists of this one room, and no one ever calls." I looked around the office, but nothing else seemed too out of place.

"Louie, why don't I brew some decent coffee? When Cazzo arrives, we can just tell him our gorgeous, well-endowed, young secretary is out making another deposit at the bank."

"Oh, yeah, glad you brought that up. Could you run across the street to The Spot and get three matching coffee mugs?"

"What?"

"We only have two mugs in the place, one's chipped, and the other is plastic. As long as we need one more, don't you think we could get three that match? And make sure they don't have lipstick on them."

Fifteen

We were staring out the window when Joey Cazzo pulled up in some low-slung, red foreign thing that probably cost more than my house. He parked across the street, and then sat in the car for another ten minutes while he appeared to berate some poor soul on the other end of the phone.

"Places everyone," Louie said as Cazzo got out of the car.

Louie hurried behind my desk, picked up the dead phone, and wedged the receiver between his chins and shoulder. He began to nod, saying, "Yes, that's correct." He had a stack of contract forms he'd pulled off the Internet piled in front of him. He began slowly paging through them, initialing a paragraph every so often, pretending to be busy.

Cazzo burst in the door a few seconds later. The energy was palpable. He was shorter than I imagined, with a hooked nose and thinning hair pulled into a wispy ponytail held in place with a silver and turquoise clip. There was a bit of a rodent look to him. He nodded at Louie. It wasn't so much a greeting as it was an indication to get off the phone, and soon.

"You must be Haskins," he said, turning and leering before attacking me with an outstretched hand. He had an East Coast accent, New York or maybe Jersey. It automatically grated on my nerves.

"Haskell, Dev Haskell," I said, shaking his hand.

"Yeah sure, whatever," he replied, giving me one of those squeeze-as-hard-as-you-can shakes.

"Get you some coffee?" I asked. I failed to mention our new mugs from The Spot.

"Is it fresh?"

"Just made. Our secretary had to run—"

"Yeah, I'll take some. Louie, come on, let's go, man. Time is money. You don't know that yet? Come on, come on."

Louie nodded at Cazzo and then said into the dead phone, "I'll review it and get back to you. I don't want you moving on this until you get my okay. Clear? All right, messenger the original documents over here, and I'll have an answer for you later today. Yes, yes. I promise. I know, the Chinese. I'll talk to you later. Goodbye," he said, then hung up the dead phone.

Cazzo stared at him like he didn't buy the act.

"I'll tell you, it's taken them two years to put this deal together and now it comes down to me, and of course they need the damn answer today. I don't know," Louie said, shaking his head. "How are you, Mr. Cazzo? Sorry to keep you waiting. Have a seat there." Louie indicated my client chair with the strip of duct tape running across the seat cushion.

Cazzo stared for a moment like he was sizing Louie up, but he didn't say anything.

"Please," Louie said, indicating the chair again with his hand.

"You get those motions and briefs filed?"

"Just like you said, Mr. Cazzo, I met with—"

"You shouldn't have to do a damn thing other than show up in court, keep quiet, and nod when they rule in our favor. Word is we've got this wired. Tommy will be hosting a victory party for Gino that night at the club. You're both invited."

I was leaning against the filing cabinet. Cazzo sat down, then turned and directed his attention over to me. He wore a white golf shirt buttoned to the top beneath a creamy colored sport coat. The creases in his black trousers looked sharp enough to shave with. He had on a pair of woven leather loafers with no socks. The shoes had little brass buckles across the front and that look of handmade Italian leather. I was sure they probably had a price tag that resembled my address. He brushed some imaginary dust from his trouser leg then said, "Be there early. Tommy wants you to meet your client before we start."

"My client?" I asked.

"Swindle Lawless."

"Swindle?"

"Lawless. She's your new and most important client." He tossed a file across the desk that landed in front of Louie. Four or five eight by ten color photos of a blonde woman partially fanned out of the file. She looked vaguely familiar from the little I could see.

"You'll be investigating her agent, local dipshit named Dudley Rockett. I want you to get the goods on him. We'll deal with it from there."

"Get the goods on him? This guy, what did you say his name was again?"

"You listening?" He raised his voice. "First name Dudley, last name Rockett. He was her agent and—"

"Swindle?" I said.

"Yeah, that's right. This douche was Swindle's agent. We're going to get her money back, the fees, well, and some interest, of course."

"So, you're going to file a lawsuit?" Louie asked, sounding like he was contemplating options. "Have you thought on what grounds? Misrepresentation? Unprofessional conduct? Sexual harassment or some unethical—"

Cazzo stared at him for a long moment, then interrupted.

"Hell no. We're not going to file a lawsuit. Haskell," he yelled, looking over at me. "You just get the info we need on Rockett. Shouldn't be too hard, it's all there in that file. Any questions?"

"Give me some time to review the file, and I'll call you with any questions," I said.

"I got a better idea. Review the damn file and then get the goods on this hose bag. I'll expect to see you both at Gino's victory celebration." He stood up from the chair and nodded at Louie. "I'll see you in court." Then he turned and exited without saying goodbye.

We watched as he crossed the street, climbed into his sports car, put a phone to his ear, and raced off.

"What a sweetheart," I said.

"Yeah, and that was his good side. Look at it this way, like I told you, more business." He picked up the file Cazzo had tossed on the desk and paged through the photos.

"Well, I'll give her this much, she seems to have enough money to pay for a plastic surgeon," he said, flipping through a stack of studio-shot prints. When he was finished, he passed the file over to me.

"I know this woman from somewhere," I said, flipping through the photos. She was a bleached blonde, sporting a surgically enhanced chest. I guessed a good deal of nose and chin work, along with a lot of Botox in that face.

"She some stripper in one of those joints you go to?" Louie asked.

I shook my head.

"Escort?"

"No, she'd be out of my price range. Just kidding. No. I've seen her recently." I was thinking hard when it hit me. "The Tutti Frutti Club, that's it. She was there that night Heidi and I were there. One of the women your pal Tommy D'Angelo had his arm around."

"You sure?"

"Yeah, she pretty much gave me the look."

"The look?"

"Yeah, but I was with Heidi, and I think this gal was pretty wasted. You know the look, that kind of an *'Interested?'* Kind of smile and glance."

"Actually, no, can't say I'm familiar with it."

"Doesn't matter. Like I said, I was on Heidi duty that night. By the way, who names their baby girl, Swindle?"

Sixteen

Aaron LaZelle spit some caramel roll crumbs in my direction as he talked. He and Detective Manning had loaded up on two rolls each along with giant Lattés to the tune of close to twenty bucks. They stuck me with the tab. I was indulging in serious chocolate overload from a large brownie. It was just after seven in the morning, and we were seated at a back corner table in Nina's coffee shop. "You're kidding, Dev, Swindle Lawless isn't her real name. That's her stage name or was. She legally changed it way back in ninety-two."

"Stage name? What the hell does she need a stage name for if she's a waitress?" I asked.

"And she's your client?" Manning half laughed. "Maybe you should sit down with her and get some background information." He handed my file with the studio shots of Swindle over to Aaron.

"Yeah, that's her," Aaron said. He quickly fanned through the photos then passed the file back to Manning. He took a sheet of paper from his suit coat pocket and unfolded it. There was a black and white image of a woman vaguely resembling Swindle's studio shots in the upper right corner, or maybe it was her mother. I guessed it was probably a booking photo, Swindle without makeup, looking hungover, burnt out, or both. Not a very pretty sight.

"Given name was Muriel Kedrowski, born in St. Paul fourteen September nineteen-seventy-four. Let's see, she's got two arrests for solicitation, one for shop-lifting, another for indecent exposure. There was an as-sault charge back in two-thousand-five." He looked up at me, smiled, and continued. "In two-thousand-six, she was charged with passing bad checks. She was nailed for driving under the influence in two-thousand-seven. Pos-session of a controlled substance in two-thousand-eight, charges dropped apparently. Another solicitation charge in two-thousand-ten, but charges dropped on that one, too."

Manning snorted then tossed the file of photos on top of what was left of my chocolate brownie. He seemed to enjoy the fact that the sticky frosting smeared all over the back of the manila file.

Aaron gave him a glance but didn't say anything.

"So what you're telling me is she's pretty much straightened up her act if she hasn't been convicted since her DUI in two-thousand-seven."

"Not exactly," Aaron said, returning to his sheet of paper. "She changed her name back in ninety-two. Up to that point, Swindle Lawless had been her stage name, and she just made it official."

"Stage name? What was she doing?"

"She was a dancer. The indecent exposure charge came when she was sixteen, performing underage at the old Buns and Roses. Sometime after that, she did a two-year stint in Vegas before she fled the scene to Hollywood and waited to be discovered."

"Was she? Discovered. I mean."

"Yeah, I guess if you call ten years of playing background roles in porn videos for fifty bucks a day being discovered. She stayed out there until she was replaced by the next generation of wanna-be's. Then she drifted back to St. Paul. Started working at the Tutti Frutti Club and got hooked up with Tommy D'Angelo or got hooked up with Tommy first and then started working there."

I picked up the file and used my fork to scrape most of the chocolate off the back. I licked the fork and stared at Manning.

"Dev," Aaron cautioned.

"Swindle's agent contract with Rockett was back in twenty-ten. Is he on your radar?" I asked.

"Rockett? Only as a bit player. He's handled a couple of bands, a singer or two, a couple of strippers with higher aspirations. Usually handles desperate folks, you know, on their last chance. Probably his biggest claim to fame was back in the late eighties. Manuel Pastori."

"Never heard of him," I said.

"Exactly."

"I'd guess Rockett saw an easy mark or maybe a desperate one with your girlfriend Swindle. Another burned-out party girl past her prime and looking ten years older than her age, hanging by her fingernails. His mistake was he didn't count on her being tied into Tommy D'Angelo," Manning said.

"So if D'Angelo is that scary, why not just give them her money back?"

"I'm guessing they want more than her money. Probably a lot more. It's been rumored Rockett owed a debt to the D'Angelos, but we could never seem to quite figure it out."

"What are we talking? A grand, ten grand?"

"No, it would be more vicious than that, they'd probably want his house, car, business, all of the above."

"Everything?"

"That sounds about right." Manning nodded. "Hey, they're your clients."

"Just she is, Swindle, and I'm not even sure about her."

Aaron shook his head and handed me the sheet with Swindle's arrest record. "Keep us posted, Dev. Let me know how it works out."

Manning crammed the last bit of a caramel roll into his mouth. "Be careful, Haskell," he mumbled, and they left.

Seventeen

Mercifully there was only one Dudley Rockett in the white pages reverse directory. I was ringing the doorbell and knocking on his front door the following morning. If Dudley was home, he didn't bother to answer.

The house, a pinkish, late fifties rambler with an attached single car garage, had a faded and unkempt look about it. Unkempt if you discounted the high tech security cameras mounted on either end of the house and over the front door. Yellowed shades were pulled down over every window. Peeling paint, untrimmed grass, weedy looking front shrubs, or maybe they were just weeds. I couldn't tell.

A mailbox stuffed with grocery store circulars hung crookedly next to the front door. Candy wrappers and a couple of plastic bags had blown up against the front of the house, looking like they had been there for quite a while.

Through the small rectangular window in the front door, I could see what looked like a television screen flickering back in a darkened kitchen. I couldn't detect any other movement. I took out my cell and dialed the phone number I'd gotten online. It rang, but no one answered, and I never got a message option.

I was back sitting in my car, trying to come up with some other idea when a kid about fifteen strolled down the street. He wandered up to the keypad on Rockett's garage door and entered a code. As the door rose up, I could see a nondescript black Toyota sitting in the garage. The kid carefully reversed the car into the driveway, climbed out, and began to walk away.

"Hey, excuse me, son. Hold up there," I called from my car. He didn't seem to hear me, and I called again. "Excuse me, young man, hey." This time he stopped and stared as I hurried across the street toward him. We were standing in front of the house next door to Rockett's. I could see a rough-looking woman in a ratty bathrobe studying us through her front window as she sipped her coffee.

"Do you live there?" I asked, pointing back toward Rockett's house.

"No."

"Do you know Dudley Rockett?"

He gave a slight nod. "Maybe."

"Do you know if he's home? I tried knocking on the door, but no one answered."

"Yeah, he usually doesn't. I back the car out for him every day. Don't know if he's home. I never see the guy."

"You get paid for that?"

"Yeah, he sends me fifty bucks every month."

"Seems a little extravagant."

"Whatever. You a cop?"

"No, I'm with the Minnesota State Lottery. Mr. Rockett is registered as the holder of a winning ticket, and we wanted to contact him."

"Cool."

I heard a car door slam. By the time I turned around the Toyota was backing out of the driveway. Whoever it was didn't waste any time.

"Mr. Rockett, Mr. Rockett, Dudley," I called.

The Toyota quickly rolled into the street and drove off.

"That him, Rockett?" I called back to the kid as I ran to my car.

"I think so. I'm not really sure. I only saw him once, but that's his car."

I pulled away from the curb as Rockett's black Toyota screeched around the corner at the far end of the block. I raced around the corner, and heard some stuff roll across my back seat and then onto the floor as I accelerated. The Toyota was a block and a half ahead of me. The taillights flashed as it approached a stop sign, but he never really slowed down and blasted through the intersection.

I approached the sign a moment later, then had to slow and finally stop while a school bus lumbered across my path. Once the bus passed, I couldn't see the Toyota. He must have turned onto a side street. I accelerated across the intersection, slowed for half a second at the cross street, looked left and right, but didn't see the Toyota. I gambled and raced ahead, but couldn't spot Rockett's car. I suddenly caught the thing in my rearview mirror as it raced around the corner behind me and took off in the opposite direction.

I made a U-turn, tearing across some poor guy's front lawn in the process. I sped up to try and catch Rockett. He was maybe two blocks ahead of me. I accelerated and blasted through an intersection with my horn blaring and my engine roaring. I was gaining on him. I'd cut the distance almost in half. I could hear the sand and gravel pinging off the undercarriage of my Fleetwood. We raced along a winding residential street as I continued to close on him. We were little more than a block apart when I first heard the siren and saw the flashing lights in my rearview mirror. I raced down the street for maybe another half block before I realized my situation could only get worse and I pulled over.

I turned off my engine and watched in the rear view mirror. The squad car stopped, the driver's door opened, and a uniformed officer knelt down behind the open door.

"Step out of your vehicle. Place your hands on top of your head," a voice blared out over a loudspeaker.

This wasn't going my way. I did as directed and waited there, standing in the middle of the street.

"Kneel down. Keep your hands on your head."

As I knelt, I could feel the pea gravel that the city used for resurfacing grinding into my knees. The street had recently been tarred, oiled, and then dusted with a coating of the gravel. The fresh oil worked its way into the knees of my jeans. They were ruined in short order, but at least I didn't have to lie down in the stuff.

"Lay face down on the street, keep your hands on your head and spread your legs."

I thought about that for a long moment.

"Face down on the street, place your hands on your head, and spread your legs. Do it now!"

I saw another squad car with flashing lights racing toward us. From somewhere behind me, I heard a car door slam. Not that it made any difference, but I guessed there were possibly four to six officers on the scene. I laid down in the freshly tarred street and ruined my shirt.

Eighteen

Manning looked across the table at me. We were seated in one of the department's interrogation rooms. Nice place if you were into brown cigarette burns worming their way across Formica, dull gray walls, and Manning's ever-present bottle of Maalox. He seemed to be enjoying himself, and his eyes literally sparkled. "I trust you found the accommodations to your liking."

"To be honest, no, I didn't like the accommodations. I would have been better off sleeping in my car."

"Except that we had to impound it. A towing fee yesterday and now today in the impound lot. Gee, it starts to add up. Funny, you didn't contact your legal representation, Mr. Laufen. I suppose—"

"Come on, Manning, quit yanking my chain. You know I called him last night. He was unable to come down here at the time, so I—"

"I believe the technical term is shit-faced."

"If you say so. Look, can I go? You know I didn't do anything."

"Speeds of up to seventy-five miles per hour on a residential street in the city of St. Paul, that's pretty serious. School kids present, that's going to cost a little additional. Four, separatc, nine-one-one calls from tax paying citizens. Resisting arrest, not the best idea."

"Resisting arrest? Come on, I didn't resist arrest. I pulled over, laid down on a freshly tarred street. I mean, look at me, my clothes are ruined. When did I resist anything?"

"Just reading the arrest report. Obviously, I wasn't present to witness this latest incident." He leaned back and smiled, attacking his gum a half dozen times, causing it to audibly snap, then he reached for his bottle of Maalox and took a gulp.

"I admit I was speeding, foolishly. But I didn't resist arrest, Manning. You know that."

He shrugged. "Mr. Rockett has filed a restraining order against you. Would you care to explain?"

"A restraining order? We already talked about this. My client—"

"Miss Lawless?"

"Yeah, Swindle is going to sue the guy or something. I just went to Rockett's house to chat with him. You can ask that kid."

"David Kenney?" he asked, reading from the file in front of him.

"If you say so. I didn't get the kid's name. He told me Rockett pays him to start his car every morning. I'm standing there minding my own business when Rockett sneaks into the car and speeds off. He's the one you should be charging."

"So you were what? Thinking citizen's arrest or something?"

"I just wanted to talk with the guy. I told you before about Joey Cazzo and my new client, Swindle. You know all this stuff already, Manning. It's not like I'm a public enemy."

"Public nuisance might be more like it."

I didn't respond for a moment. "Besides, what kind of guy has a kid start his car every morning and back it out of the garage?"

"The kind of guy who's worried about a car bomb and figures if everyone knows the kid starts his car, no one will place a bomb in there."

"No shit?" I said. It had never occurred to me.

Manning just snapped his gum a number of times, paging through the file. Eventually, he looked up at me. "Anything else you'd like to add?"

"Only that I'd like to go home so I can take a shower."

"So noted, I think that would be an improvement, by the way, a shower, I mean." He wrinkled his nose. "Would you care to comment on impersonating an officer of the state?"

"Impersonating? What are you talking about?"

Manning flipped a number of sheets of paper one by one, then ran his finger down the page like he was looking for something. "Oh yes, here it is," he said and read out loud. "The guy said he worked for the Minnesota State Lottery and that Mr. Rockett had a winning ticket."

"You gotta be kidding," I said. "So it makes sense to spend taxpayer's money just to keep me locked up in here overnight? Come on, look, you've had your little joke. Now how about letting me go home? You know there's nothing there."

Manning looked at me for a long moment, then shook his head and closed the file. "One of your many problems, Haskell, is that you just never learn. All right, go forth and sin no more." With that, he stood up, graciously bowed, and grandly swept his hand toward the door.

I picked up my cellphone and wallet at the property desk. I phoned Louie and had to leave a message. I phoned Heidi for a ride and left another message. Then I phoned Candi.

"Hi, Dev. What's up?"

"You busy?"

"Sort of. We've got to do some setup for the party tomorrow tonight. I heard you're coming."

"Party?"

"The victory party for Gino D'Angelo. I guess he's going to have charges dropped or something. I don't know. Anyway, there's going to be a big celebration. You're coming, aren't you?"

"Yeah, yeah, sure. Look, I've been busy the last day or so. Um, I'm wondering if I could hop a ride with you?"

"That pimpmobile you drive finally die?" She giggled.

"No just towed, I need to get it out of the impound lot before I get charged for another day."

"Where did you leave it parked?"

"It wasn't exactly a parking offense. Can you break away and pick me up?"

"Yeah, I guess so. Just tell me where to meet you, and I'm on my way."

Nineteen

Candi drove me to the impound lot with the windows down. Apparently, Manning wasn't kidding. I really did need a shower. On the way over, I explained to her how suddenly Swindle Lawless was my client, and I had to get information on her former agent Dudley Rockett.

She didn't seem at all surprised.

"If I might offer a little warning here. I think it's safe to say Swindle always has a number of issues on her plate at any given time and leave it at that. I'm sure whatever she's gotten herself into this time will require more than one form of professional help."

"You mean she's someone who always seems to be in trouble?"

"I mean, she's someone who always seems to be a real pain in the hole."

"Oh, great."

"So you chased this Rockett guy down, and the police arrested you?"

"Well, that's one way to look at it. I'd prefer to say I was just trying to talk with him for a few minutes, then everything went slightly out of control. Anyway, I never even talked with the guy."

“And I suppose now you can’t talk with him because he filed a restraining order.”

“I haven’t been officially served yet, so I might have a day or two to track him down. Hell, I don’t know. Maybe I should just wait for the guy on his front steps.”

“I’m not so sure that would be a good idea. Maybe just phone him,” she said, then pulled over and parked in front of the impound lot.

The zigzag sidewalk leading to the building had concrete barricades along both sides topped with about four feet of concertina wire. The place looked like something out of the Middle-East.

“This joint looks pretty creepy. You want me to wait for you?” she asked, not sounding all that sincere about the offer.

“No, I’ve done this once or twice before. It’ll be fine. Thanks again, Candi.”

She leaned over and planted a kiss on my unshaved face. “Hmm-mmm, you know I like it rough.” She smiled and kissed me again. “Okay, you better get out before I drag you into the back seat and forget I’m supposed to be at work.”

“Want to think about that? It wouldn’t take too long and . . .”

“Get out, but call me tonight, okay?” she said, then gave my inner thigh a very suggestive rub.

“I promise. Thanks, Candi.” I climbed out of the car, waved as she drove off, and then went inside to retrieve the Fleetwood. Fortunately or unfortunately, depending on your point of view, this was not my first time at the city's impound lot. Twenty minutes later, I was driving home for a long, hot shower.

I wasn't out of the shower two minutes when my phone rang.

"Hi, Dev, Louie. Hey, I had some cryptic message on my phone from you last night. You okay?"

"Yeah. No thanks to you. I spent the night locked up."

"At Candi's?"

"No, the police. Manning jacking me around on some bogus speeding charge to be precise."

"That doesn't sound like something they lock you up for. Was there something outstanding like a warrant or an old ticket?"

"Let's just say I wanted to get a jump on the Swindle Lawless deal, and it more or less backfired. I'm going over to wait for Dudley Rockett to get home and ask him a couple of questions. I'm still not sure about Swindle's case."

"Imagine that."

I hung up with Louie, got dressed, and drove back to Dudley Rockett's house. The place looked just as dead as yesterday morning. I knocked and rang the doorbell, but no one answered. When I glanced through the little window in the front door, I could see the TV playing on the kitchen counter.

I drove down the street, turned around, and parked a couple of houses away. I settled in and waited for

Rockett to appear. I must have dozed off sometime after midnight because I suddenly jerked myself awake. It was dark, close to two in the morning when a groaning muffler woke me. The pair of headlights shooting past momentarily blinded me. I got out of the car, stretched, and thought, what the hell? I walked up to Rockett's house, pounded on the door, and got the same result, nothing. The house itself was dark, and I couldn't see the TV flickering in the kitchen.

I decided to leave my card in the door. I was going to write something on it like, "call me," or "just want to talk," but thought that might not be a good idea. By the time I got home, I figured it was too late to call Candi, so I just went to sleep.

Twenty

At seven the following morning, I was once again parked across the street from Rockett's house. This time armed with four large coffees from Nina's. By eight, I was sipping the last coffee and had nibbled my way through half of what was supposed to be my lunch. Not long after that, the same high school kid came walking down the block.

Once he backed out of the garage, I started my car and pulled over to block the driveway. He gave me a funny little wave as he walked past my car, then glanced over his shoulder as he continued down the street.

I was in desperate need of a bathroom by nine and knocked on Rockett's door. When he didn't answer, I walked along the side of the house to a corner more private than not, relieved myself, then walked back out front. Rockett's Toyota was still parked in the driveway. I noticed a fairly recent oil slick on the concrete, but it didn't seem to be coming from the Toyota. I waited another hour before I gave up. By the time I got to my office, I'd finished my lunch, and it wasn't quite eleven.

"Any luck talking with Dudley Rockett?" Louie asked when I walked into the office. He was seated at the picnic table, stuffing the last of a chocolate donut into his mouth. A lone donut remained in a package that had once held six. Chocolate crumbs littered the open files scattered in front of him.

"No, I can't find the guy. Well, actually, I maybe can, but he keeps slipping away. I left him my card in the door last night, hoping he might call, but nothing. I hung around there this morning, wasting a good part of my life that I'll never get back, but he didn't so much as stick his head out."

Louie nodded, grabbed the last donut, and crammed maybe a third of it into his mouth.

"Mmm-mmm-mrumph, we've got to go to that victory party tonight. Cazzo will be there, and he's not the kind of guy who does well with disappointment."

"I don't know what to tell him, other than Rockett's dodging me. I'll think of something. By the way, I got the lowdown on Swindle Lawless from Candi and Aaron. Apparently, the woman is a first-class pain in the ass."

"No surprise there," Louie said and stuffed the rest of the donut into his mouth.

"I thought you were supposed to be in court this morning on Gino D'Angelo's hearing."

"They called and moved it back on the docket to one this afternoon. Some schedule conflict with the judge. It's a slam dunk anyway. You can ride over with me if you want."

"Actually, I hadn't planned on going. I don't want to see Cazzo any sooner than I have to. The longer I can avoid that guy, the better."

"He'll be okay. I'm heading over around noon. We can ride together."

"I'm not sure I want to be there," I said.

Twenty-one

So much for good intentions. Against my better judgment, I was sitting in the back of the courtroom when the deputy gave the "All rise."

The courtroom, one of a number on the fifth floor of the courthouse, was paneled floor to ceiling with burled wood. An oak-leaf garland was carved along the top of the panels and wrapped around the entire room. In each of the four corners, the garland was offset by a large gold wreath. The place was impressive and, depending on your reason for being there, maybe even intimidating.

Once everyone was seated, the judge looked down from the bench and spoke in a no-nonsense voice.

"In the matter of Ramsey County versus Mr. Gino D'Angelo, are you ready to proceed?"

The blonde county attorney jumped to her feet, cleared her throat, and spoke in a barely audible voice.

"Your honor, in the interest of justice at this time we wish to drop all charges against Mr. D'Angelo."

"Council for the defense, Mr. Laufen."

Louie's wooden chair scraped against the marble floor as he rose to his feet. He cleared his throat, then said, "Your honor, we have no objections."

“I would think not, Mr. Laufen.” The judge flashed a smile for all of a half-second, delivering anything but a positive note. “Very well, in the matter of Ramsey County versus Mr. Gino D’Angelo, the charges are hereby dropped. Good day,” she said, then slammed her gavel and was on her feet halfway to her chambers before the deputy called out.

“All rise.”

Tommy D’Angelo and Joey Cazzo were suddenly swarming the defense table. They quickly shook Louie’s hand then Tommy hugged Gino while Cazzo patted Gino on the back. For his part, Gino looked like he didn’t have a clue about where he was or what had just occurred.

The county attorney stuffed a stack of files into her briefcase, smiled at the D’Angelo clan like she was the only one in on the joke and strode out of the courtroom.

Cazzo continued to slap Gino on the back, laughed, and flipped the finger at her once she walked past.

That reminded me that coming down here was probably not the best idea I’d had. I followed the county attorney out the door into the polished marble hallway. Aaron LaZelle, Detective Manning, and four uniformed officers were standing outside the courtroom doors. Aaron nodded at me and then indicated with a slight shake of his head to get out of the way. Manning was focused on the doorway, cracking that ever-present wad of gum. He seemed to look right through me.

You could hear the celebratory noise growing as the D'Angelos approached the rear of the courtroom. A moment later, the ornate twelve-foot double doors burst open, and a raucous, laughing, back-slapping group flowed out into the hallway.

"You showed 'em, Tommy, you showed the bastards," Cazzo yelled above the noise.

For the first time, I noticed Swindle Lawless. She was a couple of paces behind Tommy D'Angelo desperately trying to keep up in heels that were too high and wearing a black leather skirt that was too tight.

The laughing came to a sudden stop when they came face to face with the phalanx of police officers.

"Come to say you're sorry?" Cazzo joked and then looked around for support.

Manning's face was flushed, and the top of his bald head gleamed like a stoplight. Aaron gave him a nod, and Manning stepped forward.

"Mr. Gino D'Angelo, we're placing you under arrest for the attempted murder of Dudley Rockett." Two of the uniforms moved in.

"What the fuck?" Tommy shouted and took a step toward Manning.

A very large uniformed officer blocked his progress.

"Tommy?" Gino asked, looking confused as he faced his brother.

Manning began to read Gino his rights as the uniforms took hold of his arms. "You have the right to remain silent. Anything you say can and will be used against you."

"Do something, fatty," Tommy shouted at Louie.

For his part, Louie looked about as confused as Gino.

"Come on, can these bastards do this? What the fuck? Do something now!" Tommy screamed and attempted to push Louie forward.

"Yes, they can do this, Mr. D'Angelo. We'll have to wait and see what the charges are, then post bail."

"Tommy?" Gino called as one of the uniforms slapped a pair of handcuffs on behind his back.

"You don't gotta do that, asshole. It'll be okay, Gino, don't sweat it. We'll have ya out for the party tonight. Then we're gonna sue their asses off," Tommy said, pointing his finger at Aaron.

"Can they do this, Tommy?" Swindle asked.

"Shut up," Tommy shouted. "You'll be okay, Gino, we're gonna follow you down to the station, get you out right away. You two get this moving. I don't want my brother in there overnight," Tommy shouted at Cazzo and Louie.

Swindle suddenly moved forward and tried to scratch Manning's face. He blocked her and pushed her back.

"Get him out of here," Manning said to the uniformed cops then glared at Tommy. "Don't make this any worse, or we'll haul everyone in." He held Tommy in a wild-eyed stare for a long moment.

Swindle started to take a tenuous step toward Manning again.

"Don't, bitch," Tommy shouted, and she froze.

The officers were on either side of Gino, holding him by the arms. They led him over to the bank of elevators. Manning and Aaron walked backward, keeping an eye on the group glaring at them.

"We're going to process your brother at the main station. I want you to remain on this floor for the next five minutes to avoid an incident that will do nothing but make things worse," Aaron said.

"Tommy?" Gino called, sounding like he was ready to cry.

They moved as one onto the elevator. Just as the brass doors closed, Gino called out a final time.

"Tommy, don't let—"

"God damn it, you two better figure something out and fast," Tommy screamed at Louie and Cazzo. "Come on, let's go," he said, then stepped over and began hitting the down button for the elevator a dozen times. "What the hell is taking this thing so damn long? Come on, damn it."

Tommy looked around wildly. He didn't seem to notice me at first and just glanced past. Then he returned his gaze to where I was standing and glared. "Who the hell are you?"

"That's the guy I told you about, Haskins the P.I. He's been checking out Rockett, right?" Cazzo said.

I nodded at Tommy. "Dev Haskell, nice to meet you, Mr. D'Angelo."

He seemed to be thinking for a long moment, then turned to Cazzo and Louie and said, "I want you two to post bail as soon as possible. Medical reasons. He's crazy, right?" He nodded at Cazzo.

"We'll head to my office. I've got it all laid out from last time," Cazzo said, then pulled out his cell, pushed a button, and waited.

Louie nodded, pretending he knew what was going on.

The elevator door opened and they began to file in. "No, not you," Tommy said to Swindle, then pointed at me. "You keep an eye on her," he said. Then he barked at Swindle, "Stick with him. Do whatever he wants." He stepped onto the elevator, turned, and stood in the doorway, looking very pissed off as the brass doors closed.

Swindle seemed to sag and turned around to face me. "Oh, shit," she said.

I could smell the alcohol on her breath.

"Hey, is your car here? I'll drive," I offered.

Twenty-two

We'd been sitting in a back booth at The Spot. Swindle had been attempting to impress me with her entertainment career, such as it was. In between sips from her current Brandy Manhattan, she continued to list off the various films she'd been in.

"I did *"Girls, Girls, Girls"* one thru seven. Had a supporting role in "*Babes in Toyland*" three and four. I played an elf and a toy tester in those two. I was the girl on the bar in "*Drunk and Disorderly.*" Did you see it?"

"No, I guess I missed that one too."

She shook her head like she couldn't believe it. "Well, what do you do for fun? Do you ever have any? Fun, I mean."

"Once in a while, I guess."

"I guess," she said, shaking her head in disbelief. "Kind of a drag if you ask me."

"Hey, Swindle, you sure you don't know anything about Gino and Dudley Rockett?" It was the third or fourth time I'd asked her.

"I've been with a lot of guys. Most of 'em I never even knew their name," she said nonchalantly and then drained her glass.

"You remember Gino? The cops arrested him in the courthouse today. You were there. They said he attempted to kill Dudley Rockett. Remember him? He was your agent."

"They arrested Gino, right? Not my problem then, is it?" She signaled Jimmy behind the bar with a slight wave of her empty glass.

"Hold on, Jimmy," I called. "Hey, no offense, Swindle, but I don't want to bring you back to the party tonight so drunk you can't enjoy yourself."

"I've never been that drunk," she said and signaled Jimmy with her glass again.

"No doubt, but I'm sure Tommy wouldn't be too happy."

"Tommy's never happy," she said, then slid her purse off the table, snapped it open, and pulled out a package of cigarettes. She stabbed one into the corner of her mouth, then flicked her lighter and lit up.

"Sorry, no smoking in here. It's been the law for about the past decade."

"The law," she scoffed, then shook her blonde hair back over her shoulder and blew smoke across the table in my direction.

"Come on, we can go outside if you're gonna smoke," I said and slid out of the booth.

Swindle stared up at me with bloodshot eyes, then took a long drag and blew more smoke at me. I thought of Candi describing her as *'a real pain in the hole.'* That was turning out to be a fairly accurate assessment.

"Hey, look, Swindle. I'm sorry you can't be down at the police station sitting around waiting. I'm sorry you have to sit here drinking Brandy Manhattans at my expense. I'm sure you have a very productive life, and there are things you should be accomplishing right now. But Tommy told me to keep an eye on you. You're not happy about that. Neither am I. So let's just try and get along. Maybe make the best of it."

She seemed to think about that for a moment. She took another long drag, blew the smoke toward the ceiling, and tossed her cigarette into her empty drink glass. It sizzled on the ice cubes and slowly began to extinguish.

"Yeah, sure, whatever. Look, I gotta pee," she said and slid out of the booth.

I handed Jimmy a twenty while Swindle staggered into the ladies room.

"Where'd you pick her up?" Jimmy asked.

"I didn't. She's a client."

"Business that bad?"

"I didn't think so this morning, but I'm beginning to wonder," I said.

A couple of heads in the mid-day drinking crowd turned to appraise her once she exited the ladies room taking itty-bitty steps in her heels toward the back door.

"I better drive. Give me your keys, and I'll lock up your car. I'm parked just across the street in front of my office."

Thankfully, she didn't argue. She fished her keys out of her purse and called after me. "Grab another pack of cigarettes out of my glove compartment and get that lipstick case in there too."

I had parked Swindle's purple Miata convertible behind The Spot. Based on the smashed front end, the scrape along the passenger side door, and the groaning muffler, I figured she might not be the best driver on a good day. I had a sneaking suspicion it wasn't lipstick in the silver tube with the gold top stuck in the corner of her glove compartment, but I grabbed the thing anyway.

We weren't due at the Tutti Frutti Club for another couple of hours, and I thought it might be a good idea to get some food in her. I held the door to the Fleetwood as she slipped unladylike into the front seat.

By the time I climbed behind the wheel, Swindle had reclined the passenger seat and was lounging back suggestively, sniffling and rubbing her nose.

"You missed some," I said, indicating the remnants of white powder around the base of her nostrils.

She sat up and twisted the rearview mirror so she could examine herself. She wiped up the remnants of powder with her finger, then rubbed her fingertip across her gums and slouched back.

"Happy?" She sneered.

"Not by a long shot," I said and readjusted the mirror.

She seemed to sulk for a moment, then reached into her purse and pulled out an iPhone housed in a sequined leopard skin case. She punched in a number, listened for maybe thirty seconds, then growled, “Shit” and tossed the phone back into her purse.

Twenty-three

I figured the dollar menu would serve us just fine. "What do you feel like eating?" I asked.

"Are you kidding me? I don't care, just order something for me. Nothing fatty," she groaned, slinking down in her seat and giving off an attitude.

I had a comment on the tip of my tongue but decided to keep quiet. The night was going to be long enough as it was."Three McChicken sandwiches, two small fries, and two medium cokes," I said into the screen.

"Will there be anything else?" a voice replied.

"No."

"Thank you, your total is seven dollars and thirty-seven cents. Please pull ahead to the first window."

I drove ahead to the window.

"Seven dollars thirty-seven cents," the girl said.

I handed her a ten.

"Three sixty-three is your change. Thank you. Please pull ahead to the next window."

I pulled ahead to the next window. A hand thrust out a moment later, holding a bag with our food. I took the bag and handed it over to Swindle, who didn't react. She was either asleep or passed out, so I gently set the bag on her lap. I took the two cokes, and placed them in the console tray and drove away.

The thought never crossed my mind to wake her. I cautiously lifted the bag of food off her lap and set it on mine. Then quietly began to eat as I drove onto the Interstate. I proceeded to drive along the beltline encircling the Twin Cities for the next couple of hours while Swindle softly snored in the passenger seat, and I ate all the food.

I pulled up in front of the Tutti Frutti Club a little later that evening and parked on the street about fifteen feet from the front door. As I turned the Fleetwood off Swindle groaned in the passenger seat, and half-rolled toward the door.

"Swindle, hey, Swindle, we're here," I said, shaking her gently on her hip.

"Don't touch me," she groaned.

"Come on, we're at the Tutti Frutti Club. Tommy's waiting for you."

"I said, don't touch me," she shouted and slapped my hand away.

I spanked her once across her hip, hard and shouted, "Come on, get the hell out of my car."

"Ouch! Hey, what do think you're doing?"

"Get out, Swindle, you pain, we're at the Tutti Frutti Club."

"What? Already?" she asked, sitting up, twisting my rearview mirror again, and staring into it. "Oh, God, look at me, I look like shit."

I couldn't argue with her. Her makeup had left deep dark circles under her bloodshot eyes. Her hair was a mess and pressed off to one side in a very bad case of bed-head. The red lipstick had rubbed off her lips and somehow found its way onto her front teeth.

"You can duck into the ladies room in the Tutti Frutti," I suggested.

"Oh, God, I need to pee," she groaned. It seemed to be turning into a regular theme. She grimaced, then fluttered her feet rustling the food wrappers I had tossed down onto the floor, suggesting she didn't have a lot of time to wait.

"The ladies room would probably be the best place, come on."

Twenty-four

As we entered the Tutti Frutti Club Swindle half-shouted, “Don’t touch me, Biker, I gotta pee.” She seemed to have a slight stagger to her step, and her leather skirt had shifted about four inches off-center. She blasted past Biker and made a beeline for the restroom.

Biker didn’t even blink at Swindle’s disheveled state. He stared at me, trying to place my face.

“Hey, Biker, Dev Haskell. We met before, partied with Tommy D’Angelo that night.” I lied. “How’s it going?”

He snapped back to reality with the mention of Tommy’s name. Then suddenly grew all sweet and charming, shaking my hand while he placed his left hand on my shoulder.

“Oh, yeah, knew you from somewhere. God, that was a night, wasn’t it?’ He sounded like he was still trying to remember when and where.

“One for the books, Biker, one for the books. Hey, Tommy told me to meet him at the victory party. That somewhere special?”

“Private party room upstairs. That door next to the bar, take the stairs.”

"Folks up there already? Tommy here?"

"Some of the usual crowd. Tommy and Gino got a little delayed. I guess."

Yeah, I'd seen the delay going down with Aaron and Detective Manning in the hallway of the courthouse, but didn't feel the need to tell Biker about it.

"Hey, when Swindle comes out, will you tell her I'm up in the party room?"

"Yeah, Swindle," Biker said and just shook his head.

There was a guard of sorts at the stairway. A young woman in Goth makeup, wearing black latex, and a cape stood next to the door. She was holding a spear about eight feet long and didn't react when I spoke to her.

"How's it going?" I said.

She looked straight ahead, standing at attention the way someone who'd never served in the military thought you stood at attention.

"The party for Gino up these stairs?"

Still no reaction. If I'd been drinking, I probably would have pulled some stunt like drawing a mustache on her face or worse. Instead, I just opened the door and went upstairs.

The party room was a nice enough place. There were a half dozen reclining nude portraits gracing the walls. If I recalled, prior to the Tutti Frutti Club, this place had been called Dusty's, a cowboy theme bar serving long neck beers with a mechanical bull ride in one of the corners. The nude portraits seemed to be all that remained of Dusty's.

A buffet table ran along a far wall. A number of aluminum chafing dishes held different foods and were kept warm by small flames burning beneath and what looked like heat lamps positioned over the trays. People were clustered in small groups, talking in hushed tones, not quite whispering, but almost. Next to the buffet table was a bar that seemed to draw me toward it.

"Hi, what can I get you?" She was a cheery thing, the bartender. She could have been pretty, probably was until she added fifteen pounds of metal piercing to her head. The ridge of both ears looked like a zipper had been sown onto them. I counted a half dozen jeweled bars running down the bridge of her nose. Her eyebrows looked like she'd had a bad experience with a staple gun, and her lips looked like the branch on a Christmas tree. I caught myself staring for a long moment.

"What would you like, Sir?" she asked.

"You got a Summit EPA?"

"Yes, Sir. Care for a glass?"

"Just the bottle will do." I felt like asking her something personal like how she ever cleared airport security? Or were flying magnets a danger? Instead, I just said, "Thanks," then walked away.

I was standing in the middle of the room, looking around and not recognizing anyone. I had hoped to run into Candi, but if she was around, I couldn't see her, and she wasn't the sort you'd miss.

“How in the hell did you get in here?” It was Heidi. A least, I thought it was. She was adorned with more of her fake piercings. She’d dug out her red and purple skunk wig and had pulled the thing onto her head. She was poured into a military-looking corset which was actually pretty good.

“Well, at least I didn’t have to wear a costume.”

“Very funny. Not. You certainly seem to be climbing the social ladder. How did you rate to get in here?”

I looked around the room and thought if the state medical authorities knew about this group, they’d drop a net over the entire place.

“I think all these people fell off the social ladder a long time ago.”

“I suppose you’d feel more at home in those dreadful dive bars you frequent. With people drunk and obnoxious or just passed out.”

“Probably. Hey.” I leaned in close and adopted the same hushed tone as everyone else. “What’s the deal? I thought the D’Angelos were having a victory party. This feels more like a funeral.”

“Figures you wouldn’t have a clue. Get me another drink, and I’ll fill you in,” she said, then handed me what looked like a large bathroom glass.

“You’re either drinking mouthwash or lime Kool-Aid?”

“A Green Fairy.”

“What?”

"A Green Fairy, of course, you wouldn't know. It's the latest thing, and she can really make a good one." Heidi glanced over at the zipper headed bartender.

"Be right back."

"Better give me another Summit and a Green Fairy," I said, then set my empty bottle down beside Heidi's glass. "Hey, what's a Green Fairy anyway?"

"Green Fairy? Oh, they can be nasty. Absinthe, melon liqueur, and peach schnapps."

"Absinthe?"

"It's a French liqueur. They say Van Gogh was drinking it when he decided to cut his ear off."

"Gee, better make it a double then."

"Okay."

"No, no, don't make it a double. I know where that would be headed."

"You sure? I can."

"Very sure, thanks all the same."

It was a couple of hours later when Swindle finally made her appearance. She wandered in dressed in the same outfit she'd worn earlier, so she hadn't gone home to change. God only knew what she'd been up to, but she clearly hadn't missed anything at the victory party. Joey Cazzo, Louie, Gino, and Tommy D'Angelo were nowhere to be seen.

The crowd had thinned to probably half its original size, which hadn't been a whole lot of people, to begin with. The buffet table was still in place, but the food had been on the warm-cycle for more than a few hours and appeared to have developed some dried crust over everything. Heidi was flitting back and forth between a couple of small groups and Zipper Head the bartender.

I was bored out of my mind, and even though the people-watching was great, it was beginning to get old.

Twenty-five

Swindle made a beeline for the bar the moment she entered the room. At first, I thought she might be okay. Now close up, she appeared higher than a kite with wide, unblinking eyes and dilated pupils that glared at everyone in the room. “Hey, where’s the action?” she asked.

She sniffled as she rubbed her nose back and forth and then drained the top third of her drink. It looked an awful lot like bourbon on the rocks. I prayed it was ice tea.

“Where’s the action? I don’t think there is any, Swindle. Tommy and Gino haven’t bothered to show. Half the folks have already left, and the other half will leave about ten seconds after the bar closes. The food has been slow cooking under those heat lights for the past three or four hours, so I’d stay away from that.”

“We gotta get this place moving, get some action going. There should be a band playing or something. This sucks big time,” she said, then took another gulp.

“Maybe the band is waiting for Tommy and Gino to show up. Or maybe they just canceled.”

Swindle kept moving around, shifting her weight, looking here and there, unable to remain still. She downed the remainder of her drink in one massive pour, shuddered a moment, then handed me her empty.

"Get me another I'm gonna get this place moving. This is total dullsville," she said, then staggered across the room to the stairway.

"Working friend of yours?" Heidi said in my ear.

"No, actually, my date," I replied.

"Oh, Dev. I'm sorry I didn't mean—"

"Relax, it's a business deal. She's a client."

"You're working for hookers?" she said.

"I better get her drink refilled. Need anything?"

"No, moderation is the key."

I walked over to the bar. Zipper Head was still there. "I need a Summit, and this was Swindle's, so whatever she was drinking, I guess."

She handed me my Summit, then filled a glass with ice and free-poured a large amount of Grey Goose vodka over the cubes.

"Actually, I think Swindle was drinking bourbon," I said.

"Yeah, you're right, she was." She emphasized the word "was." "But she always likes to mix things up. She usually starts with a white wine, then a shot or two of something strange, followed by bourbon, vodka, and then a gin martini. She finishes up with tequila shots if she can make it that far. Usually, there's some extra-curricular stuff in-between." She winked.

"Sounds absolutely lethal."

"That's Swindle," she said and smiled.

My client, I thought. And I was supposed to watch her? She didn't just need a keeper. She needed about five years in rehab and a team of social workers.

"Oh, oh," Zipper Head suddenly said under her breath.

"All right, everybody, let's get it going tonight. Come on, put your hands together, and start clapping."

I turned round to see Swindle with a cordless mike, circling in the center of the room. Biker was quickly setting up a sound system or something behind her, looking very flustered.

"Come on, clap with me, you bastards. Give me the clap." She giggled, shook her hips, raised her hands over her head, and clapped. A couple of the women followed suit, beginning to dance in place. Most of the guys looked toward the door.

A moment later, Biker gave her the thumbs up then quickly fled the scene.

"God, I better have another," Heidi said, coming alongside and slamming her glass on the bar.

"Come on, you pricks, let it all hang out," Swindle shouted and pulled her blouse out from her little leather skirt. That brought a couple of the guys moving in closer and joining in the clapping.

"Better make it a double," Heidi said to Zipper Head.

Swindle had made her way to the corner where Biker had set up the sound system. She stepped on a foot switch, and a light down by her feet suddenly flashed on, illuminating a section of the wall and the painting hanging behind her.

I feared the worst.

Music started to blare across the room's sound system, and suddenly, Swindle was in the throws of singing Karaoke. I don't know if it speaks to my broad range of interests or one of my many bad sides. I recognized the song. Actually, it wasn't all that tough because the title was momentarily illuminated up on the wall. Then the words to the song began to scroll across the painting of a dark-haired naked woman holding a strategically placed bottle of liquor. None of this seemed to bother Swindle as she burst, horribly off-key, into the chorus. "I just want to make…love to you."

Theoretically, she was shaking her hips in time to the beat, although she never really found it— the beat. The music stopped for a moment, and more than a little applause ensued.

"Give me another," Heidi said and drained her glass.

"You better take it easy, Heidi."

"Make that a double," she said and glared at me.

Swindle was on to the next tune, 'Rocket Queen.' Sadly, I recognized it. Everyone crazy enough to still be in the room was forming a large circle around her. Well, except for those fleeing toward what little refuge the bar provided.

"I've got a tongue like a razor," Swindle slurred and staggered a couple of steps, which just seemed to encourage the crowd.

"God, that's fucking dreadful," Heidi shouted then followed with a healthy sip.

"...but then you'll do whatever I like." Swindle roared off-key, staggering in a circle, all the while pointing at various individuals in the crowd.

From out of nowhere, someone handed her a drink. It looked like a martini. At least it was in a stemmed glass and clear. She downed the thing, spilling quite a bit across her chest in the process. That seemed to be a cause for more applause. Thankfully, some guy grabbed her empty glass just as she wound up to throw it against the wall.

Thirty minutes later and the bar was three deep with people trying to inoculate themselves. What may have been funny for the first few minutes had turned into a marathon of bad taste and off-key shouting. Swindle was in her element, an absolute mess. She'd torn her blouse open two or three songs ago and was displaying four thousand dollars worth of surgical implant expertise.

She'd completely lost the beat and was about four measures behind ACDC. "Taking more than her share, had me fighting for air, she told me to come, but I was already there."

"Dev, I'm really drunk, and I'm gonna need a little bitty ride home. But right now, you better yank the microphone away from that bitch, or someone is going to beat her over the head with it," Heidi slurred. She might have been standing too close, glassy-eyed and weaving, but she still made a lot of sense.

I approached the thinning crowd surrounding Swindle. It was largely made up of people about as far gone as she was. I stepped into the ring, gently took the microphone from her, then held on to her so she wouldn't fall as she blindly staggered three or four steps.

"Ladies and gentlemen, the fabulous Swindle Lawless," I said into the microphone.

A couple of drunks actually started to applaud, although it may have been because I'd grabbed the microphone. Swindle took a deep bow then seemed to go limp, and suddenly, she did an Amy Winehouse on me. I half hoisted her over my shoulder and carried her out the door.

Once I made it downstairs, and out of the stairwell, I set her on the nearest barstool. No one seemed to pay any attention to us. Swindle was clearly out cold. I fastened two buttons on her blouse, so she wasn't completely on display then ran back up the stairs to get Heidi.

"Heidi, we gotta go. I got Swindle downstairs passed out at the bar."

"God, thank you for taking that awful thing away."

"The microphone?"

"No, Swindle." Heidi giggled then sipped some more. I wasn't sure she could see me through her glazed eyes.

"Come on. We gotta go."

"But I just got this drink."

"I was going to make you a special one at home. Okay?"

"Oh, you're so sweet," she said. She gave me a quick kiss, then staggered back a step and glared a look that suggested there was a lot more available.

"Come on, Honey, we gotta go," I pleaded.

She grasped her drink in one hand and followed me to the stairway.

Fortunately, Swindle was still passed out on her stool. Someone had stuffed a couple of dollar bills in her cleavage, and all the buttons on her blouse were undone again, but other than that, she seemed okay.

"Heidi, can you follow us out? I've got to carry her."

Heidi nodded and sipped her drink.

"Leave your drink here. I don't want to get nailed driving with your drink in the car."

Heidi gave me a noncommittal nod. I hoisted Swindle up over my shoulder, and we headed out the door. Swindle was clearly comatose. Her arms dangled limp and lifeless toward the floor. Her leather skirt had ridden up above her hips, exposing the hint of a very small red silk thong. Heidi staggered behind me with one hand tucked into my belt and the other holding her stupid Green Fairy drink.

As we walked out, some guy coming in the door slapped Swindle across her exposed rear. "Man, you are one lucky son-of-a-bitch," he said and kept moving. I couldn't do anything except hope I would make it to the Fleetwood.

I leaned Swindle against the side of my car, opened the rear door for Heidi, and stuffed Swindle into the front passenger seat.

"Heidi, give me that thing," I said, then took her drink and set it on the sidewalk. She tumbled into my car, then sat back and closed her eyes. They were both snoring by the time I was buckled up. It suddenly dawned on me I had no idea where Swindle lived. We hadn't brought her purse out of the Tutti Frutti Club, and I wasn't going to go back in and get the thing. I put the car in drive and headed toward Heidi's house.

Twenty-six

I tip-toed back into the bedroom and laid my towel on the chair. I proceeded to dress as quietly as possible. Sometime during the ten minutes I was in the shower, Swindle had rolled over and was now spooning behind Heidi, arms wrapped around her, squeezing Heidi's boobs in either hand.

My belt buckle clanged against the chair as I pulled on my trousers, and Heidi wrinkled her nose a little. She moaned softly and ran a hand down Swindle's hip. Her eyelids suddenly popped open like she'd just discovered something very wrong. Her eyes grew very wide as she first focused on me standing in front of her and then the hands with sparkly-red nail polish visibly squeezing. She rocketed out of the bed, picked up her pillow, and hit Swindle over the head.

"What in the hell do you think you're doing?" she screamed.

"Hey, Heidi, easy, she was sound asleep," I said and grabbed the pillow out of her hands.

"She was feeling me up," she screamed.

Swindle began to blink herself into semi-consciousness.

"She was asleep, Heidi. I'm sure she didn't mean to."

"I get five-hundred for a three-way, that's two-fifty apiece," Swindle groaned, then sat up and coughed her smoker's hack.

"You perv," Heidi screamed and pushed me. She ripped the pillow out of my hands and hit Swindle with it again.

"Get out of my bed, you slut," she screamed.

"Oh, for Christ sake, I'm moving, I'm moving. Quit the damn screaming, God, my head," Swindle groaned. "What do you got to drink?"

"Get out!"

"Look, I'll give you two a discount, four hundred even," Swindle croaked, then crawled off the bed and strode into the bathroom, coughing.

"You pervert, get the hell out of my house and take that witch with you," Heidi said, turning on me.

"Nothing even happened. Will you just calm down?"

"Nothing happened? You drugged me, you perv. God, I don't even remember driving home."

"I didn't drug you. You were drinking those Green Fairy things like they were water. You did it to yourself, Heidi. And by the way, I drove home."

We heard the toilet flush and then Swindle strode out of the bathroom and stood in front of us, scratching herself. For the first time, I noticed the sunburst tattoo surrounding her navel.

"Where the hell are my clothes? Hey." She raised her eyebrows at Heidi. "Half price before noon. Want to?" she said and nodded toward the bed then started to cackle, which quickly turned into a phlegm-filled coughing jag. "Where'd you hide my damn cigarettes, Knockers?"

Heidi held the pillow up in front of her to modestly hide her body. "Dev," she whined.

"Ladies, nothing happened. We all went to sleep. Okay?"

"Oh my God," Heidi moaned.

"Please, shut the fuck up. My damn head is killing me here," Swindle said then began to crawl back into bed.

"Get out of my house. Both of you get out!" Heidi screamed.

Swindle curled into a semi-fetal position in the middle of the bed, up on all fours with her hands covering her ears. "I ain't going anywhere until you give me my damn clothes," she groaned.

I thought they might be in the living room and headed in that direction. I was wrong. They were scattered down the hallway. By the time I returned to the bedroom, Heidi had put a robe on and was attempting to pull the sheets off the bed. Swindle was still curled up on top.

"Swindle, put these clothes on while I try and find your shoes," I said.

"And get off my bed," Heidi yelled.

I went back down the hallway, walking through the living room to the front door. Heidi's latex corset was on the floor next to the front door. I scanned the front steps and sidewalk through the living room window. I could see one high heel lying in the grass out on the boulevard by the Fleetwood.

"Your shoes are out by the car. Come on, let's go," I said, returning to the bedroom.

Swindle had her skirt twisted around her waist. Her blouse was pulled on but unbuttoned. "I need a cigarette," she growled.

Heidi held a bundle of bed linen in her arms. "I'm going to burn these and then get checked to see if I need shots," she said and glared at me.

"I still need to get paid. That's two…"

"Yeah, right, Swindle, we get it. Two apiece. Come on, let's get going. Heidi, I'll call you later," I said, trying to escape before I was murdered.

"Don't bother and just get out. I'll have to fumigate this room once I take a scalding shower."

"You didn't find my cigarettes? God, I hate it when this shit happens," Swindle groaned and ran her hand through her hair.

"Dev," Heidi growled. I knew her well enough to realize her short fuse had been lit.

"We're going. We're going. Come on, Swindle, maybe button up," I said, heading for the front door.

"Your boyfriend here good for your share?" Swindle asked.

"Get out of my house, you whore. Get the hell out!" Heidi shrieked.

I didn't waste any more time and headed out the front door.

Barefoot Swindle was right behind me.

Heidi pushed Swindle onto the front stoop then quickly slammed the door behind us.

"God, my head," Swindle groaned, then shouted, "I'm coming back to collect your two hundred if lover-boy here ain't good for it."

"Come on, Swindle, get in," I said, holding the car door. "And pick up that shoe." I nodded my head in the direction of the shoe on the boulevard.

"That thing ain't mine."

"Then it must be Heidi's."

"That bitch, the one who wouldn't stop screaming?" Swindle asked, then picked up the high heel and threw it into the middle of the street.

"Come on, don't be that way."

"You buying me breakfast? I'm starving," she said and climbed into the Fleetwood.

"I'll buy you breakfast if you promise to button your blouse." I climbed in behind the wheel and caught sight of Heidi's purple and red skunk wig in the corner of my back seat.

We couldn't go to a restaurant because Swindle's shoes weren't in the car, and no one would serve us while she was barefoot. I drove over to the Tutti Frutti Club, hoping to see if we could claim her purse. The place wasn't open, but using my phone, Swindle was able to get in touch with someone on the cleaning crew, who let us in.

I searched the upstairs party room for her purse while Swindle stepped behind the bar and made herself a Bloody Mary.

"I don't see it up there. Maybe there's a lost and found or someplace where they put things that get left here. What are you doing?" I asked.

"I'm on the liquid diet," Swindle said, then set her drink down and tore open a fresh pack of cigarettes. "Oh, will you calm down, they can put it on my tab, Jesus. Hey, look, I'm going to hang here and relax for a bit. You can take off if you want."

I nodded, turned, and headed for the door.

"Don't forget you still owe me," she called after me.

Twenty-seven

My phone woke me late that afternoon. I'd been napping on the couch for three or four hours.

"Haskell Invest—"

"Dev, where the hell have you been?"

"Louie? I'm home. It's kind of a long story, late-night and all. I was babysitting."

"Babysitting? Maybe I don't want to know."

"Believe me. You don't."

"Look, meet me down at the main cop shop."

"Now? Why?"

"The cops picked up Swindle Lawless. I'm going to represent her and they're asking for you, too."

"Swindle? What's the charge, solicitation?"

"No, and don't joke Dev. They're looking at assault."

"Assault? Who is she supposed to have assaulted?"

"Dudley Rockett."

"Her agent?"

"Former agent."

"When did this happen?"

"I guess within the last day and a half. I don't have much information right now."

"Well, if it was last night, she was with me at the victory party that never happened. Probably got a hundred witnesses at least. From there, she was with me, well, and Heidi."

"That may be why your presence has been requested."

"Probably. I'm sure I'm her alibi."

"No, Dev, the police want to talk to you, too. They said you were a person of interest."

"Me?"

"Look, just meet me down there in that parking lot across the street. Do not go in until I get there. I'll be leaving in a few minutes."

"Okay, let me get cleaned up."

"Don't screw around here, Dev. I've got to represent Swindle, and I don't need you stopping somewhere for a couple of beers on the way over."

"Louie…"

"Just get cleaned up and get down there."

"Okay, okay."

Twenty-eight

I needn't have hurried. I parked in the far corner of the parking lot and hoped no one spotted me. I sat in the Fleetwood, waiting for close to forty-five minutes before Louie's faded blue Geo Metro rumbled into the lot.

The lot was supposed to have been repaved a couple of years ago. But as a result of city-wide budget cuts, it was pretty much just sand, gravel, and potholes, a whole lot of potholes. Louie seemed to find just about every one of them as he bounced and banged to the far corner where I was parked.

He looked reasonably good as he climbed out of the car. Good, at least for Louie. He wore a pin-striped suit coat, only moderately wrinkled, and pin-striped trousers. On closer examination, the pin-stripes on the trousers and coat didn't quite match.

"Nice job, I'm guessing you got another suit like that at home."

"What?"

"The stripes, they don't match up. The ones on your coat are thicker than the ones on your trousers."

"Whatever." Louie shrugged. "Listen, they mentioned you as a person of interest. Please tell me you can account for your activities last night, and you've got witnesses."

"We're in luck. I was with none other than Swindle from the courthouse yesterday until about ten-thirty this morning. And we were at that so-called victory party for Gino D'Angelo. A lot of people saw us there. I left with Swindle and Heidi, so both of us are covered."

"Swindle and Heidi?"

"They'd both been over-served, so I drove them home."

"Mmm-mmm." Louie nodded like it made sense. If Detective Manning was involved, I knew things were going to be pushed a lot further than just a nod.

"What was up with Gino? How did that deal shake out?" I asked.

"He's out on bail and wearing an ankle bracelet now, but it was close to one in the morning before we got him out. Tommy was ready to kill just about anyone and everyone."

"Careful how you say that," I cautioned.

Louie nodded.

"What was the charge? Attempted murder of Dudley Rockett?"

"Yeah, I think they were just yanking his chain. Sounds like a business misunderstanding that went bad. Rockett apparently filed a charge or something."

"Gee, join the club. Sounds like Rockett's filing charges against everyone," I scoffed.

"Yeah, well, you're Swindle's alibi, and you got witnesses to corroborate, so, all in all, it's turning out to be a pretty good day."

"Maybe for you. I'm never too excited to be called down here."

"I think we got a pretty air-tight defense, Dev. Just answer truthfully, and we should be out of here in short order. Let's get in there. The sooner we get started, the sooner—"

"You just watch my back. You know Manning isn't the biggest fan."

We were ushered up to the fourth floor and left to sit in one of the interrogation rooms for close to an hour. I could feel Manning's hand in all this and figured he was probably watching us through the mirror, hoping to see me break down in some tearful confession to Louie. Even though I had nothing to hide, I was still worried. I thought one of Manning's unfulfilled goals in life was to see me resting comfortably behind bars for a very long time.

At about the one hour mark, the door burst open, and Manning bubbled in, followed by a uniform and a plain-clothes woman. The uniform remained against the door. The plain-clothes woman took the seat next to Manning and then sat there looking like a pissed off grade school principal.

"Gentlemen, sorry to keep you waiting. Busy, busy, busy," Manning chirped. He attacked the ever-present wad of gum, viciously biting the thing like some red-faced mad dog. The top of his bald head glistened pink. His blue eyes shone like lasers that seemed directed at me.

"How are we doing?" He smiled and looked from me to Louie, then back at me for a long stare.

I was determined not to say anything if I could help it. His cheery attitude did not bode well for my options. I gave him a polite nod then just held his stare.

He set his Maalox bottle on the corner of the table, opened a file, and said, "Let the record show that..." He read off a series of form lines listing himself, Detective Clara Gutnacht, the uniformed officer, Louie, and me as present. Then he stated that we were there of our own free will, etc., etc. Of course, if I'd protested in any way, it would have been a strike against me, so I sat there quietly and waited for the other shoe to drop.

I didn't have to wait long.

"Mr. Haskell, at this time, you are not being charged and let the record state again that you and council are here of your own free will. There are a couple of items we think you might be able to help us clear up."

I was focused on the previous day, reviewing in my mind everything from when I arrived at the courthouse with Louie until this afternoon when I left Swindle drinking behind the bar at the Tutti Frutti Club. At no time was I ever out of sight of someone who could vouch for me. There wasn't a five-minute block of time when I could have made it to my car, let alone drive somewhere to harass Dudley Rockett, then somehow drive back and not be missed. I was just thinking of how I could come up with the guest list from Gino's disastrous victory party when Manning got my attention.

"Do you know a gentleman named Gary Ruggles?" Manning asked.

I was so focused on Dudley Rockett I had to have the question repeated.

"Excuse me?"

"Gary Ruggles, do you know him?"

It was ringing a distant bell, but my mind was still in the Dudley Rockett universe.

"No, I don't think I do. At least, I don't recall anyone by that name at this time." I added that last bit just as a safety net. Who said you couldn't learn something from watching sleazy congressmen on TV?

"Have you ever known or had dealings with a woman named Melissa Marie Ruggles?"

"No, not that I'm aware of. To the best of my knowledge at this time."

Manning's eyes seemed to sparkle. Clara what's-her-name blinked.

I was wondering what the hell? Then all of a sudden, things started to sink in.

Manning grinned at me like he was reading my thoughts, which wasn't very hard to do just now.

"Wait a minute, Detective. I know, or rather knew a Bunny Ruggles. We had a brief acquaintance. If it's the same person, I didn't recognize her name when you said, Melissa Marie. Not to get too far ahead of things here, but you were at my office a few days ago and wanted to examine my vehicle. I believe this was in relation to a hit and run accident I stated I knew nothing about. I believe you said Gary Ruggles was the victim."

"And you still stand by your earlier statement that you have no firsthand knowledge of the accident involving Mr. Ruggles?"

"I do stand by my earlier statement. The only knowledge I have is a news report I heard on the radio and a brief newspaper article I read online just after you left my office the other day."

Manning made a note in the open file in front of him. Clara sat next to him and didn't blink.

"How brief was your acquaintance with Mrs. Ruggles?"

"Very brief."

"Define very brief. Does that mean a year, a month, or did you just meet at a church function?" he asked, then smiled.

A principle tenet of law. Never ask a question you don't already know the answer to. I thought I had better be truthful.

"We met for an evening."

"An evening. Where?"

"A concert, actually, and then we got together at an establishment over in the Como area."

"An establishment…do you mean a bar?"

"Yes."

"And the name of this establishment?"

Here we go, I thought. "The establishment is a bar called Charlie's."

"Hmm-mmm, interesting."

"If you're suggesting it's interesting because that's the same place her husband was drinking the night he was killed in a hit and run, you're correct. But the coincidence stops there. You examined my car, there was not then, nor is there now, any damage relating to a hit and run accident on my vehicle. And, as a matter of fact, if you're interested, I was with another individual on the night in question, a Miss Candi Slaughter. We were at my home until the following—"

"Have you driven any other vehicle in the past ten days, Mr. Haskell?"

"No, no, I have not."

Suddenly, there it was, looming up on the distant horizon, Swindle's purple convertible. The Miata with the smashed front end and the scrapes along the passenger side. I wondered how much Manning knew.

"Mr. Haskell, are you acquainted with a woman by the name of Swindle Lawless?"

He knew more than me.

"Yes, I am. She is a nominal client of mine. Now that you mention it, I did drive her car yesterday. If you'll recall, I was in the courthouse hall when you and a number of officers arrested Mr. Gino D'Angelo. Miss Lawless left with me. We took her car, and I drove. I parked her car in the parking lot of The Spot bar. I took her to dinner and then to the Tutti Frutti Club."

"And her vehicle is still at The Spot Bar?"

"As far as I know. We couldn't find her purse when it was time to go home last night. Miss Lawless didn't seem to have a spare set of keys, and she appeared to possibly be a bit over-served."

I wasn't sure, but I thought I heard a door slam from behind the two-way mirror. It really didn't matter. I had more than enough on my plate just now.

"You took her out to dinner, really? Where did the two of you dine?"

"Dine?"

"Yes, where did you take her to dinner?"

"McDonald's, I guess."

"You guess?" Manning raised an eyebrow and shook his head. He seemed to be enjoying my discomfort.

"McDonald's," I said.

"Define nominal client," Manning said.

"Just that, a client of Mr. Laufen's here." I nodded at Louie, sitting next to me. "He asked me to look into a matter involving Miss Lawless and a former business agent."

"And that agent would be?"

"A gentleman named Dudley Rockett."

"Hmm-mmm, that seems to ring a bell," Manning said and then slowly, deliberately pawed through a series of forms in the file. He seemed to be softly humming to himself.

"Ah, yes, here it is, Dudley Rockett. Is that the same Dudley Rockett who filed this restraining order against you?" he asked and held up a copy of the restraining order against me, pointing to a signature that read Dudley Rockett.

"Possibly. I mean, it's a common name."

"And most likely not the only restraining order filed against you. If I recall, weren't you incarcerated for an evening recently? Was it something to do with your harassment of Mr. Rockett? Do I recall a resisting-arrest charge somewhere in there, too?"

"Come on, Manning cut the bullshit. You jacked up the paperwork, so I had to spend the night here under your loving care. We discussed it in this very room the next day. I should have filed charges against you guys and the city. I pay taxes just like—"

"May I speak with my client privately for a moment," Louie interrupted as he stepped on my foot under the table.

"Yeah, sure. I'm going to get a cup of coffee. Either of you care for one?" Manning asked.

"No, thanks," I said. Louie just shook his head and waited until the door closed behind them, so we were alone in the room.

Then he looked at me and asked, "What the fuck are you doing Dev?"

"I'm doing what you told me. I'm telling him the truth."

"No, you're not. You're giving him a lecture, you idiot. You were screwing that Ruggles guy's wife? Shit. And I gotta tell you, that line about driving Swindle's car just yesterday sounds pretty damn bogus. If you want me to help you, Dev, you have got to work with me, not against me."

"Louie, I never even met Swindle until yesterday. As for that guy's wife, it was a one-nighter. I didn't know she was married. There I am trying to regain my strength in her bed, minding my own business, and she kicks me out just before he walks into the bedroom. I had to hide under the damn bed for about a week. Then sneak out of the place once he fell asleep. Hell, she picked me up, not the other way around. I haven't seen her since that night."

"Oh, God. You complete, absolute idiot. Look, whatever you do, don't bring the D'Angelos or Joey Cazzo into this. It won't help your cause one damn bit, and it's bound to screw things up for me."

"What? Now I'm supposed to lie to Manning to cover those creeps?"

"No, now you're supposed to use the pea-sized brain inside that thick skull of yours."

Twenty-nine

Manning stuck his gleaming pink head back into the room. "Hope I'm not interrupting. All right to come in and pick up where we left off?"

Louie nodded.

Manning seemed barely able to contain himself and began rifling questions before he'd even sat down.

"I believe we were discussing Mr. Rockett. How well do you know him?"

"I think I saw him once or twice from a distance, but I have never actually spoken to him. At least that I know of."

"Ever been in his home?"

"No."

"What about his office?"

"I didn't even know he had one. To the best of my knowledge, I've never been there," I said.

Manning nodded, but then seemed to switch gears.

"So, Swindle Lawless, your client. I thought she was an item with your friend Joey Cazzo?"

"If you say so. He's not really my friend. I was just doing him a little favor," I said and shrugged.

“Oh. I see, a little favor for someone you really don’t know? How very nice,” Manning said, nodding like it all made perfect sense.

I could hear Louie give an exasperated exhale.

“Miss Lawless mentioned to us that you owe her a five hundred dollar debt. Is that correct?” Manning asked.

Louie turned to look at me as his mouth dropped open.

I looked stunned and couldn’t think of anything to say.

“Mr. Haskell? The matter of five hundred dollars owed to Miss Lawless? Was she correct about that amount?”

“I think she’s mistaken. I’ll have to check with her.”

“Not a problem on this end, Mr. Haskell. I’m sure it was a simple good faith arrangement on your part, and she just probably misunderstood,” Manning said. “Of course, I hate to be the bearer of bad news. But, I believe she suggested she was planning to file rape charges against you.”

“I don’t know anything about that.”

“Probably just another misunderstanding then. I’m sure once she completes the rape examination, any questions will be cleared up. They’re very efficient and thorough.” Manning flashed a predatory grin.

Louie shook his head and let loose a frustrating exhale. From underneath the table, he gave me the finger.

"Now, Mr. Haskell, can you account for your whereabouts between the hours of nine o'clock last night and ten o'clock this morning?"

"Yes, I was at the Tutti Frutti Club until maybe midnight. I drove a friend home, Heidi Bauer. At approximately ten the following morning, I drove Miss Lawless to the Tutti Frutti Club to look for her purse. She decided to remain there, and I returned to my home until my attorney, Mr. Laufen, phoned, and told me that I should come down here for this interview."

"I see." Manning nodded and flipped a page in the open file in front of him. "You drove Miss Bauer home. Had she been drinking?"

"Yes."

"Were you drinking?"

"I may have had a beer, possibly two, over the course of five hours."

"Only two beers, that is very commendable. So you acted as the sober cabdriver for Miss Bauer. That pretty much it?"

"Yes."

"Would you state you weren't under the influence at any time during the evening?"

"Yeah."

"And Miss Bauer, she was perhaps not in the best of shape to drive. Would that be a fair statement?"

"Yes, it would. In fact, she slept on the way home."

Louie stepped on my foot under the table.

"Passed out?"

"I don't know, it may have been a long day, and she was just tired."

"I see. And Miss Lawless?"

"Miss Lawless?"

"She seems to think she may have been hired by the two of you for the purpose of a bit of late-night sexual entertainment."

"Yes, I mean no. She wasn't hired, but come to think of it, she was in the car."

"I see. Did she end up in bed with you and Miss Bauer?"

"I believe she may have slept there, yes."

"In the same bed?"

"Well, yes, but nothing happened."

"Was she clothed?"

"Not exactly."

"Would you care to elaborate on 'not exactly'?"

"She may have removed some of her clothing."

"Care to define some?"

"Maybe all."

"I see, so she was naked?"

"Yes, pretty much."

"Were either you or Miss Bauer wearing clothes?"

"I…I don't think so."

Manning flipped a couple more pages and pulled out a pink sheet from the file. "Based on our toxicology report, the levels of alcohol and cocaine still in Miss Lawless' blood workup approached the lethal level. Interesting. It sounds like she was severely drugged, forced to consume a large quantity of alcohol, and then raped, repeatedly. What do you think?"

"I don't have any idea what you're talking about."

"And yet you admit to being naked in the same bed with both Miss Lawless and Miss Bauer. Is that correct?"

"Yes, but…"

Louie placed a hand on my wrist to quiet me.

"I never realized you could muster up so much restraint, Mr. Haskell. One for the books." Manning smiled, but his eyes betrayed his mood.

"Is Mr. Haskell being charged with rape? You know as well as I do there may be some questions regarding the character of Miss Lawless. The fact that she remained in a drinking establishment after Mr. Haskell last saw her certainly suggests she may have consumed more alcohol and possibly other substances after his departure. It would seem your toxicology report is therefore, null and void. At least, in relation to my client."

"Perhaps," Manning said.

"You know it is, Detective. Unless you have something more besides a blood sample with levels of alcohol and cocaine from an individual you picked up in a bar, I think you're grasping at straws. Thus far, the only crime my client would appear to be guilty of is providing an impaired individual a safe place to spend the night."

"In the same bed with another individual and your client, who proceeded to rape her." Manning shot back.

"Let's see what the evidence says."

"We intend to do just that," Manning said and closed the file.

"Are we free to go?" Louie asked.

"Maybe just a couple more questions," Manning said, and then held his hand out as crabby Clara Gutnacht seemed to pull another file out of nowhere.

Thirty

We were out in the parking lot, talking. It was dark by now. Louie was seated in his car with the door open while I was standing in a pot hole. We'd been in the interrogation room for four or five hours. My head was pounding, and Louie was pissed off, really pissed off.

"I don't know, you tell me. I finally get a dream client, the D'Angelos. So many legal problems they'll never find their way out of the court system. I got Joey Cazzo, a creep, I admit, but the bastard tells me everything I have to do and pays for the privilege. I can work part-time and make full-time money, and somehow you, in just twenty-four hours, have managed to fuck everything up."

"Louie, I'm telling you I didn't do anything."

"I don't know, maybe you've heard this before, but you never do anything. It's never your fault. It's always someone else. Guess what? I'm the poor bastard up to his neck in shit. Your shit! You better get this mess cleaned up and fast, Dev."

"Louie, I—"

"No. The first thing you are going to do is pay Swindle the five hundred for the three-way."

"I never touched her. There wasn't any three-way. We all just went to sleep."

"I don't care. Look, Dev, make it go away. Figure it out, douche nozzle. If this charge remains, me or someone else unfortunate enough to represent you is gonna ream your ass for a good fifteen hundred in legal fees just to deal with this mess, and that's just for starters. So your best option is to pay her five hundred bucks, make the charge go away, and consider yourself a thousand bucks ahead of the game."

"Louie, don't you think—"

"No, Dev, you're not thinking. Next thing you do, you better find out if Swindle's car was involved in that hit and run. I'll lay you odds they towed that thing from The Spot once you cleverly told them where it was parked, and they're tearing the God damned thing apart piece-by-piece right now."

"Maybe she picked it up and—"

"You dropped her off at the Tutti Frutti Club around noon. That's where they picked her up later in the afternoon. Do you really think she stopped the party to go get her car like any normal, responsible adult? We're talking Swindle Lawless here, Dev. You had better find her, figure out a way to land on her good side, and make this mess disappear before it gets any worse."

"Her good side? You mean she has one?"

"You'd know better than me. You were the one in bed with her. No," Louie said, holding up his hand. "Don't say another word. Now, the next little bit of a problem is Dudley Rockett. You better figure something out on that deal and fast. The restraining order Rockett filed against you does not help. Anything happens to him. Manning is going to come after you full speed."

"Louie, all I did was—"

"No, I don't want to hear it," he said, then slammed his car door. He turned the ignition, lowered the window, and yelled, "All you did was fuck things up royally. Get them fixed, pronto. Oh, and I want chocolate donuts tomorrow morning." With that, his car belched a cloud of black exhaust. I had to jump out of the pothole to avoid being run over as he raced away.

"God damn, Swindle," I swore, as Louie's taillights bounced across the potholes and a cloud of dust and exhaust drifted over me.

Thirty-one

So much for my legal representation. I thought it might be a better idea if I called Heidi and asked her to maybe make a phone call on my behalf. I figured she could sign a statement to the effect we didn't participate in any sexual activity with Swindle. At least, it was a start.

"Hi, Heidi, Dev."

I figured the call must have dropped because I didn't hear anything.

"Hello? Hello, Heidi?"

"Funny, I was just about to call you."

"Oh, look, sorry about the way things worked out this morning. I didn't have Swindle's address. She didn't have her keys. I couldn't just leave her at the Tutti Frutti Club last night and—"

"So you decided to drug the two of us and bring us both into my bed? In my bedroom? You absolutely horrible, disgusting sleaze ball," she screamed.

"Heidi, that's not what happened."

"Oh, really? Gee, must have been my imagination playing tricks on me. I guess there wasn't another naked woman squeezing my boobs this morning. I guess you weren't there watching and enjoying the whole thing."

"Well, that wasn't really what was going on. She just —"

"I guess I misunderstood her when she said we owed her five hundred dollars. I guess the detective who phoned this afternoon and asked me to come down tomorrow morning at nine for an interview called the wrong Heidi Bauer."

"Manning phoned you?"

"How could you, you pervert? And after all I've done for you. The times I bailed you out. All the times we—"

"Heidi, will you calm down. Hey, look, I know is Swindle is a little crazy."

"Listen, you jerk, she's gift-wrapped garbage. A little crazy? She's certifiably nuts and apparently underpaid. You're gonna pay a lot more than five hundred to have your worthless butt in my bed ever again." Click.

"Hello? Heidi, did we get disconnected? Hello."

That hadn't exactly gone my way. I checked my contact list. Fortunately, I'd been enough on the ball to put Swindle's number in there, so I phoned her.

"The subscriber you have contacted is unable to accept calls at this time." Meaning idiot Swindle hadn't paid her phone bill. I phoned Candi.

"Hello."

"Hi, Candi, Dev."

There was a long pause, but at least she wasn't screaming when she said, "Sounds like you've been a busy boy."

"Let's just say it hasn't been my best day. You working?"

"Yeah, been here for a while. I guess I just missed the police hauling Swindle away."

"What did you hear?" I asked.

"Well, knowing Swindle, I'm sure she didn't go quietly. Anyway, she went down to the police station, and from what I understand, she apparently filed charges against you."

"That's just a big misunderstanding," I said.

"All I know is, she filed charges. After that, the thing apparently takes on a life of its own."

"I'll say. No good deed goes unpunished."

"You mean your three-way?"

"There was no three-way, Candi. Nothing happened, honest. I just took her to a friend's house. I couldn't leave her passed out on the street. I didn't want her at my place in case she got the wrong idea. I couldn't find you, so I took her to the safest place I could think of. God, I should have just dropped her at some fleabag hotel that rents by the hour."

"Wouldn't be the first time for her." Candi laughed.

"Is Swindle back there at the Tutti Frutti Club?"

"I think so. I saw her about a half-hour ago."

"Can you keep her there for fifteen minutes? I want to talk with her."

"I'll try, but I can't ever promise anything where she's concerned."

"I'm on my way," I said and hurried over to my car.

Thirty-two

On the way to catch Swindle at the Tutti Frutti Club, I drove past The Spot. The only sign of her purple Miata was the oil slick that had dripped onto the pavement where I'd parked it. I could only hope she found her keys and picked the thing up.

Swindle was sitting at the bar as I entered the Tutti Frutti Club. She was basically in the same spot as the last time I saw her, except now she was on the customer side of the bar. Our eyes met at the same moment, and she waved me over, looking all happy to see me.

"Hi, Dev, get you a drink?" She smiled and shrugged in a little girl kind of way.

"No, thanks, Swindle. Hey look, no offense, but what the hell is going on? You filed charges against me? I told you nothing happened between us. Not a damn thing happened with you or me or Heidi."

"Yeah, I kinda figured that out."

"You figured it out? Then why in God's name are you filing rape charges against us?"

"Five hundred bucks. That's my price. I was there for the taking. It's certainly not my fault if you couldn't take advantage of the situation. You took me to bed, so I certainly put in the time."

"You were passed out. We all were. See, we were actually doing a good deed. We took you there so you'd be safe, and you pretty much abused our kindness."

"Look, Dev, did you sleep with me? Did what's her name, the chick that kept freaking out, did she sleep with me?"

"Her name is Heidi, but that's not the point. See—"

"Actually, it's exactly the point. You slept with me, right? Both of you?"

"Yeah, I suppose, technically, but I mean we actually slept."

"There you go, five hundred bucks."

I didn't know what to say. I remembered Louie's gentle advice. *"Figure it out, douche nozzle. If this charge remains, me or someone else unfortunate enough to represent you is gonna ream your ass for a good fifteen hundred in legal fees dealing with this, and that's just for starters."*

"Could I write you a check?"

"You got a credit card?"

"You take credit cards, Swindle?"

"No, but there's an ATM back by the restrooms, and I do take cash. Let me buy you a beer while you're back there getting things organized."

"And you'll drop all the charges?"

"You bet, lover boy."

"The other thing, Swindle. In light of all this, of course, I'm going to resign from your Dudley Rockett case. Obviously, it doesn't make any sense for me to continue now."

"Whatever," she said, then sipped and shrugged like she couldn't have cared less.

On my way to the ATM, I ran into Candi.

"Hi, Dev, did you see Swindle? I told her to wait for you. She was up by the front of the bar."

"Yeah, believe me, I saw her."

"Everything okay?"

"It will be in about five hundred dollars."

"Five hundred? Whoa, must have been some night."

"Don't even go there, Candi. Nothing happened, and it wasn't supposed to happen. She lost her keys, passed out, and I couldn't just leave her."

"I would have."

"I should have. Anyway, she'll drop the charges for five hundred bucks."

"She's your client, right?"

"She was. I just told her I resigned."

"Do I feel some additional expenses coming her way on your final invoice?"

"To tell the truth, I'm not even going to invoice her. I just want to get as far away as possible from that whole crowd."

"Look, I'm off in an hour. Free tonight?" she asked.

"Free? No, but I'll charge you five hundred."

"I could probably get Swindle to join us," she said.

"Don't."

Thirty-three

I was up, showered, dressed, and about to head home when I heard the news on the flat screen in Candi's kitchen. A story described as "evolving" had a reporter standing with neighbors behind a half dozen squad cars. They were all parked outside a grey looking rambler. The place had a faded and unkempt look about it. Someone had been found dead in the home in the background, and the police were treating the circumstances as questionable.

The reporter went on to say, "An anonymous source said the deceased was found drowned in the bathtub. Amazingly, this house has gone into foreclosure and has been unoccupied for a number of months."

"Dev, quit pacing and sit down for God's sake, let me make you breakfast."

She was leaning against the granite countertop, sipping coffee and wearing a white Terrycloth robe that she hadn't bothered to tie. As enjoyable as the breakfast view was, I wanted to get to the office and Louie. I was sure Manning wasn't finished gunning for me, and I wanted to be prepared. Then there was the other problem.

"I can't sit."

"Oh, will you just calm down."

"No, it's not that," I said, nodding toward the flat screen mounted on the wall. "It was last night."

"Last night? Oh, you mean your little spanking? God, I really enjoyed that."

"Little? Yeah, you must have enjoyed yourself, but I was the guy on the receiving end."

"I didn't hear any complaints."

"Candi, you had me gagged and handcuffed."

"Don't forget the five or six Jamesons you had. You were more like passed out. You slept like the proverbial baby except for the snoring. Like I said, I didn't hear any complaints. I'd say things seemed to work out all right for you over the course of the night."

"Yeah, they did, thanks for that. Sorry to pass out, get spanked, and run, but I better meet with my lawyer. There's probably going to be more questions."

"You sure?" she said and then opened her robe a little wider and stood there, smiling at me.

"I gotta go."

"Can't keep up, can you?"

"That too."

It was more than a little uncomfortable driving to the office. I'd checked myself out earlier in Candi's bathroom mirror. The bruising on my butt looked like someone had applied zebra stripes. I noticed a pink rectangle over my mouth where Candi must have applied the duct tape. Not pretty.

* * *

"Man, thanks for doing that, and thanks for these, too," Louie said, then licked the chocolate off his fingertips.

I'd shown up with chocolate doughnuts as instructed and had just finished telling him about my payment in full to Swindle and my resignation from her case.

"Like I said yesterday, it's your cheapest option. Believe me, Dev, I know nothing happened, but it'll cost you an arm and a leg to prove it. Not to mention you'd have your pal Heidi going after your scalp."

"Yeah, that's another problem I'm going to have to deal with."

"Well, charming as that may be, your bigger headache is going to be Dudley Rockett."

"I just told you, I resigned from Swindle's case last night. I'm not going to go to the guy's house, or follow him, or anything. I'm done with it. It's just better for everyone this way."

"Dev, didn't you hear?"

"Hear what?"

"They found him drowned in the bathtub of some abandoned house early this morning."

"Rockett?"

"Yeah, and with that restraining order, you can count on Manning fingering you as his main suspect numero uno."

"I was worried about that hit and run."

"Gary what's-his-name? Yeah, maybe, but with Rockett washing up on shore dead, I think you are really going to have Manning's undivided attention."

"Why does that guy have such an in for me?"

"Maybe because it's logical, and you seem to figure prominently into both circumstances. Does this ring a bell? You were with the hit and run guy's wife. What, you were just holding hands? And Rockett filed a restraining order, and now he's suddenly drowned in a bathtub. In both cases, you're floating out there, pardon the pun, not too far from the edge. Anyone with any brains would have to wonder, and even though you may not like the guy, Manning is no one's fool. By the way, I've got a call into him, Manning, but I haven't heard back."

"This is too weird. Rockett's found drowned in an abandoned house. How did they even know he was in there if the place was empty?"

"I'm gonna guess the old anonymous tip," Louie said and licked another fingertip.

"You know what the common denominator in all this is?"

"Yeah, I just told you…you."

"No. Well, yeah, but I mean the real common denominator behind the scenes is…Swindle Lawless."

"Swindle? God, Dev, she's so pickled and fried most of the time she's incapable of remembering her own name on any given day, let alone doing any of this."

"Think about it. Rockett was jacking her around, and now he's dead. And Ruggles was killed in a hit and run, and Swindle's car is all smashed up."

"Her car? That's what you're going to hang your hat on? Her car? Given that leap of faith you should be nailed as a pimp or a pusher for tooling around in that bomb you drive. And will you please sit down. You're driving me nuts standing there."

"I'm more comfortable standing right now. I think I did something to my back."

Louie looked at me for a half moment.

"And what's with your face? Either a new razor or it's time to get one. You're all pink around your mouth. You having an allergic reaction to your new love interest?"

"No, just shaved a little too close. No big deal."

Louie gave me a look like he didn't buy my excuse, then just shook his head. "Anyway, I want us to get to Manning first, offer to go down there and talk with him. At the very least, you're a person of interest. Let's show him you've got nothing to hide, and it's all just a bit of unfortunate coincidence."

With that, Louie's phone played the theme song from the movie 'Jaws'.

"Manning?" I asked.

Louie put his finger on his lips to silence me before he said, "This is Louis Laufen. I'm unable to take your call. Please leave a message, and I'll get back to you just as soon as possible." Then he made a beep sound, frowned, and set the phone down.

"Who was that?"

"Cazzo. He just yelled, *'Call me, damn it.'*"

"Maybe you should have taken the call?"

"I'd rather have him thinking I'm really busy. I'll get back to him in a bit. I always like to collect my thoughts before I talk to that guy."

Thirty-four

I got a text message from Heidi saying she was on her way home from her interview with Detective Manning at the police station, and she was in the process of blocking my phone number. Then she was going to delete me from her list of Facebook friends.

Manning phoned Louie about ten minutes after that. It was pretty much a one-sided conversation.

"I see," Louie said.

"What does he want?" I whispered.

"I see."

"Do we have to go down there?"

Louie waved me off, then turned his back and said, "No, I fully understand, Detective."

I wrote, "Did Swindle drop the rape charge?" on a note pad and passed it over to Louie.

He gave it a quick glance before he tossed the pad off to the side. "I absolutely understand, Detective, just as long as we're on the record as offering our full cooperation in your on-going investigation. I look forward to hearing from you when you've more facts, and we can help set the record straight. Yes, yes, thank you for returning my call. Fine. Yes. Goodbye."

"So, I'm off?" I asked as Louie set his cellphone on top of a stack of fake files.

"Not exactly. They're waiting for lab reports on Swindle's car and some items recovered from Rockett's house this morning. You sure you were never in the place?"

"Rockett's house? No, never. Closest I got to being inside was knocking on the front door."

"I don't know. I got the feeling they're looking at something. By the way, it sounds like your girlfriend, Heidi Bauer, was none too happy. She pled too drunk to remember but suggested you were off her radar screen forever. You're sure you weren't inside Rockett's?"

"Scout's honor."

Louie drummed his fingers on the desk, thinking for a moment. "I just have the feeling there's something we don't know. Anyone you can check with to see what they got from the Rockett crime scene? Be nice to get a clue what's up, rather than have Manning springing a surprise on us."

"I might know someone, let me check."

I remained standing and leaned against our file cabinet when I made my phone call to Krystal. She'd worked as a processor at the BCA, the state's Bureau of Criminal Apprehension. We'd dated a few years back before she dumped me for the man of her dreams and actually married the guy, but we're still on friendly speaking terms. It was Louie's turn to listen.

"Hi, Krystal, Dev Haskell, long time no talk. Yeah, I know I should have answered, but I was on a case and really going twenty-four-seven for a while. You know how it gets. What? Really? That's great. When are you due? Terrific, I'm happy for both of you. Hey, I'm wondering if you can give me any help. I'm doing a tangent investigation on a guy who— well, I think you folks might be processing some items. Name is Dudley Rockett, suspicious circumstances just this morning if it's the same guy. I don't want to screw anything up, but I'm wondering if you have any idea when that crime scene is going to be open? My client's going to subpoena files or something, and I just want to give them the word on timing, so it doesn't goof up your investigation."

"Really? No kidding." Krystal then proceeded to expound at some length, giving me the details. "Okay, I'll pass it on. Great chatting, you'll make the world's best mom. Good luck, and give my best to Bill."

"So?"

"So a couple of things...suspicious circumstances? He was beaten pretty badly and was found drowned in the bathtub."

"Could he have fallen, maybe hit his head?"

"Not a lot of folks I know bathe fully clothed with a garden hose coiled around them. Apparently, someone held his head underwater while he was kneeling on the bathroom floor."

"Not good."

"No, it seems they got an anonymous call from a neighbor around four in the morning. The front door was wide open when they got there. Their team is still processing the site. The thought is there might have been some sexual interaction that got out of hand, but she didn't go into any detail."

"You thinking what I'm thinking?" Louie asked.

"Swindle?"

"Yeah, except for the beating and drowning the guy. She strikes me as someone who can barely find her car keys on a good day, but she might be tied in somehow. Can you check her out?"

"I can try," I said. "But I'd really prefer to stay away. Trouble seems to never be too far away from her. Besides, finding her might be kind of tough. Her act never really seems to be together."

"Just see if you can track her down, and stay available just in case we hear from your friend Manning."

My phone rang. It was Heidi's number. Probably calling to apologize now that she'd calmed down a little. I could understand her being upset, but I was glad she'd seen the light.

"Hi, Heidi, are we feeling a little better, dear?"

"Shut up, you slimy piece of toilet scum. I just want you to listen to this," she screamed. There was a slight pause before something crashed or shattered.

"Heidi, are you okay?"

"Those were your flowers, you disgusting, low life rapist. How dare you think you can ply me with flowers after what you did to me. I hate you, hate you, hate you," she screamed.

"Heidi, for God's sake, calm down. What the hell are you— Hello? Heidi, hello?"

She had hung up, and I knew her well enough not to call back. I'd been on the receiving end of her temper more than a few times in the past, and the wise decision was to just give her some time. Besides, it wasn't like I didn't have enough to deal with already.

Thirty-five

I tried Swindle's phone and got the same message as the last time, "The subscriber you have contacted is unable to accept calls at this time." Swindle was probably wondering why no one phoned her, forgetting she had to occasionally pay the damn bill.

I phoned Candi.

"Hi, Dev, I knew you'd change your mind. Coming back for more?"

"Actually, as fun as that sounds. I better not." I was still unable to sit, and I felt like someone had taken a belt sander to my rear. "Hey, I was wondering if you know where I might find Swindle."

"Not another three-way." Candi laughed. "Sorry, I just couldn't resist. What? Looking for a refund?" She chuckled.

"Oh, I'm sorry, did I call the comedy club? Let me know when we get to the funny part."

"Relax, Captain Crabby. No, I don't know where Swindle is. You might try the club."

"The Tutti Frutti? I didn't think they opened until around four."

"They don't, but that's never stopped, Swindle. If you call, someone will eventually answer. Believe me, they'll know if she's there, everyone tries to keep their distance."

I phoned the Tutti Frutti Club and then listened to about three dozen rings before someone picked up. By the heavy accent, I guessed it might be a guy on the maintenance staff or cleaning crew.

"Yes."

"Hi, sorry to bother you. I'm calling to see if Swindle Lawless might be there, maybe at the bar."

"She here sleeping."

"Sleeping?"

"Si."

"Thank you…er, ah gracias," I said, then hung up and climbed into my car.

I parked next to the dumpster in back of the Tutti Frutti Club. There were two other vehicles in the small parking area. A non-descript faded red Chevy van I guessed was maybe a '97 and a spotless, gleaming black Mercedes CL600. The Mercedes rested at an angle across two parking spaces. I guess to prevent the more common folk like myself from getting too close.

The back door to the Tutti Frutti was open, and the hallway that had been dark the night I was with Heidi was brightly lit. The jail cell door at the far end of the hall was wide open, and as I approached, I heard the hum of what sounded like a vacuum cleaner.

There were two people, a man and woman, working as a cleaning crew in the bar area. The woman was vacuuming around the tables and booths, while the guy took stools down from the top of the bar then lined them up against the brass rail. They quickly glanced over at me then just as quickly returned to their work.

I approached the guy, and using my best Spanish, asked if he spoke English.

His smile suggested my best Spanish wasn't that good. "Yes," he said, then pulled the next stool off the bar and positioned it against the brass rail.

"I'm looking for a friend of mine. She told me to meet her here, Swindle Lawless."

He sized me up for a moment then pointed to a booth toward the front of the barroom. A pair of feet dangled out the end of the booth, one foot was bare while the other had a red high heel hanging from it.

"Yeah, that looks like her, thanks," I said and made my way to the front of the room. He didn't seem phased by the situation, and I had the distinct impression it wasn't the first time he'd dealt with her. I could hear Swindle's rhythmic snoring as I approached.

I grabbed her bare foot and shook it gently. She had fire-engine-red polish on her toenails and a gold ring around each one of her toes. "Swindle, hey Swindle. It's time to wake up."

She groaned and tried to kick my hand loose.

I held on tightly and shook her foot a little harder. "Swindle, come on, it's time to get up. Let's go."

She kicked her foot again and rolled forward off the booth letting off a high pitched shriek just before she hit the floor. "Ahh-hhh, God, what in the hell do you think you're doing to me?" She screamed, landing on all fours amidst paper napkins, swizzle sticks, and a cardboard bar coaster or two.

I grabbed her ankles and pulled her out from under the table. Her skirt rolled up over her waist, but she seemed oblivious and just twisted around until she was sitting on the floor. I noticed her thong matched her toe-nail polish.

"Okay, okay, damn it, enough with the dragging me. Jesus, I just closed my eyes for a minute. You don't have to…oh, you, what the hell do you want?" she said, then sucked her tongue over her teeth and smacked her lips.

I thought I'd seen her at her worst the other morning at Heidi's, but she looked a couple of rungs below that right now. Her hair was a mess, and smeared mascara formed deep rings under her eyes. It looked like blood had dripped down the front of her cream-colored blouse. She sported a black eye that had swollen and a puffy upper lip.

"Swindle, what happened? Are you okay?"

"I was until you came in and manhandled me, Jesus. Come here, help me up damn it."

"Just don't charge me, okay?"

She gave me a look suggesting she was thinking about it, but I pulled her up by her arms, anyway. She staggered a bit, but that might have been because she just had the one heel on. I looked under the booth but didn't see her missing shoe.

"You okay?" I asked again. There was crusted blood around her nostrils and, of course, the fat lip and that eye. Someone had beaten her up pretty good.

She tugged her skirt back in place then said, "I gotta pee." It seemed to be the main theme in her life.

"I'll wait for you. Then I'm gonna get you out of here. I'll look for that shoe while you're in the ladies room."

"Ladies room," she scoffed then limped off in the direction of the restrooms, still wearing just the one heel. "You could make me a Bloody Mary if you want to be useful," she called over her shoulder.

The couple on the cleaning crew shot one another a quick glance then acted as if she wasn't there. They gave the distinct impression they were familiar with Swindle, very familiar.

I found her other red heel about three booths down. I stepped behind the bar and made her a Virgin Mary, just like a Bloody, but without the alcohol, then I waited. After twenty minutes, I went to the ladies room and pushed the door open.

"Swindle, you coming out?"

"I need you to find my lipstick case. It's silver and has a little gold top. I really need it."

I remembered the lipstick case and its contents. I didn't think it was lipstick she was after.

"Come on out, I got your drink ready, and I'll look for the lipstick case while you're sipping your Bloody Mary. Come on."

That seemed to do the trick, and she hobbled out on the one heel.

"Here, slip this on. It'll make walking a lot easier," I said, handing her the missing shoe. "I've got your drink at the bar."

She slipped the shoe on and followed me to the bar. She slid onto the stool and drained a good portion of the drink in one long swallow, then smacked her lips and looked around. I noticed she hadn't bothered to clean her face.

"I'm gonna look for your purse while you finish that drink. You just sit here and do what you're doing."

"Find that lipstick case. I really need that," she pleaded.

I didn't find her purse or her damn lipstick case. I stopped looking when she slid off her stool to go around the bar and make herself a new drink.

"Swindle, come on, let's get you out of here," I said.

"Is Tommy okay with that?"

"Tommy?"

"He doesn't like me doing anything unless I check with him first."

That probably explained the shiny Mercedes in the parking lot. I had about a hundred different lectures and responses on the tip of my tongue, none of which would have been worth the effort.

"Yeah, Tommy said it was okay. He sent me," I lied.

"Did you find my lipstick case?"

"I'm thinking you left it in my car, come on."

That got her moving, and she rushed out to the rear parking lot ahead of me. By the time I got out to the parking lot, she was frantically pulling on the locked door of the Mercedes. She'd set the alarm off on the thing, but seemed oblivious to the noise.

"I can't open this damn door," she screamed, then took a half step back and attempted to kick the side of the car. She fell over in the process and bounced her head off the pavement. That either calmed her down or left her only semi-conscious. Either way, I was able to shepherd her into the front seat of my Fleetwood, buckle her seatbelt, and leave before Tommy D'Angelo or some other thug responded to the car alarm blaring from the Mercedes.

Thirty-six

We were arguing in my kitchen. I was standing, Louie was seated on a kitchen stool, and Swindle was asleep on my living room couch. "I only have one thing to say. Are you 'f'ing crazy! Dev, I love you, but this is not a good idea."

"Keep your voice down, Louie, you'll wake her."

"Let me spell it out for you, dumb-shit. You are most likely the main suspect in one and possibly two murder cases. You are hiding the other potential suspect in your damn house. She is a drunken, drug-addled, nut case, opportunistic, hooker slut who has filed rape charges against you. At the very least, she should probably be up on the psych wing of Regions Hospital, occupying a padded cell and wearing a straight jacket. But of course, you thought your living room couch made more sense."

"Louie, someone beat the shit out of her. You saw what she looks like."

"Dev, hard lesson here. It's most likely, not the first time. God, this is really going to screw things up with Cazzo and the D'Angelos if they find out."

"Cazzo and the D'Angelos? Are you kidding me? They're probably the ones who beat her up."

"You don't know that, Dev."

"Well, someone did it. She's rarely out of their sight. You heard the way that jack-ass Tommy talked to her at the courthouse the other day."

"That was a high-stress moment for everyone. Yeah, she's rarely out of their sight, except when she ends up with you for a twenty-four hour period, or apparently goes off on a bender and sleeps till noon in the back booth of a bar. Come on, she was probably drunk out of her mind, all coked up or both, and she got in a battle with the street curb or a sidewalk," Louie said.

"I don't know—"

"Stop right there. That's about the only sensible thing you've said so far. Did you ask her what happened?"

"Yeah, but she isn't sure."

"She isn't sure? Damn it, Dev, you'd better get rid of her. I'm telling you, the cops get wind of this, you might as well lock yourself up and throw away the key."

"Louie, I can't do that. She's, I don't know, vulnerable."

"She's nuts is what she is. Look, Dev, I'm speaking as a friend and as your attorney. This is a bad idea, a very, very bad idea."

From the kitchen, we could look out through the dining room to the living room window and the couch where Swindle was passed out. Much as I hated to admit it, Louie had a point.

Just then, his phone rang. He stared at me for a long moment before he pulled the cell out of his pocket.

"Oh, great, God damned perfect timing," he said, looking at the number.

"What?"

He waved me off with a glare and then answered the phone. "Hello. Oh, Detective Manning, how are things going?"

I felt the color drain from my face.

"Yes. Yes. All right, I'll have to try and locate Mr. Haskell. Can I phone you back in say a half-hour or forty-five minutes?" Louie shot me another glare.

I mouthed the word, Manning. Not so much a comment as it was an acknowledgment of my lousy luck.

"Thanks, Detective, be back to you just as soon as I locate my client, Mr. Haskell," he said, then hung up.

"Well?"

"I'm trying to think what else can go wrong," Louie said, then stared out into my living room where passed out Swindle snored. "Manning would like to chat, his words. I don't know what, but he's got something. I can just feel it."

"I don't have anything to hide, Louie."

"Jesus, Dev, except your new best friend Swindle passed out on your couch. The restraining order murdered Dudley Rockett filed and your love connection with that hit-and-run Gary something's wife."

"Ruggles."

"Did I leave anything out, miss anything?"

"Swindle's car?"

"Shit. I don't know, Dev, we need a break here."

Louie's phone suddenly went off, playing the theme from 'Jaws' again. That meant Joey Cazzo.

"Christ, not the break I was hoping for."

Thirty-seven

It was late in the afternoon— hours since Manning had called Louie. Once again, we were sitting in my favorite interrogation room. Manning had been asking a few thousand questions about my whereabouts over the past few days. Louie was seated next to me. Manning sat across from us with crabby, unsmiling Clara Gutnacht sitting statute-like next to him.

I was damned uncomfortable. It was bad enough being interrogated, *'just chatting'* as Manning liked to refer to it. But the love taps Candi had delivered with a riding crop last night were still sore as hell, and sitting on a hard plastic chair being cross-examined was doing nothing to improve my disposition.

"You stated earlier that you had never been inside Dudley Rockett's home. Is that correct, Mr. Haskell?"

"That is correct."

"And you continue to maintain you have never been inside Mr. Rockett's home?"

"That is correct."

"I believe you mentioned you had knocked on his front door once or twice."

"That's correct."

"And on one of those occasions, you placed your business card in the door, correct?"

I nodded.

"I'm sorry, as I mentioned this is all being recorded, would you be kind enough to reply with an audible response."

"Yes, that is correct."

"Any other contact at Mr. Rockett's home?"

"I spoke to the young man who started his car and backed it out of the garage."

"David Kenney," Manning added without looking at the file. He took a swig from his Maalox bottle, swallowed, and grimaced.

"Yeah, that's the kid. I think I actually spoke to him on the sidewalk in front of the neighbor's house, but it may have been in front of Rockett's house. I can't really be sure. Then one morning, after that kid started his car, I pulled my vehicle in front of Rockett's driveway in the hopes of preventing him from driving away."

"And were you successful?"

"Maybe. I sat there for a couple of hours. His car remained in the driveway. At no time did I see him. I finally concluded I was wasting my time and decided to return to my office."

"What time would that have been?"

"I believe I returned to my office sometime after midmorning, maybe ten, ten-thirty."

"So again, just for the record, other than sitting in your vehicle, a red, 1995 Fleetwood Cadillac, knocking on his front door, and possibly chatting with David Kenney on the sidewalk, you were not in or around Mr. Rockett's house."

"That is correct."

"Detective, my client has been very clear on this matter. Is there a point here?" Louie finally asked.

"I'm not sure," Manning said, then directed an open hand toward crabby Clara. She handed him a manila file. Manning dramatically placed the file on the table, looked up at us and stared for a long moment, then slowly opened the file so both Louie and I could view the contents together. We stared down at a grainy eight by ten photo.

"Is this you, Mr. Haskell?"

It was a picture of me peeing against the corner of Rockett's house.

"Well, yes, I guess I forgot about this, but I can explain."

"Please do." Manning smiled, but his eyes remained icy blue.

"See, I was sitting in my car for a long time and drinking lots of coffee." I looked over at crabby Clara. "A real lot of coffee," I said, hoping to play to her sympathetic side. "I probably drank at least five or six cups, large cups. Anyway, I knocked on Rockett's door to see if I could use his bathroom."

"Really?" Manning said, sounding surprised like he genuinely couldn't believe my sheer stupidity.

"Yeah, and when he didn't answer, I went around the corner to relieve myself. You know how it is," I said in Clara's direction. Based on her complete lack of reaction, I'm not sure she did know.

"I'll admit, perhaps not the most proper thing to do, but other than drinking too much coffee and finding himself in an unfortunate situation, is there anything else here?" Louie asked.

Manning smiled coldly, and this time, crabby Clara had a manila file which she placed in front of him before he even asked for it.

"A bit of a delicate situation here, but I wonder if you might care to explain these?" Manning asked then once again dramatically turned the manila file around on the table to face us. He waited a very long moment before he slowly opened the file.

Crabby Clara suddenly had a slight gleam in her eye.

"I believe this is you, Mr. Haskell. We'd be interested in any comment you may have."

"Where in the hell did you get these?" I asked, stunned. The images, there were five, were me all right. I was handcuffed to a headboard with what looked like a strip of duct tape over my mouth while someone holding a riding crop issued punishment. If I was uncomfortable before, I was really beginning to feel the pain now. There was something else. While it was clearly me, the images appeared to have been doctored. The bed wasn't Candi's, nor was the room, and it was impossible to tell who was on the business end of the riding crop. The images were blurry and grainy like they'd been shot through a cloud of fog.

I was confused, to say the least.

Louie slowly pawed through the photos, exhaling loudly each time he turned over an eight by ten and viewed the next one.

"Jesus," he said, giving me a side glance. "This would seem to indicate nothing other than my client was photographed," Louie stuttered. "These could have been taken anywhere at any time."

"True, I grant you to a point, councilor. But they were found on a pay-as-you-go cellphone in Mr. Rockett's possession at the time of his death. The bed seems to be Mr. Rockett's or at least amazingly similar. We recovered a riding crop, as well as a pair of handcuffs in Mr. Rockett's house."

I was speechless.

"These two photos were found on the same phone," Manning said as Clara placed another manila file in front of him. He went through his dramatic routine once again, slowly opening the file and revealing two eight by ten images. He was beginning to get on my nerves.

"Would you happen to know this woman, Mr. Haskell?"

"I'm not sure that I do. She looks vaguely familiar, but…"

"Maybe focus a bit more on the face, Haskell," Manning growled. He was in his element, enjoying himself.

The photos were crisp, sharp, and looked studio perfect. It seemed obvious to me that the naked blonde with the glassy-eyed stare was completely out of it. She was seated on the edge of a bed, holding a riding crop and giving the thumbs up. She had one of those intoxicated stares on her face that suggested she couldn't remember her own name. The surgical implants and the sunburst tattoo around her navel eliminated any question. Drunk, coked-up, or both, it was none other than my worst nightmare, Swindle Lawless. Her upper lip looked swollen, but there was no hint of the bloody nose or the black eye that would follow.

"Like I said, she looks familiar, but I'm not sure I can place her at this time."

"Once again, I have to insist that these images could have been taken at any time in any place. Quite honestly, they could have been downloaded off the Internet for all we know." Louie sounded a lot less than convincing.

"I'd say she shows a remarkable resemblance to one of your clients, Haskell. I believe this could be Miss Lawless. You recall Miss Lawless? She recently filed a rape charge against you," Manning said.

"That charge is in the process of being withdrawn, a simple misunderstanding," Louie replied.

"Perhaps. She seems to have left her purse behind at Dudley Rockett's home as well. We found it along with a pair of her shoes. Apparently, Miss Lawless is a fan of red heels. Is that correct, Detective Gutnacht?"

Gutnacht smiled and nodded. "Yes, with red soles, Christian Louboutin."

"A virtual treasure trove of sexual deviance," Manning said, patting the photos of Swindle.

"I'd say it's pretty obvious these were doctored. They're grainy, blurry. I was never in that house," I said, then pushed the eight by tens staring up at me back across the table toward Manning.

"Oh, really? Yet here you are, along with your client, Miss Lawless. Maybe Mr. Rockett was just a fan and wanted to start a collection." Manning smiled.

"I can't explain that. These could have come from anywhere," I said, genuinely confused.

"They came from the pay-as-you-go phone found in Rockett's possession. Did I mention that the phone was registered to Miss Lawless?"

"What?"

Manning abruptly changed direction. "Tell me, Mr. Haskell, would you consent to us photographing you? It would just be a couple of photos."

"Photos? I'm not sure what you mean," I said, afraid I knew exactly what he meant.

"Photos of you just standing. Nothing like your earlier activity." Manning looked down to indicate my images replete with duct tape and riding crop. His eyes sparkled while he cracked his ever-present wad of gum and smiled.

"I don't know. I think it might not be—"

"We can do it under the heading of full cooperation," Manning said to Louie. "Or we can place Mr. Haskell in custody and hold him overnight until we get the authorization to take the photos. Your choice how you want to do it, Counselor, but in the end, we're going to have the photos taken."

"Look, if it will help set the record straight and exonerate my client, we're all for it. Can we have a moment's privacy to discuss?" Louie asked.

"Certainly." Manning smiled gracefully before he and Clara stood up and headed out of the room. He stopped at the door just before he stepped out of the room. "Just knock when you're ready to proceed," he said, then pulled the door closed behind him.

"Jesus Christ," Louie hissed. "Are you kidding me? I told you to ditch her, told you she was nothing but trouble, God damn it."

"Louie, I don't have any recollection of this, honest. Any of it. I don't want to take those photos for Manning."

"Why not?"

"Because I've still got some marks on me from that beating with the riding crop. Only it was from Candi, at her place. At least, I think it was."

"Oh, for God's sake, what the hell were you thinking?"

"Hey, look, something's not right here."

"Gee, really? You're telling me! Okay, they're going to get the photos one way or the other. I can fight it, but we're talking holding them off no more than about twelve hours, tops. Manning's probably got the paperwork already signed and set to go. Are those marks going to disappear within the next twelve hours?"

"Probably not."

"Are they going to look any better tomorrow morning than they do now?"

"Not really."

"So why spend the night in jail, Dev? Christ, they'll just lock you up overnight and be photographing you before breakfast tomorrow. Besides, need I remind you about your living room couch?"

"No." I could only hope Swindle was still passed out at my place.

"Then let's get this over with so you can get home and deal with that problem before things get any worse."

Louie went over and knocked on the door.

Manning opened it a second later and smiled. "Any decision?"

"We'll agree to be photographed," Louie said, sounding resigned to the situation.

"Excellent. We'll take the photos right in here and have you both on your merry way in no time flat."

He was sounding way too cheerful for my tastes. He strode back into the room, followed by a crew-cut guy in jeans and a T-shirt, carrying a camera. Manning picked up a small remote off a shelf and, after pushing a couple of buttons, adjusted the lighting to better illuminate a corner of the room. There were a number of lines taped on one of the walls about six inches apart, each one indicating different height.

"Mr. Haskell, if you would kindly step over into that corner." Manning absently waved his hand like it was no big deal and then went back to pushing buttons on the remote.

I walked over to the corner, turned to face everyone, and secretly prayed they just wanted to document my height.

"Would you remove your shirt, please?" the cameraman asked.

I gave a quick glance toward Louie, who frowned and nodded back.

The cameraman fired off one shot of me facing him, then instructed, "Turn round, please." I heard the camera click three times. "Lower your trousers, please." Three more clicks. "Lower the boxers, please. A little bit more. More, please."

I heard a gasp that sounded like it could only have come from Louie.

"Good," the cameraman said and then followed with a half dozen more clicks of his camera. "All right, that should do it, Mr. Haskell."

"Did you get enough?" Manning asked.

"More than enough," he replied.

I wasn't thrilled with the sound of that.

“Very well. Gentlemen, thank you for your cooperation. Mr. Haskell, you remain, as always, a person of interest. I need you to sign this release form for the photos before you go. You are not, I stress not, at this time under arrest. I would request that you plan on remaining in the area, and should anything come to light, please let us know. Do either of you have any questions?”

“No, Detective, we do not,” Louie said.

Louie may not have had any questions, but I, for one, had a ton of them I wanted to ask. None of which I thought Manning would be able to answer. Besides, I had a little more pressing matter, hopefully still passed out on my living room couch.

Thirty-eight

We had just pulled to the curb in front of my place after a silent drive from Manning's little modeling session at the police station. "No, don't even think of asking. Believe me, it's best if I don't come in," Louie said, cutting me off before I'd had a chance to even ask him.

"I wasn't going to ask you in," I lied. "I just wondered what you thought we should do next."

"Probably the best thing to do would be for you to sign a full confession and throw yourself on the mercy of the court."

"What?"

"I think right now, you better get Swindle at least semi-sober and straight so you can try and get a semblance of an answer from her." The "Jaws" theme suddenly erupted from Louie's coat pocket.

"Is that—"

"Shit, Cazzo," Louie said. "I'm gonna have to take this, you better get inside and deal with Swindle." He pulled the phone out of his pocket then motioned for me to get out of his car before he half-shouted, "This is Louie Laufen."

I opened the door and waved good-bye, then watched as Louie drove off. I took a deep breath of the still settling exhaust fumes and went in to deal with Swindle.

No need to rush. She wasn't there. I ran upstairs in the hope she might have adjourned to a bedroom or the bathtub, but there was no sign of her. I even checked the closets, where I noticed a sawed-off twenty gauge I kept in my bedroom closet was missing. Her red heels were still under the coffee table. One of the cushions from my living room couch lay halfway on the floor. The door to my liquor cabinet was open, and a kitchen stool was tipped over.

About the only conclusion I could draw from these facts was that Swindle was apparently barefoot and armed when she left.

I was thinking of the photos Manning had shown us. He said the photos had come from a cellphone in Dudley Rockett's possession at the time of his death. The phone was registered to Swindle, but a pay-as-you-go didn't seem to describe her sleazy leopard skin iPhone.

Hell, as far as I could remember, I'd never even been inside Rockett's place. Based on her appearance in the photos, Swindle looked to be incapable of even leaving her name, let alone taking photos. I sure didn't take those photos. I was pretty sure Swindle didn't take them. But I had a pretty good idea who did, the only person I was with that night.

"Hi, Dev," Candi cooed. "Interested in a little giddy-up action after I get off work tonight?"

"You at the Tutti Frutti Club now?" I asked.

"Working till close, honey. How's my spank baby?"

"Eager to see you, Candi. Feel like giving me some of your extra-personal attention if I come over?"

"Ooo, you are so bad. I didn't think you'd be ready to go so soon. I'll be home about two-thirty, maybe three this morning. Is that too late for you?"

"No, that'll work. It gives me some time to rest up. Can't wait to see you," I said.

Actually, I wasn't kidding. I couldn't wait to see her, but not for the reasons she thought. That, plus Swindle seemed to hold a key too, as frightening as that sounded, and Candi was the closest chance I had to finding Swindle. I thought back to Heidi, screaming at me about the flowers I'd left in her kitchen. What if she wasn't having one of her lunatic moments? What if there really were flowers left in her kitchen?

I attempted to call her and got a recording, "The subscriber you have attempted to reach has requested that no calls from this number be accepted." Apparently, she really did block my number. I walked down the street to a payphone outside of Fern's bar and phoned her.

"This is Heidi," she answered a few minutes later, sounding very professional and relatively sane.

"Heidi, please don't hang up."

"I told you to never, ever call me again, Poopy," she said, but she didn't shout, and she didn't hang up.

"Heidi, I'm in a bit of a mess, and I'm hoping maybe you could help. I—"

"I knew it. You need bail money again, don't you? Well, guess what? The First National Bank of Heidi is closed to you forever. Do you hear me? For-fucking-ever!"

"Will you quit screaming and just listen for a moment? It's not about money, but it concerns you, too."

"If I picked up some STD from you and that Swindle slut, I'm going to cut off your little—"

"Heidi."

"I'm telling you, Dev. So help me—"

"Heidi, this isn't about STDs and Swindle. Well, it might be about Swindle."

"Oh, I can just hardly wait."

"Are you ready to listen?"

"So help me, Dev."

"Heidi, remember when you phoned me about the flowers, and then, I don't know, there was a crash, and you hung up?"

"I threw them out onto the patio, along with that disgustingly cheap vase, you low life little weasel. I didn't want your shitty flowers anywhere in my home after what you and your slut, hooker, low-life girlfriend did to me."

"Okay, for the umpteenth time, nothing happened, Heidi. Was it a good idea? Probably not my brightest, but nothing happened. Besides, I would never want to share you."

A long pause followed.

"You really mean that?" she asked.

"Absolutely. Of course, I mean it, but tell me about the flowers."

"The ones you put on my kitchen counter? Totally bad idea, totally. I was pretty upset, and by the way, that creepy card you enclosed did nothing to help. I was gonna get the locks changed so you couldn't get back in, but I haven't had time, and I guess I've pretty much calmed down."

"Heidi, I didn't leave any flowers on your kitchen counter," I said.

"Well, if you didn't, who did?"

"What did the card say?"

"Some gross line about the three of us giving and getting or something. I was so pissed off I didn't even finish reading it. What do you mean you didn't leave the flowers? Unless, don't tell me, it was that slut Swindle, your pal?"

"Swindle? I don't think so. She's got a number of problems she's dealing with right now, and I don't think she could actually find the time, let alone your house. Where were they sent from?"

"They weren't sent. I told you they were on the kitchen counter. I came home from that stupid police interrogation, thanks for that by the way, and there they were sitting in my kitchen."

"On the counter?"

"Are you listening? Yes, on the kitchen counter. The flowers, little roses, by the way, cheap ones, in some dreadful glass vase. I just called you and tossed the whole thing out onto the patio so you could hear it crash."

I could sense her getting worked up again.

"What are you saying? It wasn't you who left them in my kitchen?" she asked.

"I didn't leave flowers or anything else for that matter."

"So who did? And how the hell did they get in here? I still think it may have been that dreadful slut."

"I'd say it's a pretty slim chance. Besides, I'm not sure she can even read, let alone write something on a card."

"Charming. You sure you didn't leave them? Cause that means someone broke into my house and left me flowers, which doesn't make a whole lot of sense."

"Seeing anyone else?"

"None of your business, Dev. Besides, neither one of them is really the flower type."

Thirty-nine

I closed my eyes about ten that evening with the idea I'd catch a few winks before I dealt with Candi. I couldn't sleep and found myself sitting in the Fleetwood in front of her place a little after midnight. I was casing the joint. She came down the street and gave me a wave as she pulled into her driveway a little before three in the morning.

I wasn't sure what I was going to do, but I was sure of one thing— she'd set me up.

"Hi, Dev, how long have you been sitting out here?"

"Not long, just a few minutes."

"Silly, why didn't you just let yourself in?" she said, then gave me a kiss on the cheek and a little rub on my back. "Missed you."

"Let myself in? You don't lock the place?"

"No, your key," she said as we walked up to her front door. She placed her key in the lock, unlocked the door, stepped in, and hit the lights.

"You never gave me a key, Candi."

"I thought you took the spare. It was hanging in the kitchen. Besides, you left me those flowers. They were so beautiful. See? I put them on the table," she said and turned on the dining room light.

There, in the center of the table, was an unattractive glass vase with small red roses. They looked like a discount dozen, a bit dark along the edge of the petals like maybe they wouldn't last more than another half day. A number of petals had dropped and lay scattered around the vase on the table.

"Thank you, they're beautiful, and you didn't have to do that. You are so sweet," she said and gave me a kiss on the cheek, then lingered against me suggestively.

"When were they delivered?"

"What are you talking about, delivered? You left them in the kitchen, remember? On the counter. Look, I even put your card on the refrigerator. You want a drink?" she asked, walking into the kitchen. She opened the freezer door, pulled out two chilled glasses, and the ever-present bottle of Grey Goose Vodka.

"Let me see the card."

She gave me a funny look, then pulled a little note card from behind a refrigerator magnet and handed it to me.

"Had a great time! Ride 'em cowgirl! Dev"

"Just wanted to make sure I spelled everything correctly," I said.

"It was so sweet, Dev. To tell you the truth, I haven't gotten flowers from someone for so long. Well, almost since forever. Here's to you." She smiled, then handed me my frosted glass, and we toasted.

"I wasn't sure if you liked roses," I fumbled, wondering what in the hell was going on.

“You kidding? Like I said, it’s been so long since someone gave me flowers. You could have given me dandelions, and I would have been thrilled. It was really sweet of you. You are a wonderful, wonderful man, Mr. Haskell.” Her eyes suddenly watered, and she looked away.

“What’s wrong?” I said.

She just waved her hand and turned farther away. Her shoulders began to shake. She was crying.

“Candi?”

“It’s been so long since somebody cared. Oh, damn it, why am I being such a big baby? Thanks, Dev, thank you so much,” she said then kissed me. She looked at me for a moment, then took a big sip, grabbed my hand, and led me upstairs to her bedroom.

* * *

“You feel like some breakfast? I got bacon and eggs,” she said but gave no indication she was interested in rolling off my shoulder. It was sometime past mid-morning. I’d been lying next to her for quite a while, trying to figure out what in the hell was going on and coming up with absolutely nothing.

“Breakfast sounds good. Be okay if I grabbed a shower?”

“Take your time, I’ll bring some coffee in to you,” she said, then rolled out of bed and slipped on a short black robe that left nothing to the imagination.

I laid there for a minute or two longer, then quickly looked under the bed. I checked her closet. I peered into the heating vent. I stood on the bed and examined her ceiling light, searching for some kind of recording equipment. I didn't find any. I did find the riding crop, along with a mask and set of handcuffs under the far corner of her bed. Who knew she was a superhero? She'd apparently forgotten to remove the price tag on the riding crop. Eventually, I hopped in the shower.

We chatted about nothing specific over breakfast. I noticed a larger pile of rose petals littered her dining room table, but didn't mention anything. We kissed good-bye at the door.

"Thanks for coming over, Dev."

"Thanks for having me."

"Thanks for being had. Now, don't be a stranger," she said and flared her eyes.

"Not to worry," I said and went out the door. About halfway to my car, she called out my name, and when I turned around she smiled, opened her little robe, and flashed me.

I laughed, waved, and wondered what in the hell was going on?

Forty

I phoned Detective Manning. Usually, when he knew it was me, he'd leave me hanging on the line for ten minutes before he'd come on to say he was too busy to talk and hang up. Today he picked up after about thirty seconds.

"Haskell? Ready to come in and sign a full confession?"

"Actually, Detective, I was wondering if Swindle Lawless has withdrawn the rape charge she filed against me."

"Not that I'm aware of. But, then again, I've had a few more things on my plate to deal with other than the status of your personal relationship with Miss Lawless."

"I was under the impression she was going to drop all charges sooner rather than later," I said.

"Gee, I can hardly wait. I'll be sure to alert everyone in the department. Anything else?"

"No, not at this time, thank you. You've been extremely helpful, Detective." My tone suggested otherwise.

Manning hung up.

"Did she withdraw the rape charge?" Louie asked through a mouthful of chocolate doughnut.

“No.” I put the binoculars back up and took a moment to study the three women getting off the bus.

“Does it make sense to you that someone is giving these women flowers with my name on it? I mean, what the hell?”

“Nothing makes sense to be quite honest.” Louie was in the process of picking up chocolate doughnut crumbs one by one off his picnic table and placing them in his mouth.

“Why would someone do that?” I wondered out loud.

“Why? I guess to set you up, but then you’re back to the same question. Why? I mean, if someone has an in for you, it seems to me there are better ways to get at you than sending flowers to women.”

“They weren’t sent.”

“Fine, whatever. The question still is, why? Well, and then who? Whoever it is can get in and out of at least two homes, apparently without a problem.”

“Maybe three if he placed that doctored stuff on Rockett, plus took the photos of me and Swindle.”

“And, don’t forget, had the time and ability to drown your pal, Rockett. I don’t know, it sounds like an awfully busy individual, and I still don’t get why.”

“What about Cazzo?”

“Cazzo? No, he’s capable of doing a lot of sleazy stuff, but this isn’t his style. Would he beat Swindle up? Maybe, if Tommy D’Angleo gave him the okay, but murder Dudley Rockett? No, I'd say that's out of Cazzo's league."

"Then, the D'Angelos?"

"Perfectly capable of all of it, especially the violence. The only problem is Gino has a monitor on. They can track him. And Gino can't go anywhere without Tommy taking him there. Hell, the poor guy would never be able to find his way back home. The cops know where and when the guy goes anywhere. He probably has a limited amount of places he can be, and I'm guessing he's required to be home after hours." Louie sat back and put his feet up on the picnic table.

"By the way, the monitoring company also contacts him at random times. Some standard message he has to respond to within a certain time so they can check to see that he's where he should be. No, Gino's on a short leash. Tommy rarely, if ever, let's him out of his sight, so they're both essentially under lockdown. Call your pal LaZelle. He'll tell you."

I thought that was probably one of Louie's better ideas.

"You aware you're a person of interest in an on-going investigation? That means I really can't talk with you, Dev," Aaron said.

"That's why I'm calling."

"Because I can't talk to you? The person you should be talking to is Detective Manning?"

"Actually, that's not such a good idea. I just had a question."

"And I'm jammed. Like I said, if you were paying attention, I'm not at liberty to discuss your involvement in an on-going investigation. Look, Dev, we've been friends since we were kids, but you're over the line on this one. Like I said, you should talk to Manning."

"Aaron, I just wanted to know if Gino D'Angelo was wearing a monitor bracelet."

"Gino D'Angelo? No offense pal, but maybe you should be paying a little more attention to your particular horse shit situation. Don't let the person-of-interest line fool you. Manning is getting all his ducks in a row, and then he is going to lower the boom. And he's good, Dev, very good."

"Great. What about Gino?"

"Yes, your friend Mr. D'Angelo is wearing a monitor. By the way, he's one of about twelve thousand individuals currently being monitored. Look, Dev, concerned citizen that you are, please forget about Gino D'Angelo. In fact, here's some free advice, stay as far away from him and his brother as possible. Hey, I know. How about just getting your own act together?"

"My act?"

"Yeah. Because right now, Dev, all roads in the Rockett and possibly even the Gary Ruggles case seem to be leading to you."

"But I haven't done anything."

"Then help us out by proving it, Dev. God damn it. It would sure be nice if we had photos of you going to church services or helping an old lady across the street instead of a rape charge, bondage photos, and a security camera shot of you pissing on Rockett's house."

"All that shit is bogus."

"Well, then there certainly seems to be a lot of bogus items piling up. Damn it, Dev get this straightened out. You're running out of time. and there is nothing I can or will do to help if you're guilty. You hear me?"

"Thanks, Aaron. Thanks a hell of a lot."

"Nice chatting," Aaron said and hung up.

"Anything?" Louie asked.

"Nothing we didn't know. Gino D'Angelo is wearing a monitor, and I'm in deep shit. Aaron said all roads in the Rockett murder and maybe even that Ruggles hit-and-run seem to lead to me."

"And maybe Swindle," Louie offered.

"Yeah, Swindle. If you were Swindle, where in the hell would you be right now?"

"She seems to be incapable of functioning on her own for more than about thirty minutes. If I were looking for her, I'd try and find Tommy D'Angelo. Swindle will most likely be in the immediate neighborhood."

Forty-one

Swindle wasn't just in Tommy's immediate neighborhood. She was in his pool.

I had left the office, debated about wasting time in The Spot, but instead, ended up driving down Summit Avenue to Tommy D'Angelo's home.

Tommy's place was a long, rambling, two-story brick structure encompassing three very pricey wooded lots on the Mississippi River Boulevard. The house sat along the river bluff, a little south of Summit Avenue, overlooking the Mississippi and the city of Minneapolis. The front of the lot was surrounded by an eight-foot high wrought iron fence sporting very sharp-looking spikes. The fence was posted with "Private Property" and "No Trespassing" signs placed about every ten feet.

I rang a buzzer at the front gate, then looked up and smiled kindly into the security camera when the green light blinked. I rang the buzzer and smiled four separate times, but never received an acknowledgment.

I drove around to the far side of the lot. The rear area was walled off by a wood fence that matched the height of the wrought iron out front. Just like a grade school kid, I peered through a knothole that looked into the lavish backyard and an elegant pool area.

There, floating on an air mattress in the far corner of the pool, was a topless female figure that looked an awful lot like Swindle Lawless.

I groaned, grunted, and hoisted myself up to the top of the fence, then wobbled a bit before I dropped to the brick patio. I landed next to a round, glass-topped table sporting an umbrella. Any noise I made didn't seem to have an effect on the woman in the pool.

What remained of a drink tray sat on the glass-topped table. Next to the tray was a bowl of sliced limes looking less than fresh, an almost empty bottle of vodka that had probably been sitting in the sun for a couple of hours, and a silver bucket with about three inches of water that must have held ice cubes at one time.

I remained crouched next to the table, waiting for a watchdog, a security guard, or the D'Angelos to come storming out after me. But nothing happened.

Swindle remained napping on the air mattress as I quietly approached. Closer examination had me reassess my evaluation. She wasn't napping, she was passed out and snoring. Based on the scarlet sunburn blistering her figure everywhere but her postage stamp thong area, she was going to be in some real pain whenever she finally regained consciousness.

Her knees hung off the air mattress so that her lower legs were submerged in the water and remained lily-white. The position she was in as she lay there had exposed her inner thighs to the rays from the sun and made the thought of her walking in the immediate future a painful proposition.

Her eye was only slightly swollen, and the bruise had faded from mostly purple to more of a yellow-brownish cast. It still did nothing to improve her appearance.

Her air mattress had apparently drifted into the sunny corner of the pool, and Swindle had lain there comatose for God knows how long. She rested a large, empty stemmed glass directly over her navel and her sunburst tattoo. The glass had apparently deflected the sun's rays, leaving a white area the size of a small doughnut surrounding her body art. The rind from a slice of lime was nestled in her hair alongside her neck.

Her implanted breasts rose up from her chest like two large mounds of dessert that had been slathered in a scarlet, sunburned glaze. She must have been passed out here for hours.

I double-checked the open sliding glass doors leading into the house for any movement before I gently called her name.

"Swindle, hey, Swindle, wake up. You're getting sunburned."

She wiggled her nose but gave no indication of regaining consciousness.

"Swindle, Swindle, wake up. It's time to get out of the sun. Come on, honey," I said and gently shook her knee.

She batted my hand away. Then, like déjà vu all over again, she made to roll over as if she were in a large bed, only she wasn't, of course. Instead, she rolled off the air mattress and down toward the bottom of the pool before I could even attempt to catch her.

She surfaced a second later, looking like a boiled lobster and shrieking.

"What in the hell are you doing? Are you crazy? Get me out of here, God. I feel like I'm on fire," she screamed.

I reached for her outstretched arms and hoisted her up out of the water onto the brick patio.

"You maniac!" she screamed. She coughed a couple of times, stumbled to her knees, and moaned, "Oh no," just before she vomited.

"Nice, Swindle. Gee, I really missed you."

"Oh, God, blick." She groaned and coughed a few times. "Blick, blick, blick, get me a drink, quick."

"Yeah, right, a drink is just what you don't need. Come on, get up. Let's get you out of this sun. You're really sunburned."

"I don't feel so good," she whined.

"Go figure. How long have you been out there?"

"I just had a little pitcher of martinis."

"A little pitcher?" I looked around the patio for the thing and finally caught sight of the pitcher resting on the bottom of the pool. I gently took her by the hand and led her into the house.

The house felt like it would have been nice and cool in the air conditioning if Swindle hadn't left the double glass doors open. I closed the doors behind us as Swindle staggered toward a flowered upholstered couch. She stumbled over the leg of a coffee table and landed on the floor.

"I feel like I'm burning. My skin's on fire."

"You passed out in the sun, Swindle, and earned yourself one hell of a sunburn. You got any cream around here we can use to cool you down?"

"Down that hallway. There's a bathroom off of my room, the pink bedroom. Maybe check the medicine cabinet in there," she said and half-pointed toward the ceiling.

I walked down the hallway until a nuclear pink bedroom exploded into view. The bed was unmade. There was a vodka bottle on the dresser with maybe an inch of vodka sitting in it. An empty bottle had rolled halfway under the bed. A couple of empty drink glasses sat on a nightstand. Dirty clothes were strewn all over and covered the floor. Swindle's room, no doubt. I wondered how anyone could go to sleep with the pink walls in the place, let alone wake up and still remain sane. Then again, we were talking Swindle here.

The bathroom was the same violent pink color with white subway tiles halfway up the walls. The vanity boasted two sinks set in an eight-foot length of white marble. The marble was completely hidden beneath a variety of makeup containers, hair driers, about twenty different makeup brushes, and some dreadful silk kimono with a modern art design that looked more like splattered paint. About a dozen prescription bottles were mixed in amongst all the clutter. Three different sandals lay scattered across the bathroom floor next to a towel dropped over the bathroom scale. One-half sheet of tissue was all that remained on the toilet paper roll.

I couldn't locate any skin cream amongst the debris on the marble vanity counter. But I did find a medicated sunburn spray in the medicine cabinet. Apparently, this wasn't Swindle's first time to burn. I grabbed the spray and the ugly kimono.

I sauntered back down the hallway, looking in various rooms. All were nicely appointed and uninhabited. I wandered up the large staircase, looked into a nice den, five different bedrooms, a billiard room with a bar, some large flat screen type of theatre, another den, and an office. All were devoid of human life. One of the bedrooms held a wheelchair and a pair of crutches in a far corner. A large Sesame Street poster hung on the wall above the bed, but other than that, nothing unusual.

Apparently, Swindle was the only one home.

By the time I returned to the flowered couch, she was across the room on all fours pawing through a cabinet that held liquor bottles, a lot of liquor bottles.

"God, we can't be out of vodka. I know there's some in here. What the hell did you do with it?" she half yelled. She was pulling liquor bottles out of the cabinet and tossing them off to the side. They clanged against one another as she tossed them, but thankfully none had broken.

"Swindle, come on, get up. Let me get this spray on you so you can cool down. I brought you this thing so you can cover up afterward. Here, stand up," I said.

Amazingly, she followed my direction and stood facing me.

"Okay, put your arms out and close your eyes," I said, shaking the aerosol can lightly. Once she assumed the position, I sprayed her. The white ring around her navel and her sunburst tattoo looked even more ridiculous as she stood there. Her legs were scarlet down to just below her knees, then almost snow-white where they had hung in the water. While I sprayed her skin, I detected the slightest hint of a smile creep across her face.

"Better?" I asked.

She nodded, kept her arms extended, and her eyes closed.

"Here, put this on," I said, handing her the ugly kimono. She slipped into the thing and tied it loosely around her waist.

"Swindle, do you remember being photographed the other night?"

She looked at me blankly and shook her head.

"You were naked with a riding crop."

She smiled, and a sense of recognition or memory gradually spread across her face. "It'll cost you another fifty bucks if you want to take pictures."

I knew where this was going. "I didn't take any pictures of you, Swindle. Do you remember what happened to your eye?"

"My eye? Who the hell knows? Besides, what difference does it make? I've been hit a lot harder."

"Who hit you this time?"

"I think I must have been kinda drunk, cuz I can't remember. I just woke up and had a black eye." She extended her arms out, palms up, and then gave a shrug as if to say it happens all the time.

"Did you have fun with Dudley Rockett?"

Her smile suddenly turned to a frown as she stared at the floor before glancing up at me with a confused look. She brushed her wet hair away from her face. "Dudley Rockett? Did he have a party?"

"Maybe, I don't remember being there either," I said. "Come on, let's get you out of here."

"What'd Tommy say?"

"He said I should take you to a safe place so you can relax and take care of that sunburn."

Forty-two

Louie's face grew red and he half screamed, "Are you crazy? No, no, no."

"It'll just be for a little while. Maybe over night until I can get something else lined up," I said.

"No, Dev. Come on, this will absolutely end everything with the D'Angelos and Joey Cazzo. They're my meal ticket, man. Besides, to tell you the truth, honorable idea that it may be, I just don't want to have anything to do with her," Louie said. He looked over my shoulder as Swindle half stumbled out of my car. His eyes seemed to get wider with every step she took. She had the kimono half-way on. The belt around her waist had come undone and was trailing on the ground behind her as she walked unsteadily toward us. The kimono hung open, exposing her sunburned figure, the lily-white spot of skin surrounding her tattooed navel, and the postage stamp sized thong.

"Oh, hi, Swindle," he said, giving a little wave and sounding very unsure.

"Hey, I gotta pee."

Of course, I thought.

"Oh yeah, let me show you the bathroom," Louie said and then glared at me while he held the door for her.

"Just down that hallway, it's the second door on your right. No, your right side, Swindle. No, the next door. Yeah, there you go, that's it."

"Absolutely not," Louie said, coming back out to the porch. "Dev, I don't need the hassle. She's gonna get up in the middle of the night, turn on the gas burner on my stove, then pass out, and I'll get blown up. Or she'll smash up my car, or pass out and leave the water running in the bathtub and the ceiling below will collapse. Believe me, I've been around too many folks like this. I know you want to help, but they're just a disaster waiting to happen."

I couldn't argue with him.

"Maybe check her into Detox," Louie suggested.

"She said she has no memory of being photographed and no idea who beat her up. She said it wasn't the first time she'd been hit."

"Probably not. People only have so much patience, after all. Besides, she could have done it to herself for all we know. Maybe she just fell down or bounced off a wall or something."

"You're not sounding too sympathetic," I said.

"Dev, I've been here before. I know where this is going. She's on a race with herself to hit rock bottom, and she'll inadvertently destroy anyone who gets in her way. Stay away from her. You should probably just take her back to wherever you found her."

"The D'Angelos and—"

"Oh, shit."

"And I can't take her back there. She holds the key. Whoever photographed her holding that riding crop is most likely the same person who murdered Dudley Rockett, and maybe even the same person who ran over Gary Ruggles."

"She might have held the key at one time, but believe me, she's lost the thing by now. It's impossible for her to remember. It's hidden in her alcohol and drug-induced haze. Hell, she can barely remember her name, let alone getting photographed. Dev, she's just damaged goods."

I couldn't argue, but that still didn't provide any new options for me.

"What about your pal, LaZelle?" Louie asked.

"Yeah, great idea since it obviously worked so well when I spoke to him just a couple of hours ago. Man, now why didn't I think of calling him?"

"Can it hurt?" Louie asked.

Just then, Swindle staggered into Louie's front hall with her kimono wide open. She clumsily brushed her hair back, causing her to stagger a half step before she attempted to focus on Louie and I. "Hey, fellas, how 'bout it? You wanna party? I'll give you a discount, two for one. What do ya say? Maybe get this little lady another drink."

"Get her into Detox," Louie said under his breath.

I had to wait about ten minutes until Aaron finally came on the line.

"Yeah, Dev, now what?"

"Look, Aaron, Swindle Lawless—"

"We're looking for her. There's a warrant out for her arrest."

"A warrant?"

"We got the initial test results on her car back from the BCA lab. They found bits of Gary Ruggles on her front bumper and right front quarter panel. The paint is an exact match to samples taken from his body. At this point, any help you can give would be advantageous to your situation."

Swindle was standing in Louie's front hall, whining and begging him for a drink.

"I think I might know where she is, but if I bring her in, she should probably go into Detox."

"Tell me where she is. I think it might be better if I sent a squad."

"I can get her to Detox in less time. Besides, the squad may present other problems. Let me give it a shot."

"Okay, you got ninety minutes to get her down there. After that, all deals are off."

"Look, I'll get her down there. Can you alert them we'll be coming in? I don't want to give her a chance to flee the scene."

"You gonna show up with her?"

"I'm almost a hundred percent sure I can do that."

"Call me when you're on your way, Dev, and don't let me down. I'm counting on you."

By now, Swindle was leaning against the wall in Louie's front hall. She'd crossed her arms tightly over her chest like she was holding herself. She was swaying back and forth as Louie continued to try to reason with her.

"Thanks," I said, but Aaron had already hung up.

"Come on, you'll have a good time. You can ask anyone. I'm really good. Please, please, please," Swindle pleaded to Louie.

He looked at me for help as I stepped in the front door.

"Go ahead, Louie, give her some vodka. Swindle, close your kimono and tie it shut," I said.

Swindle pulled her kimono together, then gathered the belt around her waist and cinched it closed. Louie stepped back into the hallway and handed her a glass with a couple of shots of vodka in it. She immediately downed the glass, then closed her eyes, titled her head back, and seemed to visibly relax.

"Look, Louie, we'd like to stay, but I found a party, so we're going to go. You up for a party, Swindle?"

She opened her eyes and nodded vigorously.

"Sorry we can't stay," I said. I had Swindle by the arm and began to lead her to my car.

"The party with your pal, LaZelle?" Louie asked.

I didn't want to halt our progress toward my car, so I just nodded and kept moving with Swindle in tow. "Yeah, I'll keep you posted," I called over my shoulder.

I phoned Aaron about ten minutes later to tell him we were just a few minutes out from the Detox center.

"They're waiting for you. A doc named Maxine Washington is your point of contact. She's got the paperwork already started. Dev, you know, once she's in there, we're going to have to place her under arrest."

"I know. Tell you the truth, Aaron, it's probably the safest thing for her." I glanced over at Swindle slunked down in the passenger seat on the verge of passing out.

"We almost there?" She moaned but kept her eyes closed.

"I'll call you after we're checked in," I said to Aaron and hung up.

"Is the party at a hotel?" Swindle asked a couple of minutes later.

"Yeah, everyone is waiting for us. It'll be a lot of fun," I said, then put my blinker on and turned into the entrance to the Detox unit.

The Ramsey County Chemical Dependency Unit, was a modern structure of three stories with separate dorms for men and women. The entrance was a one-story double door affair jutting out from the center of the building. The double doors sat beneath a curved red roof, which seemed to serve as the only nod to any architectural inspiration on the entire building. In a way, I supposed the place did look like a no-frills hotel.

"And they got a bar here, right?" Swindle asked. She was attempting to rally and come awake.

As we pulled up, two large men stepped out of the entrance, rolling a gurney. They were dressed in white and were followed by a short black woman in a blue lab coat holding a clipboard. I couldn't read her name tag, but I assumed she was Doctor Washington.

I pulled to a stop, and Swindle stared at the gurney for a moment before she looked at me. "What the hell is this?"

"Just a little kinky thing they like to do, but it's good, Swindle, very good. You'll have fun."

Her sunburned face stared at me for a long moment before she slowly seemed to accept my explanation and carefully climbed out of my car.

Forty-three

Manning shook his head and said, "You're still a person of interest."

"Yes, sir, I'm aware of that," I said, trying hard to act like I was on my best behavior.

We were parked next to my Fleetwood in the Detox parking lot. Aaron was sitting in the passenger seat. He watched me in the rearview mirror, but I couldn't read his look. Manning sat behind the wheel and stared straight ahead like I wasn't worth the effort of a backward glance. I was sitting in the middle of the back seat of their unmarked car, groveling.

"She'll be here for at least seventy-two hours. Depending on what we learn, she'll either go to county or a rehab facility after that," Aaron said.

"I think she's probably been drunk for so long I don't see how she could be capable of doing any of this," I said.

"Well, her car is definitely the vehicle that struck and killed Gary Ruggles. Whether she was driving or not is another matter, although her lifestyle doesn't do much to plead her case. And by the way, don't forget, your DNA was found on the wheel, too."

"And she was definitely a player in your little bronco busting event. We're waiting for DNA results on the riding crop and handcuffs," Manning said, sounding just a little too cheerful.

I thought I caught the hint of a smile from Aaron.

"Actually, about all those cellphone images prove is that someone photographed her. It's really not conclusive evidence," I said.

"No, but it helps build a case one image at a time," Manning replied. He was still staring out the windshield, acting like this was a big waste of his precious time. I had the feeling he was commenting more on the images of me, rather than the two featuring Swindle.

"I'm telling you guys, the D'Angelos are mixed up in this."

"So you say, Haskell, but we've got Gino hooked up to a monitor, and he hasn't been anywhere in the past week. He's never left the house even once. Tommy might be one of the bigger crooks in town, but he doesn't like to get his hands dirty. I was there when they slipped that bracelet around Gino D'Angelo's ankle. If either of those two idiots even thinks of screwing with the monitor, we're alerted immediately," Manning said.

"Yeah, I've had the pleasure of wearing one before," I replied absently.

"Any other ideas?" Aaron asked.

"None that make any sense," I said.

"Okay, for now. Keep us posted, Dev, and thanks for bringing Swindle Lawless in. It's for the best."

"Yeah, hopefully she's hit bottom, and she can begin to put things back together. Now, if we could just figure out why she's been set up."

"How 'bout *if* she's been set up," Manning scoffed.

I phoned Louie after Aaron and Manning drove off.

"Hey, Louie."

"Dev, guess who I just got off the line with?"

"The IRS? They said it was all a mistake, and I can forget about the fines?"

"Don't get your hopes up. No, Joey Cazzo."

"What'd that jerk want?"

"Swindle."

"Swindle?"

"Yeah, he was looking for her. He said she hadn't answered her phone, and they wondered if you or I had seen her."

"Why didn't he call me?"

"Maybe because he doesn't like you. Besides, based on what I saw, she was incapable of answering her phone. You get her into Detox?"

"Yeah, she's safe and sound for at least the next seventy-two hours. If Cazzo called her phone, it was ringing in the evidence room at police headquarters. I think it's in custody with all those photos on it. Remember? They grabbed the thing off Rockett's body or from his house or something."

"Yeah, it all seems just a little too convenient."

"You think? I'm telling you the D'Angelos, and probably Cazzo are all involved, Louie. I just can't quite figure out how or why?"

"Look, Dev, if you're thinking Swindle can help, forget it. It would be like looking into a very deep, black hole."

"She's involved somehow, but I'm pretty sure she doesn't know it. Anyway, she's just a distraction. I'm missing something, somewhere."

"Probably common sense for starters," Louie said.

"Let me ask you something. You saw Swindle this afternoon, and she was totally out of it."

"That's putting it mildly," Louie said.

"That's close to the condition she was in when I left her at my house, and we went down to view Manning's little picture show at the police station."

"Yeah?"

"How does someone who forgets her shoes at my place, and is that screwed up ever find her way back to Tommy D'Angelos?"

"Maybe she called a taxi?"

"She doesn't have her phone. She doesn't even have her purse."

"Hitchhike?"

"Possibly, but it's pretty slim. I don't think she could tell them her name, let alone where she wanted to go. So is it possible the same person who left flowers at Candi's and Heidi's house broke into my place and stole Swindle?"

"Anything's possible, but why? Well, and then who?"

"Tommy and Gino are my guess. I just can't figure out why."

"Except that they have that monitor bracelet on, or at least Gino does. The police can track them all day long," Louie said.

"And Gino never goes anywhere without Tommy. Yeah, I keep running into that. It's gotta be Cazzo," I said.

"I just don't figure him. Like I said before, it's too low even for a weasel like Cazzo."

Forty-four

I phoned Aaron the following morning and left a message. I left another message at noon. Manning called me back around mid-afternoon.

"I'm returning your call, Haskell."

"I never called you."

"Yeah, well shit rolls downhill, and you're pretty much at the bottom. So what did you want to bother the good Lieutenant about?"

"I just had a question about the D'Angelos."

"Gee, that line is long. I'm sure you do have a question, and if I recall, the Lieutenant's response is something along the lines of getting your own shit cleaned up before you get concerned with the D'Angelos, right?"

"Here's the deal, while I was being interrogated by you and Officer Friendly, that blonde who doesn't know how to smile . . . "

"Gutnacht?"

"Yeah, anyway, Swindle Lawless was passed out at my place on my couch. When I got back home, she was gone. I thought at first she may have left under her own power, but now I'm thinking she may have been forcibly removed. You know, someone took her."

"Or maybe it was half-a-dozen sailors who'd just gotten paid, and she ran off with them. So what's your point? Other than I can add perjury to the laundry list of charges I intend to file against you."

"Thanks. My point is, can you check your monitor records and see if Gino and Tommy D'Angelo were at my house? I'm guessing you can track them off cell-phone towers or something."

"We can, and no, they weren't anywhere in the vicinity of your lair. I checked the reports personally. And like I told you earlier, they haven't left their home for the better part of the past week."

"The past week?"

"Correct. Anything else?"

"You're sure?"

"Haskell, I want you to listen to this very carefully," Manning said and hung up.

I thought about what he said; they hadn't left their home for almost a week. I had a tough time picturing Swindle making it out of my place barefoot, on her own, while carrying a sawed-off twenty gauge. I phoned Louie back.

"Yeah, Dev."

"Your clients have another home in town here?"

"My clients, the D'Angelos? No, they got the joint on the River Boulevard, a lake place up north, some condo thing out in Vegas, but as far as I know, they haven't been out there for the better part of a year. I think they're renting out the Vegas condo on a timeshare program."

"No separate condo for Gino here in town? Maybe a trailer or something?"

"No, they live together. Have for maybe the past eight to ten years. Why?"

"I'm talking to Manning just now, and he told me they haven't left the house for the better part of a week."

"Yeah, they're not supposed to. Well, unless it's been cleared with the cops. They got the monitor—"

"Screw that. If they aren't supposed to leave the house, then where the hell were they when I pulled Swindle out of the pool? Louie, I could have ransacked that house, and they weren't around to stop me. I walked through the entire place and, believe me, she was the only one home. I took her out of there, and Cazzo called you looking for her, right?"

"Yeah, that's what he said. That house is a pretty big place. Maybe they were just in a different wing and didn't know you were there."

"They didn't know I was there, that's for sure. I never would've been able to get Swindle out of there if they'd been anywhere near the place. It's just that Manning said they were home and hadn't left for the better part of the past week, but they sure as hell were gone when I went through the place. It doesn't make any sense."

"It's a big joint," Louie suggested.

"It ain't that big. And they're definitely not my biggest fans, so they wouldn't put up with me wandering around the place, looking in rooms. I'm not kidding. I walked through the entire house and didn't see anyone else. I think they got a way to beat that ankle bracelet monitor."

"Dev, the thing is programmed to send an alert the moment they try to screw with it. It's impossible for them to remove it. Believe me, better guys than those two have tried and been nailed."

"Well, something ain't right."

"Probably, but this time I don't think it has anything to do with the D'Angelos."

Forty-five

I phoned Candi to see if she was working. I arranged to meet her at the Tutti Frutti Club toward the end of the evening, which gave me plenty of time to check out her place. I pulled up in front of her house just after dark. I walked around the side, through the gate, and into her backyard. I carried a bouquet of flowers from the grocery store, just in case someone questioned what I was doing. I was hoping she might have a spare key hidden near her back door.

I found the key, but it took me the better part of an hour. The thing was cleverly hidden along the edge of a flower garden in a Styrofoam rock made for hiding keys. I unlocked the back door and stepped inside, my ears perked for an alarm system, although there hadn't been a little sign out front and there weren't any stickers on her windows from an alarm company. I really didn't need a breaking and entering charge added to my laundry list of trouble, so I remained just inside the kitchen door for the better part of five minutes.

Some lights were on around Candi's first floor. They looked like the lights you would leave on when you left the house to make it look like you were still home.

Once I was convinced the place was empty, I left the flowers on the kitchen counter and started to go through the place. Candi had a nice home, a lovely home actually, and it suddenly struck me that even with the tips she made, it was pretty pricey for someone slinging drinks in a bar three or four nights a week.

I peeked inside her attached garage. The place was spotless and had some shiny coating on the garage floor that looked to be mopped and scrubbed regularly. There was a silver car parked in the second space. I panicked, thinking someone might be in the house. I quietly walked over and felt the hood. It was cold to the touch. If someone was home, they'd been here for a while.

I looked at the logo on the front of the hood, a small shield, red and black in the upper right and lower left corners— a Porsche. I walked to the rear and checked. It was a 911 Carrera 4S. I didn't know the cost, but I thought they started in the six-figure neighborhood and headed north. The thing was too expensive for my budget. I wrote down the license number on the back of a dollar bill and stuffed it back in my wallet.

I tiptoed back inside and stood in the kitchen, straining my ears. I failed to pick up any telltale sounds in the house. I cautiously moved to the front staircase and stood listening again, but didn't hear anything. I crept up the staircase as quietly as possible and stopped at the top of the stairs to listen again. The only thing I could hear was my heart pounding.

I remained alert as I quietly checked each room, just to make sure no one was in the house. When I had satisfied myself I was indeed alone I began to search, although I didn't know what it was I was searching for.

I started with Candi's room. I looked under her bed, expecting to see the infamous riding crop and handcuffs. Nothing was there. I went through her dresser drawers. Found the usual thongs and bras in the top two drawers, blouses, and tops neatly folded in the next two drawers. The bottom drawer contained jeans and a bottle of lubricant. No real surprise until I did a closer look at the jeans. They were men's jeans and folded next to them a Patriots jersey, a Boston Celtics T-shirt, and a couple of golf shirts from clubs I'd never heard of. None of it would have fit Candi.

I checked her closet. The usual thousand plus garments on hangers crammed into too small a space, and shoes, lots of shoes. At the back of the closet, there were two sport coats that looked to be fairly expensive on dark wooden hangers with brass hooks. One coat was a creamy color, the other black with a subtle check pattern. Each coat had two pairs of pressed slacks hanging from the horizontal bar and black belts hanging from the brass hook.

Next to the coats was a plastic bag from the dry cleaners with five pressed and starched men's shirts hanging inside. The tag had been removed from the plastic bag. Two pairs of men's shoes sat on the floor in a far back corner, a pair of loafers that looked handmade and

Italian with little brass buckles. Next to them sat a pair of lace-up shoes that looked like they cost a lot more than I would pay. Both sets of shoes were black and highly polished.

I checked the other rooms and didn't find anything out of the ordinary. I wandered into what served as an office, again maybe strange for a woman who served drinks three or four nights a week, but maybe not. There were no paper files in the file cabinet, which might just suggest Candi paid everything electronically. I turned on her computer, but it asked me for a password the moment the screen lit up, so I turned the thing off.

There was nothing out of the ordinary in the bathroom. Her medicine cabinet held the usual array of aspirin, bandaids, toothpaste, and some creams. There were two electric toothbrushes in a drawer in the double sink vanity, but nothing else that suggested another individual. Maybe the clothes were her father's when he came to visit?

I went back down to the first floor, looked through the rooms, and didn't see anything that suggested nefarious activity. The basement had a large finished room off of a laundry room work area. All the laundry consisted of Candi's clothes, all neatly folded on a table. There was an exercise bike in the corner near the dryer, but based on the half dozen hangers holding blouses arrayed along the handlebar I guessed it hadn't been used in quite a while.

Against one wall was an olive drab metal shelf affair. Miscellaneous tools, laundry soap, and basically just junk littered the shelves. The second shelf held a couple of glass vases like the cheap one I'd seen on her dining room table the other day.

In the finished basement room, a large flatscreen television was mounted on a wall opposite a Jacuzzi that could fit four to six comfortably. I guessed the flat screen was at least sixty inches across. There was an extremely well-stocked bar holding, among other things, eight bottles of Grey Goose Vodka.

Whatever I was looking for, I was pretty sure it wasn't here. The men's clothing was interesting, but Candi was certainly entitled to a personal life before I showed up. There was a fresh bouquet of flowers in a cut crystal vase on the dining room table.

I'd been there for the better part of an hour and figured I was close to wearing out my welcome. I locked the door and returned the key to its hiding place, then went to meet Candi at the Tutti Frutti Club.

Forty-Six

It was Biker at the front door of the Tutti Frutti Club. He waved me up to the front of the line, then gave me a suggestive little wink and let me in, so I didn't have to pay the cover charge. I was able to dodge the requisite greeting spank by giving him a hug.

"Thanks, Biker."

"Just let me know if you need anything, anything at all. I mean it, Dan." He smiled.

I let the wrong name thing pass. "Actually, I'm looking for Candi."

"Candi? Oh, sorry, I didn't recognize you. I mean I thought you were— hey, look, I'll send her over when I see her." He appeared more than a little disappointed.

I settled in at the far end of the bar and searched the room for Candi, but couldn't see her. She tapped me on the shoulder a number of beers later.

She was wearing her standard too-small latex outfit with the zipper pulled three-quarters of the way down, revealing her bottomless grand canyon of cleavage. A thick wad of bills was nestled in there comfortably between the hillsides.

"Hi, Dev. Been here long?"

I was at the point where I really couldn't remember how long I'd been at the bar. "No problem," I said, thinking that covered a multitude of sins and hoped I hadn't slurred my words too much.

"I'm just going to log out. You hungry? We could maybe grab a late bite somewhere, or we could just go back to my place and rustle something up." She winked.

"Your place sounds more fun."

She smiled, squeezed my arm, and said, "Give me a couple of minutes, and I'll be back."

It was more like forty minutes or two more beers, take your choice.

"You all set?" she asked.

I nodded. "Let me just pay my tab," I said and handed the bartender my card.

"Maybe I should drive," she said.

I thought that sounded like a pretty good idea. The bartender was back in half a minute. "Sorry, sir, but your card has been declined," he said, not sounding all that surprised.

"Declined? You gotta be kidding. Better run it again. There must be something wrong."

"Well, what's wrong is it's been declined. If you had another one, I could try that."

"You must be doing something wrong. That card is perfectly good."

He looked over my shoulder at Candi and shrugged. "I ran the thing twice, sorry."

"I'll sign off on his tab, Petey. Don't worry about it," she said.

"Hey, look, the card is good, pal," I said, maybe just a little too loud.

"Relax, Dev. Here, Petey," she said, pulling the wad of cash from her cleavage and peeling off a couple of twenties. "Sorry for the hassle."

"Candi, I think I can pay my own damn bar bill."

"Dev, no need to get upset. My treat, come on. Besides, I know how you can work it off."

We headed out the back door to her car. I forget what we chatted about on the short drive to her place. But all of a sudden, we were on her street, and the next thing I knew, she pulled into her driveway and parked.

"Do you ever park in your garage?" I asked, careful to annunciate clearly.

"Yeah, in the winter, I guess, or if it's raining. Otherwise, I just don't need the hassle of hitting the wall when I pull in, or backing out and snapping off a side mirror. As long as the weather stays nice, I just park in the driveway."

"Maybe it'll rain tonight. Might be a good idea to pull in," I said.

"Dev, hello, anyone home?" she asked, climbing out of the car. "In case you forgot, we've been in a drought for the better part of two and a half months. Rain?" she asked, looking up into the clear sky. There was a half-moon up there and lots of stars. "I don't think so. Come on, I'm hungry."

I couldn't put my finger on it, but as we walked into Candi's house, I had that feeling I'd forgotten to do something. I reflexively checked my fly. It was zipped up.

"Grab a stool and let me throw something together. Chicken sandwiches okay with you?"

"Yeah, sounds great," I said, following her into the kitchen. I realized what I'd forgotten the moment I saw the four-dollar flower bouquet I'd left on her kitchen counter earlier.

Candi spotted the flowers the same time I did and moved toward them, quickly acting like they belonged right where they were.

"I better put these in some water. You want another beer?"

"Oh, I don't know."

"Yeah, right, let me get you one," she said. She tore the cellophane off the flowers I'd left behind. She opened the refrigerator, grabbed a beer, and handed it to me. She tossed the cellophane in the trash, opened a cup-board, and took down a nice looking vase, which she proceeded to fill with water. It took her about five minutes to prepare our sandwiches.

"Another beer?"

"Better not," I said.

She reached into the refrigerator, took out another beer, and handed it to me.

"I was thinking I should be on my game tomorrow."

"Sure you should." She smiled.

"Nice flowers," I said, giving the nod to the vase she'd put on the kitchen counter.

"Yeah, I love flowers. I always have some in the house. It just seems to brighten up the mood of the whole place. You know how it is."

Did I know? Not really. Had she meant to buy flowers and thought she did? Flowers struck me as an item you didn't forget, whether you purchased or not. A bar of soap, lettuce, dinner? Yeah, I might not remember if I bought that stuff. But flowers? Really? I don't think so. I felt pretty sure I'd remember. Yet, here she was, acting as if everything was normal. I kept thinking this wasn't making sense.

"Ready for bed?" she asked, snapping me back to reality.

I drained the remnants of my beer bottle and pushed the empty across the granite counter.

She took my hand and led me upstairs to her bedroom. Everything looked the same as I'd left it. I was still curious about the men's clothing in the bottom drawer of her dresser and the sport coats hanging in her closet, although right now, there were other things on my mind. I crawled onto her bed then watched her undress.

She stripped down to her black thong, winked, and pulled on a pair of knee-high boots with spiky heels. She flashed a wicked grin and said, "I'll be right back." She wasn't kidding. Just when I thought I heard the TV go on in the other room, she was back with two crystal glasses filled with a thick amber liquid.

"Little something to get us started. God, no matter how hard I try to stop it, you just seem to have this effect on me," she said. She bent down and kissed me along the side of my face. She pulled back a little and held the glass to my lips. I attempted to just take a sip, but she kept raising the glass, forcing me to gulp until I'd drained the thing. All the while, she knelt over me and giggled.

"What the hell is that stuff?" I gasped. It burned on the way down and felt like it was taking the enamel off my teeth.

"Like it?"

"It's hot or strong or something. It must be about a thousand proof."

"Got this in Mexico. It's pretty strong, but you're gonna need it to get through what I have in mind." She laughed then pushed me back on the bed and slowly unbuckled my belt, nibbling her way through my jeans.

I remembered thinking this was going to be great, then wishing I maybe hadn't had all of those beers. I thought I heard the TV again and was vaguely aware of the thing playing in front of me. Were those real people? It was hard to tell, and I couldn't seem to find the remote or reality. The sound wasn't very good, and I looked at one of them and tried to say something clever like, "She's with me," only I couldn't seem to get the words out and then everything just went black.

Forty-Seven

I was uncomfortable. Let me rephrase that. I was in a hell of a lot of pain. I was slowly regaining consciousness, gradually becoming aware of a conversational rumble from some distant corner. My hands were secured behind my back, and I couldn't seem to move them.

I was seated on a wooden chair that seemed vaguely familiar. I stared at a concrete floor that rang a distant bell. I shook my head a couple of times in an attempt to clear it. Not that it really worked. The voices sounded like a bad recording on slow speed. They were deep, drawn-out, and unintelligible.

I blinked and tried again to move my arms, but couldn't. The floor seemed to come more in focus as I glanced left and right peripherally. The area gradually began to take shape. I was in my basement. I recognized the mountain of laundry on the floor in front of my washer waiting to be attended to. I looked up and recognized the bare light bulbs with pull chains hanging from the white enamel fixtures. Then I noticed the red-painted wooden stairs that led up to the first floor and my kitchen.

The voices seemed to be growing more intelligible.

"… for another couple hours 'til it clears his bloodstream and looks like an accident…"

I shook my head in an attempt to clear the cobwebs and realized I was alone. I was still tied to the wooden chair, but whoever had been down here with me was gone. I'd no idea how long I'd been alone in my basement. I could tell by the light making its way through my grimy basement window that it was daylight. I was also aware that my head was throbbing.

I was guessing I'd been drugged, and my sense of self-preservation strongly suggested I had better get the hell out of there and fast. I could stand, if I hobbled bent over.

The chair was a rickety, antique oak thing. I'd promised to strip, re-glue, and refinish it for a pretty brunette named Kylie about two years ago. She dumped me before I ever started the project and never asked for the chair back.

I hobbled toward one of the solid timber supports that held the massive floor beam running across the basement ceiling. The support was about a foot square, and my thought was to smash the chair against it and flee the scene. It took some time. I hobbled for a couple of steps, then had to sit for a moment to rest, hobbled a few more steps, and sat again until, eventually, I got to where I was going.

I swung my back to smash the chair against the timber. It didn't work, and the chair just bounced off innocently. I sat down again and used my foot in an attempt to break one of the horizontal pieces between the chair legs. After a good deal of effort, I heard the piece crack and felt the chair legs splay slightly.

I shifted to the side a little and applied pressure to another horizontal support. It suddenly snapped audibly, then one of the front chair legs cracked, causing me to fall to the side and come to rest against the large timber. I inched my way back onto my feet and then swung the chair back and forth against the timber. I began to feel the chair come apart a little more with every swing. One of the back legs snapped off, then the other with part of the seat. Finally, the turned dowels connected to the pressed wooden back began to fall apart. I was able to get my fingers on what felt like tape around my wrists and was in the process of pulling that off when I heard faint voices and then footsteps overhead. A moment later, the basement door opened, and more than one pair of legs began to descend the wooden stairs.

I wiggled my hand out from the tape and picked up one of the turned wooden legs from the pile of chair kindling on the floor. I smashed a bare light bulb hanging overhead, hoping to darken the room.

"The bastard's loose," a voice yelled.

"Damn it," another voice shouted and stormed down the last three steps.

I swung the chair leg and caught Joey Cazzo across the bridge of his nose just as he began to raise a shotgun in my direction. The thing fired just as Cazzo went down, and a light bulb shattered somewhere behind me.

My ears were ringing, and I was seeing stars from the blast. My hand seemed to work, and I grabbed the barrel as Cazzo crumbled to the ground. Through the cloud of gun smoke, I could just make out feet as two figures stopped and turned on the stairs. I could taste the acrid smoke in the air.

"Fuck! Come on," one of the voices shouted as they both raced up the basement stairs. I fired the shotgun without aiming. I just half pointed in the general direction and pulled the trigger. The blast forced a scream from the last figure on the stairs, and the lower portion of his right leg, just above the ankle, seemed to disappear as he turned into the upstairs hallway. I waited but didn't hear him fall. I didn't even hear him scream again.

Footsteps pounded on the wooden floor overhead and seemed to race out my back door. I waited for a very long time, shotgun at the ready, pointed toward the basement door. Eventually, my attention was drawn to some groaning from the bloodied figure of Joey Cazzo lying on the floor, beginning to regain consciousness.

I spotted what was left of a roll of duct tape sitting on my dryer, grabbed it, and, keeping one eye on the stairs I taped his wrists. I was just wrapping the tape around his ankles when he began to blink his eyes.

Blood was splattered down the front of his formerly spotless golf shirt. The bridge of his nose sported a vicious looking split and seemed to swell as I stared. Blood had run down the sides of his face and into his ears as he'd lain unconscious on the basement floor. His eyes were already darkening, and he was going to sport two beautiful black eyes in short order. He coughed a few times and spit a mouthful of blood, splattering more on his shirt than on the basement floor. With the broken nose, his voice sounded like he suffered from a severe head cold.

"Oh, God, what the hell do you think you're doing?" he groaned. He coughed and spit some more.

"You better work at improving your aim. You're spitting all over that expensive shirt," I said.

He attempted to sit up, and I slammed his head back down, causing it to bounce off the concrete floor.

"What the hell do you think you're doing? Jesus, are you crazy? We were coming down here to save you, and you attacked me, I mean us. What the hell is wrong with you? Get me out of this shit," he half screamed. He shook and attempted to wiggle his wrists free from the duct tape.

I couldn't resist and kicked him in the ribs.

"You are certi-nuts-fiable, Haskens," he screamed, then shook some more.

"It's Haskell. And Cazzo, you prick, you're going to tell me what in the hell is going on, and then I'm calling the cops."

"The cops? Don't do that. We can work something out here." He coughed and spit again. This time his aim was better, and he hit the floor.

"I don't think so."

"You call the cops, you got any idea the kind of trouble you'll be in? Don't be stupid. Come on, think about it."

"Think about it? You come storming down here with a shotgun—"

"We were going to rescue you."

"From who, me? Hey, wait a minute, this is *my* shotgun. You piece of shit, you took this from my bedroom closet the other day, didn't you? You came here and grabbed Swindle off the couch."

"I don't know what the hell you're talking about. Besides, she said she wanted to go with Tommy," Cazzo said.

"Whatever you had planned, it doesn't look like it was going to bounce my way. The D'Angelos, that's who was with you, right? Gino and Tommy, those two fuck sticks. Well, I got news for you, the cops are going to be able to trace those two idiots from the monitor bracelet. You're finished, Cazzo. I don't know what your deal is, but it's done, finished as of now."

"You dumb shit, you got no idea what you're up against here. You know what's good for you, you'll cut me loose right now. We can make it worth your while. Think about it, pal. Think about it," Cazzo yelled, then coughed and spit more blood onto my basement floor.

"Yeah, I have thought about it," I said. I fished my cellphone out of my pocket and pushed a couple of buttons.

"Don't be stupid. Just think for a minute. Don't—"

"Lieutenant Aaron LaZelle," I said into the phone and stared at Cazzo. He sat on the floor and slowly shook his head back and forth.

"It's an emergency, assault in progress, shots fired," I said, then looked down again at Cazzo. He half coughed and spit more blood.

"No, I'm not joking. Get me Lieutenant LaZelle, now. If he isn't available, I'll even talk to that prick, Manning. What? Oh, Haskell. Dev Haskell. I'm holding one of them at gunpoint right now. Yeah, no, I want to talk with LaZelle or Manning, please. Tell them it's an emergency. I'm holding this guy at gunpoint, an intruder. What? No, I'm not kidding," I half yelled.

Manning was on the line about ninety seconds later.

"This had better be good, Haskell," he said, then made a noise that sounded like he had just bit into an apple.

"Manning, I got Joey Cazzo in my basement. He broke in here, was going to shotgun me, and I disarmed him. I've got him tied up."

There was a long pause before Manning said, "So help me, Haskell, if you're doing some comedy routine on this, I will lock you up and throw away the key."

"What the hell does it take to get you guys to come here? I guess I'll just have to . . ." I lowered the shotgun at Cazzo down on the floor. "Count to three, Cazzo," I said and pretended to sight down the barrel.

"Jesus, God, don't shoot," Cazzo screamed. "Please, please, don't shoot, please don't."

"Manning?"

"We're on our way," Manning said, suddenly sounding breathless like he may have been running. "Don't shoot him, Haskell. Please don't. We're there in about four minutes, you hear? Just stay calm, stay calm."

"Then hurry up." I chuckled. I hung up and looked down at Cazzo. "You are about to be placed under arrest, my friend. Anything I can come up with, I plan to use against you. You have the right to remain silent, but I wouldn't if I were you. I intend to do everything I can to see you hang."

Forty-eight

Once again I was in my favorite interrogation room. Louie had arrived a few minutes earlier and was seated next to me. Manning and unsmiling Clara sat across from us. She seemed to be busily taking notes and never looked up once. In defense of Manning, he seemed to be unconvinced by Cazzo's claims, but none the less he was going through the motions.

"He's filing charges? Against me? You gotta be kidding."

"No, I'm not kidding, Mr. Haskell. In fact, he claims you forced him into your basement at gunpoint."

"I told you. I was at Candi's house. She gave me something to drink, and the next thing I knew, I was duct-taped to a chair in my basement."

"Yeah, that would be the chair Mr. Cazzo claims you used to assault him with, correct?"

"Correct, and I can support that claim one hundred percent. I was drugged, taped to that chair, and was in the process of escaping from my own basement when Cazzo returned with two guys and a shotgun to finish me off."

Humorless Clara kept her head down, but she stopped writing for a moment like she couldn't believe her ears.

"The shotgun you refer to is the weapon you were carrying when we arrived, correct?"

"Yes."

"And I believe that shotgun is registered to you."

"Yeah, exactly." I nodded and glanced over at Louie, who was shaking his head ever so slightly like I was telling some kind of unbelievable tale.

"And you had returned to your home from the Tutti Frutti Club is that correct?"

"Yes, I mean…well, no. Look, we've already been over this a number of times. I went there to meet Candi. To the Tutti Frutti Club, that is."

"And you had been drinking rather heavily." Manning flipped a couple of pages in the file in front of him then looked up at me.

"I guess it depends on what you consider heavy."

"We have a statement from one of the bartenders at the Tutti Frutti Club. He said you became belligerent when your credit card was declined."

"I don't know that belligerent is correct. Yeah, I was upset, who wouldn't be? But belligerent? I don't think so."

"You were belligerent to the point where another employee felt compelled to pay your bill."

"Not belligerent and, actually, Candi paid my bill."

"And she is employed by the Tutti Frutti Club?

"Well yeah, but . . . "

"So then you departed with her and?"

"And I'm not sure. I had a beer, no two beers, and I think a late dinner or an early breakfast and another drink, and that's all I remember."

"You did this where?"

"At her place. In her home."

"And you left her home sometime prior to sunrise before she was awake?"

I had a hazy memory of Candi driving home and some vague conversation about her parking in the garage. The whole thing wasn't making any sense to me.

"I think she drove me from the Tutti Frutti Club to her home. We took her car. I had been over-served, and having her drive seemed to be the wisest choice."

"And so your car got to her house how?"

"I have no idea. I have no memory of leaving her house. The last thing I remember is her wearing a smile and a pair of these black knee-high boots. Kinda sexy," I glanced at humorless Clara, but she remained focused on her notebook. "Candi gave me a drink. I don't know what the drink was. I just know that it burned when it went down. I remember that. Oh, and she said she got the stuff in Mexico."

"Tequila?"

"I don't know what it was."

"Are you in the habit of drinking drinks that you don't know what they are?"

"Sometimes."

"Then you woke sometime before Miss Slaughter and left her home?"

"I'm not sure. All I know is I woke and found myself duct-tapped to a chair in the basement of my house."

"But your car was parked in your driveway, right? That Fleetwood thing with the blue door? That's your car, isn't it? I believe we saw it there. It's being processed now as we speak."

"I don't know how it got there. That's not how I park it."

"You don't park in your driveway?"

"Yeah, I park in my driveway, but not there. I always pull up to my garage."

"So you woke tied to a chair in your own basement?"

"Yes." Finally, he was getting it.

"And then you assaulted Mr. Cazzo?"

"Not exactly, I was in the process of freeing myself when Cazzo returned with two other guys. They were coming down the basement stairs as I was trying to get out of the chair. Cazzo tried to shoot me with the damn shotgun."

"The one registered to you?"

"Right. He missed me, narrowly. I hit him with a chair leg and got the shotgun away from him. The other two guys ran up the stairs. I fired the shotgun at them. I'm sure it was the D'Angelos, and I'm sure I hit one of them, that idiot Gino most likely. If you arrest those two jerks, all your questions should be answered. You can track them, right? You've still got that monitor bracelet on Gino, don't you?"

Manning nodded imperceptibly.

"Do you have a money dispute with Mr. Cazzo?"

"A money dispute?"

"Yes, for fees he owes you. He claims he hired you to do some investigation."

"He hired me to check out a former agent for an acquaintance of his." I suddenly felt on very thin ice.

"Do you recall the name of this acquaintance?" Manning asked. There was no point in trying to dodge. It was obvious Manning already knew the answer. I felt myself crashing through the thin ice.

"Yeah, it was Swindle Lawless. She was or is the girlfriend of Tommy D'Angelo, and the guy I was checking out was her former agent, Dudley Rockett."

"Did you invoice Mr. Cazzo?" Manning asked, almost as an afterthought, and then began slowly flipping through pages in his file.

"No, I never sent him an invoice."

Manning looked up at me, feigning surprise. "Really? Never sent him an invoice? Are you working as a non-profit now?"

"No."

"Do you recognize this?" Manning asked as he flipped a final sheet of paper, then turned a plastic envelope toward me and pushed it across the table. It held a business check from the Tutti Frutti Club made out to me in the amount of two thousand dollars. The thing was dated yesterday and was signed in a completely illegible scrawl that vaguely resembled a coiled slinky.

I studied the check for a long moment before I slid it over toward Louie. "I've never seen this before in my life," I said and shook my head.

Manning nodded, but it was a noncommittal nod as if that was exactly what he had expected me to say.

"So you didn't demand more money from Mr. Cazzo?"

"No, I've never had a money conversation with Cazzo, ever. I've barely had any conversation with him to tell you the truth. He just yells a couple of things and storms out of the room. I've only met him maybe two or three times." I glanced briefly at Louie for support. "Quite honestly. I hadn't planned to charge him, Swindle Lawless, or the D'Angelos for that matter. I just wanted to get as far away as possible from all of them. You already know the Swindle story."

Manning didn't react but continued with his questions. "Mr. Cazzo stated you demanded he bring a check to your home this morning and that once he got there, you insisted on more money."

I shook my head no.

"Then you forced him to go down into your basement at gunpoint."

I continued to shake my head no.

"He said you fired your shotgun twice to emphasize just how serious you were."

"Does Cazzo strike you as the kind of guy who would run over with a check for two grand just to make me happy and then let me force him into my basement?"

Manning didn't respond.

"You think I fired that shotgun at a light bulb in my basement, then turned around and fired another blast up the basement stairs just to make my point? Look, Detective Manning, I know we've had our differences, but do you really think I'd be dumb enough to do this? Check out the D'Angelos or, better yet, check the blood at the top of my basement stairs."

"There isn't any."

"What? Well, look, at least talk to Candi. She could help clear this whole thing up."

"We're trying to contact her so we can do just that."

"What do you mean trying to contact her?"

"Well, it seems she hasn't responded to any of our requests."

"Hasn't responded? Oh, Christ, arrest the D'Angelos now before they do something to her, and keep Cazzo locked up. Honest, Manning, they're the guys you want. If they're still running around, she's liable to be in some serious trouble."

"We have a monitor on the D'Angelos and know exactly where they are at all times."

Forty-nine

Louie was driving. We were headed to his place since my house was apparently still an active crime scene, and I couldn't get back in there. The windows in the car were all the way down, but there was still the hint of exhaust lingering in the front seat of his Geo Metro. The exhaust did nothing to help my headache.

"Jesus Christ, I have one hell of a headache. Maybe it would be a good idea to swing by Candi's?" I suggested. I could feel jack-hammer pounding just behind my eyeballs.

"Maybe it wouldn't since both Manning and LaZelle specifically told you to stay the hell away. Besides, I'd say they probably have someone parked outside in the event she shows up. What the hell are you doing?"

"I'm calling Candi. I'm worried."

"You idiot, they'll be able to track that call."

"I don't care. I want to know she's okay," I said. Then I listened to the recording that said her message center was full and hung up.

"I suppose I could call the Tutti Frutti Club and—"

"What part of *no contact* do you not understand? No, Dev, we're going to my place where you can crash on my couch for a couple of days until we get this straightened out."

"What's to straighten out? Cazzo and the D'Angelos, your great clients, are setting me up for Rockett's murder, and maybe that hit and run on Gary what's-his-name."

"Ruggles? The guy whose wife claims you got her really drunk and then took advantage of her?"

"It was a two-way street, but just forget that for the moment. What about the D'Angelos?"

"The D'Angelos?"

"Yeah. They got Swindle so pickled she can barely remember her own name, and now they've probably grabbed Candi. Perfect."

"Dev, we don't know that they've grabbed anyone."

"Seems to be pretty convenient for them that Candi suddenly can't be found just when I need her as my alibi. Hell, she works for them. They probably called her in to work a shift and then grabbed her. Maybe you could call the Tutti Frutti Club just to see if she's there?"

"Me?"

"Yeah, you. Manning just told me no contact. He didn't say anything about you. Besides, I wouldn't be in this mess if I hadn't been so pressured to help you and your cash-cow clients."

"Yeah, well, not to worry. I'd say that deal has probably run its course for both of us."

"So you'll call the Tutti Frutti Club?"

"I suppose at this point, it's not like it's going to hurt any future business."

"Thanks."

Louie placed the call as we stepped into his kitchen and put the thing on speaker. It turned out to be a waste of time.

"No, sorry, Candi isn't here tonight. Can I take a message?" I guessed it was some bartender on the other end of the line. I could hear a hum of conversation, lousy music, and the clink of glasses in the background. I pictured the guy with a phone tucked between his ear and shoulder, pulling beer taps with both hands.

"Is she scheduled to work tomorrow?" Louie asked.

"I'm sorry, even if I did know I can't give you that information. Maybe stop in tomorrow night to see if she's here. We've got a three for one special on tequila shots between four and seven."

"I'll keep it in mind," Louie said and hung up. "There, that didn't help. Besides, I swore off tequila. I need a beer. You want one?"

"No, better not. At least we know she's not working. I don't know, maybe she's shopping or out with girlfriends. I mean, what would you do?"

"What would I do? I'd get about as far away from you as possible," he said, walking into the kitchen. I heard the refrigerator door open, then the clink of a beer bottle. "You sure you don't want one?"

"No, not the best idea just now. Maybe we should call Aaron, let him know Candi isn't at the Tutti Frutti Club."

"Good idea. That way, when the cops find out you attempted to make contact with her after they told you not to, they won't be surprised," Louie said. He was leaning against the kitchen door frame and proceeded to guzzle a good half of his beer. When he finished, he burped audibly, then wiped the back of his hand across his mouth.

"Yeah, maybe you do have a point."

"You think?" he said, then drained the rest of his beer and walked back into the kitchen. "Sure I can't talk you into one?" he called. I heard the refrigerator door open again.

"No, thanks."

Louie walked back into the living room and collapsed on the couch. He drained about a third of his new beer, then looked up at me. "Dev, a couple of beers ain't gonna hurt. I don't need you going all responsible on me here. We'll find her, don't worry."

Fifty

I didn't have a beer. I spent the night on Louie's couch, tossing and turning, worried sick about Candi. I'd made coffee and was in the process of warming up some breakfast pizza in the microwave when Louie stumbled into the kitchen.

"What the hell time is it?"

"According to the clock on your stove, it's either three-twelve in the afternoon or the morning. Take your pick."

"Very funny."

"It's a little after ten. Want some breakfast?" I asked, holding up a slice of pizza.

"Where'd you get that?"

"It was in your fridge."

"It was?"

I set the piece back down on the plate. I wasn't really hungry anyway. "Tell me if you think this is a bad idea. I'm going to call Aaron and offer my services to help locate Candi."

"I think that's a bad idea, a very bad idea."

"Why?"

"Because it is. You are suspect number one in two murders. I don't doubt your story about Cazzo yesterday, but you've got to admit it's pretty strange. So look at it from their point of view, use your head and just stay out of their investigation."

"I could at least tell them she wasn't at the Tutti Frutti Club last night."

"Another bad idea, for the same reasons it was a bad idea last night when we talked about this. They told you to stay the hell away."

"But, I've got information that could help their investigation."

"No, Dev, you have information that proves you are meddling, that you are not following their instructions, and confirms the fact you are an idiot."

"Hmm-mmm, maybe I could call and just check to see if they located her, that she's all right."

"The bad ideas just keep on coming."

"Maybe I could call to see if I can get back into my own house?"

"Now you're talking. You want anything in that coffee?" As he asked, Louie pulled a bottle holding maybe an inch-and-a-half of Jameson out of the cupboard.

"I'll take a pass," I said and punched in Aaron's number on my cell. Amazingly, he answered after the second ring, catching me off guard.

"LaZelle."

"Aaron, Dev. Ahhh, just wanted to check and see if it was okay for me to go back to my place today."

"Your place? You mean your house?"

"Yeah."

"No, not for at least a couple of days. Where are you now?"

"Louie's kitchen. I'm having some pizza for breakfast."

He didn't seem to blink at my pizza line. "I want you to remain very available for the next few days, Dev. If we have a question for you, I don't want to be running around town trying to find you. It's for your own good."

"I'm available for you guys twenty-four-seven," I said.

"Good, and I don't want you contacting the D'Angelos, Cazzo, Candi, or even Swindle Lawless for that matter."

"Not a problem."

"Good. See that it stays that way."

"Say, that reminds me. Candi. It occurred to me that I don't think she was scheduled to work last night. At least that's what I think she said when we last chatted."

"Last chatted when?"

"Oh, a few nights back. I think she just mentioned it in passing."

Louie's back was to me, and I watched his neck grow red as he shook his head then proceeded to empty the Jameson bottle into his coffee mug.

"Please tell me that wasn't you who phoned the Tutti Frutti Club last night asking for her. Someone called a little after nine. Was it you?"

"No, I didn't call the Tutti Frutti Club last night."

Louie turned around with a shocked look on his face then gulped down the contents of his coffee mug.

"Good," Aaron said. "We'll have the phone records soon enough, and we can check on it. We'll track the number that phoned in. Anyway, stay the hell away, got it?"

"Yeah, relax, I know all that shit. You guys run into the D'Angelos?"

"That's the beauty of the monitor system. We can check from here and never have to deal with that kind of slime in person. They haven't left their house for days."

That was a red flag, I knew differently, even if Aaron didn't.

"Sounds pretty dull to me. Maybe you should pay them a visit," I suggested.

"You just let us worry about that, and make sure you stay the hell away, got it?"

"Not to worry."

"Anything else?" he asked.

"Well, now that you mention it, I just think it might be wise if you guys…" but Aaron had already hung up.

"You idiot," Louie said. His back was to me as he pawed unsuccessfully for another bottle of Jameson in the back of the cupboard. "Why did you even say that? They probably already know it was me who called to see if she was working."

"Yeah, well, they also know that the D'Angelos haven't left their house for days. Bullshit. That just proves Tommy and Gino are up to something, and those two fools have found a way to beat the system. God help the two of them if they hurt one hair on Candi's head."

Fifty-one

Louie let me borrow his car provided I first made a run to the liquor store and replenished his supply of Jameson. It quickly became apparent why he always drove with the windows down. Even roaring down I-94 with the accelerator pressed to the floor and the needle inching up toward fifty miles per hour, I was worried about asphyxiation.

I was on my way to Candi's, hoping to find her sunbathing in the backyard, asleep with her head under a pillow, or listening to music wearing a pair of headphones. I needed something, anything that might serve as a logical explanation for why the police couldn't contact her. I was hoping she just didn't hear the phone ring or the knock on the door when the police had attempted to reach her. Let's be honest. I was grasping at straws.

I didn't see a police presence as I came down her street, so I pulled into her empty driveway and rang her doorbell. Louie's Geo Metro still continued to cough and sputter before gasping to a stop. I went around back, retrieved her key from the Styrofoam rock then pounded on her back door before letting myself in.

"Candi? Candi, its Dev. Are you home?"

The stillness in her house was not the answer I'd been hoping for. I did a quick walk through the first and second floor, then started in the basement and methodically went through every room in the house, looking for something, anything. Whatever it might have been, I didn't find it.

I did find the knee-high spiky heeled boots I last saw her in. They were neatly placed side by side in her walk-in closet, along with a couple hundred other pairs of shoes and boots. I noticed that the sport coats, slacks, shirts from the dry cleaner, and the men's shoes were gone. I checked the bottom drawer of her dresser. The jerseys, jeans, and golf shirts I'd seen before had been replaced by Candi's shorts and some cotton tops, although the bottle of lubricant was still there.

Nothing else seemed amiss. There was no sign of a struggle. No blood-splattered carpet or bullet holes in the wall. I checked her garage…empty. The silver Porsche was gone. Next stop, the Tutti Frutti Club.

I thought it only appropriate that I parked Louie's car next to the dumpster. The same faded, red Chevy van from a couple of days ago was parked two spaces over. The rear door to the club was open, and I could hear the hum of a vacuum as I walked down the hallway toward the bar. Just like before, the same couple was working. She was vacuuming, and he was pulling stools off the bar and lining them up against the brass rail.

"Excuse me," I said.

The woman quickly began vacuuming the carpet up toward the front of the bar, getting as far away from me as possible.

He nodded, pulled another stool off the bar, and in a heavy accent, said, "I have not seen Miss Swindle for many days. I don't know where she is."

"Lucky you. Actually, I was looking for Candi Slaughter, the waitress. Do you know her? She's—"

"Of course I know Miss Candi, she our boss lady. She not here," he said, shaking his head back and forth.

"Not here? She told me to meet her here," I fished.

"I no see her. You should wait maybe, Señor," he said, then pulled another stool off the bar.

"Thanks," I said. I wandered toward the front of the room. In an effort to avoid me, the woman seemed to frantically vacuum herself into a corner up near the fire-base area where Heidi and I had sat that first night a thousand years ago. I walked past her, around the end of the bar, and the corner stool where I'd deposited drunken Swindle the night she said Heidi and I raped her. I climbed up the stairs to the private party room. It was empty.

If anyone was upstairs, they did an awfully good job of hiding. I saw no sign of life. There was a storeroom crammed with stacks of chairs and long folding tables, a unisex employee restroom, and a small office with the lights turned off.

I flipped on the lights and entered the office. Once again, I didn't have the slightest idea what I was looking for. There were the usual stacks of invoices, order forms, and brochures along with a laptop and a printer on a credenza. Next to the laptop was a State Of Minnesota liquor license form. The signature in the applicant's block was the same coiled slinky-like signature that had been on the two thousand dollar check Manning had shown me. The typed name below the signature block read Candi Slaughter.

That didn't seem to make sense. Why would a waitress sign the liquor license form? Maybe Cazzo had forged the signature? Maybe they had forced Candi at gunpoint to sign the check? Maybe I was kidding myself?

I went back downstairs, nodded at my pal pulling down the last barstool, walked through an empty kitchen, and back out to the rear parking lot.

I had one option left— the D'Angelos.

I parked on the river boulevard in front of their mansion and then walked another twenty yards to their front gate. I pushed the security button and smiled into the camera as soon as the green light began to flash.

I waited for what seemed like a long time and was set to drive around back when a voice barked, "Yeah."

"Oh, you're home. Dev Haskell to see Tommy and Gino D'Angelo."

"What about?"

"I'll tell that to Tommy when I see him in person."

"This is Tommy. What the hell do you want?"

"No offense if you're Tommy, but I don't know that for sure, and I'm only talking to him."

"Then you're out of luck, jackass, cuz you ain't getting in."

"Okay, suit yourself." I shrugged and turned to leave. I was taking a gamble.

"Wait a minute, wait a minute, okay, I'm buzzing your ass in. Jesus Christ," he growled. A buzz sounded, followed by an audible snap, which I took to be the lock on the gate releasing. I pushed the gate open and walked up the brick path to the front door. Tommy opened the door just as I was about to ring the bell.

"What the hell do you want?"

"Gee, fine, thanks. I wanted to check on a friend of mine. She told me I could find her here."

"You can save yourself the trouble, dumb shit. If you're looking for that worthless slut Swindle, she's run off again. We ain't seen her for almost a week. Check the bars, if you find her, tell her not to bother coming round cuz she ain't getting back in."

"Actually, I'm looking for an employee of yours, Candi Slaughter."

"Candi? And she told you she would be here?"

"Tommy?" A voice from somewhere behind him called out.

"Just a minute, Gino, I'm dealing with a jerk."

"Gino?" I called. I wondered if he was in a wheelchair after I shot him yesterday. To tell the truth, I was shocked he wasn't in intensive care after I blew part of his leg off with the shotgun.

Tommy pulled the door open, and there was Gino, walking across the massive entryway toward the front door. He didn't seem to have a problem walking, didn't seem to be injured. He smiled, bobbed and weaved back and forth, waved at me, and flashed his idiotic grin. He was dressed in pajamas with a powder blue Terrycloth robe pulled over them. He wore white socks and fuzzy blue slippers with "Cookie Monster" emblazoned across the top of the slippers.

"Hi, I'm Gino," he said.

"He knows who you are. You finally up, sleepy-head?" Tommy said, and directed his attention back to me. "Look, pal, we been home all week, and we ain't seen no Candi. You want anything else?" He seemed to smirk, or was I just imagining that?

Looking at Gino, I was too stunned to answer, so I just shook my head.

"Maybe you should just call the cops. See ya," Tommy chuckled and then slammed the door in my face.

I stood there staring at the front door, replaying the scene of the two of them racing up my basement stairs. I'd fired the shotgun, actually saw the leg shatter. I was sure it had been them. Was there someone else?

Fifty-two

Louie had pretty well worked his way through the fifth of Jameson I'd purchased that morning. Things had gone full circle, and there was maybe just an inch and a half left in the bottle. He was stretched out on his couch, propped up by some mismatched threadbare pillows, still sipping from his coffee mug, which had ceased to hold coffee hours ago.

"Great, that's just great! So you're telling me I've lost my best clients of all time, and they weren't even down there in your basement?"

"Best clients of all time? They're crooks, for God's sake."

"Exactly, eternal clients," Louie whined.

"I must be losing what's left of my mind. Who in the hell was with Cazzo if it wasn't the D'Angelos and, more importantly, where the hell is Candi?"

"Yes, you are losing your mind. By the way, you're driving me crazy, too," Louie said, then took a healthy gulp from his mug.

"Jesus."

"Look, Dev, I'm not doubting you on the Cazzo thing. I mean, the three guys. I don't think the cops are doubting you either because they let you go. But maybe you were just wrong, and it was two other scum bags and not the D'Angelos."

"Something isn't right here," I said.

"Brilliant. But I don't know that we're going to figure it out. The cops said they've been stuck in that house for a week. D'Angelo told you the same thing today. It was probably someone else with Cazzo."

"No, it was the D'Angelos, and they've done something to Candi. I just know it."

"Well, if you're so sure, call Manning or your pal LaZelle. Better yet, since you're so clairvoyant, you can pick the winning numbers for me on the lottery ticket you're gonna buy while you're out getting me a refill, here," he said then held up the almost empty Jameson bottle.

"Too late, the liquor stores are closed."

"Already? What the hell time is it?"

"It's after eleven, Louie."

"Oh, no wonder I'm tired," he said, then snuggled down, closed his eyes, and promptly began to snore.

I waited a bit longer and then got in Louie's car and drove past Candi's. It was dark, and you couldn't have done a better job of making the place look like no one was home. I sputtered past the D'Angelos' house. The lights were on in a couple of second-floor rooms, and through partially closed blinds I could just make out colors flashing on a flatscreen TV.

I was really worried about Candi, but there seemed to be absolutely nothing I could do. I decided to park on the side street back beyond the D'Angelos' garage and wait. If they decided to go anywhere, I could follow them.

The birds woke me up. The damn things were chirping happily. It looked to be just before sunrise, growing a brighter grey to the east with every minute. If the D'Angelos had gone anywhere, I'd slept right through it.

I coaxed Louie's decrepit Geo Metro to life and sputtered my way around the corner. When I got back to Louie's, he was still asleep on the couch, clutching his almost empty bottle of Jameson like a security blanket.

I was drinking coffee at the counter when he stumbled into the kitchen. I'd spent the past couple of hours planning to write down all the ways I might find Candi. So far, the only thing I'd written down was her name.

"You look like I feel," he grumbled.

"Did you tell me the D'Angelos have a lake place up north?"

"Yeah, and a condo they rent out in Vegas."

"You got a location on the lake place?"

It turned out the place was in the middle of St. Louis County, way up north. I knew a guy in the sheriff's department up there and called him. I had to leave a message, but unlike Candi, Aaron, Manning, and just about everyone else I knew, he returned the call a few minutes later.

"Dev, long time, man. How they hanging?"

"Good, Tony. Hey, calling to see if you can give me a hand. I got a client down here looking for someone, and we're wondering if maybe she isn't at a cabin up there and out of cellphone range or something. Is it possible you could maybe check the place out see if she's there?"

"Is it on a lake or in the woods?"

"On a lake?" I asked Louie.

He nodded yes.

"A lake."

"Cool, I got my boat hooked up, and maybe I can get some fishing in."

"I'm sure they wouldn't mind. Call me if you see her. Maybe keep it on the quiet side if you catch my drift," I said.

"Yeah, I get it, probably just another woman trying to get as far away from you as possible."

I ignored the comment and gave him the address.

"Nothing else comes up I'll call you later this afternoon. I'd like to get the boat in by four-thirty, walleyes been biting all week."

"Glad you got your priorities, Tony."

"You betcha," he said and hung up.

"Sounds like you're grasping at straws," Louie said.

"It's about all I got. I been sitting here racking my brain, and I can't come up with anything. I'm really worried, Louie. I can't figure out where in the hell she would be. Why she wouldn't get in touch with me? Unless she can't."

"Maybe she just needs some space, and she's, I don't know, driving around town or something."

"That reminds me," I said. I pulled my wallet out and fished the dollar bill from the back. I'd written down the license number of that Porsche I saw parked in Candi's garage, but never checked it out.

I punched in a number on my cell and listened to four rings.

"Department of Motor Vehicles, this is Donna. How may I help you?" a cheery voice said.

"Hey, Donna, Dev Haskell."

There was a slight pause, just long enough to turn things icy, before she whispered, "You said you'd never call me here."

"No, I said I wouldn't call you unless it was an emergency."

"What do you want?"

I had a vision of her sitting in a grey office cubicle with her hand over her mouth as she spoke on the phone, trying to look innocent and failing miserably.

"Look, I just need you to run a license plate for me. I want to find out who the car is registered to, and then I'll let you go."

"Promise?" she didn't sound too sure.

"Scout's honor."

"Okay, give it to me?"

I read the number off the dollar bill. I could hear the keys clicking on her computer, and then I listened to her breathing while she waited.

"Registered to Rockett, Dudley. One one four two Dorthea Avenue, Saint Paul, Minnesota. Anything else?"

"Dudley Rockett?" I said, lost in thought.

"Anything else?"

"No, no thanks, Donna appreciate your help," I said, but she'd already hung up.

"Who was that?"

"I woman I know down at the DMV. She owes me a favor for the rest of her life."

"What the hell? Did you have photos of her with someone other than her husband?" Louie joked, then saw the look on my face and said, "Oh, Jesus. So what's up?"

"I saw a really pricey car parked in Candi's garage and wrote down the license number. Guess who it's registered to?"

"I heard you mention Dudley Rockett. What the hell does that mean?"

"I'm not sure."

Fifty-three

I could say something wasn't right, but that would be the understatement of the year. A super expensive car registered to that low life Dudley Rockett parked in Candi's garage? Cazzo or the D'Angelos must have parked it there, and now she was tied up in this mess. I was more worried than ever.

Tony called me back a little after five with a report that the D'Angelo lake place looked like it hadn't been occupied for months, and the walleyes weren't biting.

Much later, I left Louie happily ranting in front of the TV watching a rerun of *Teenage Mom*. I drove back to the D'Angelos'. I parked on the side street, armed with a couple of high octane coffees, and settled in to wait. A little after midnight, the garage door opened, and a shiny black Mercedes pulled out.

There were two people in the car. Tommy was behind the wheel and looked past me, checking for oncoming traffic before he turned. Gino sat in the back seat. I had slouched down as their garage door went up, but was able to catch a blank stare from Gino just before they drove off.

Once again, I had to coax Louie's car to life, then nearly floored it to get the thing going. It shuddered around the corner, belching black clouds of exhaust. I could see the taillights of the Mercedes a good block away. There wasn't any other traffic at this hour, so I was able to follow from a distance and not be recognized.

They drove along the river bluff and then crossed over the Mississippi on the 35E Bridge. Tommy took the first exit, and maybe a mile down the road turned into an exclusive condo development. I drove past the entrance, then pulled a U-turn farther down the road and doubled back.

The condo units were attached three-story brick and timber affairs. They had separate entrances set beneath steeply peaked slate roofs and tall fireplace chimneys. Every home had an attached double garage with a smaller third garage set back slightly that probably served to house a golf cart. They looked like a series of English cottages, which I guess fit since the sign coming in identified the development as Buckingham Estates.

At this hour most of the units were dark, although a number of cars were parked in front of the last place at the far end of the street. The Mercedes flashed its taillights, and I coasted to the side, maybe ten lots behind. I turned off Louie's car and waited.

About a half-minute later, Tommy climbed out of the front seat, then opened the rear door for his brother. Gino stood in the street, bobbing up and down until Tommy took him by the arm and led him up to the front door. Other than being led, Gino seemed to have absolutely no problem walking. Once they stepped inside the condo, I waited a brief minute before I walked down the block to get a closer look.

The place was dark. The blinds or drapes were tightly drawn. I counted a total of nine vehicles in the driveway and parked along the street. All were pricey rides, including one that was very pricey, a silver Porsche 911 Carrera 4S. The license plate rang a bell. It was the same number I'd called on this afternoon. the vehicle registered to Dudley Rockett.

I took out a couple of business cards from my wallet and wrote down the address. Then I took down all of the license plate numbers. When I finished, I resisted the urge to check out the back of the house and instead walked back to Louie's car, rumbled the thing to life, and putt-putted my way back to his house.

* * *

I phoned my close pal Donna down at the DMV before nine the next morning.

"Hi, Donna, Dev."

There was a pause before she hissed, "Oh, God, now what?"

"Just need a little help. I've got some plates I'd like you to run."

"I did that for you yesterday. I can't be doing this all the time. Somebody's going to find out, and I could lose my job," she whispered.

"Okay, look, you're right. I don't know what I was thinking. Hey, did I mention those photos of you and that young intern from your office? Was he in college or just high school? Hard to tell with that baby face. Was he even eighteen?"

"Okay, okay, I'll do it. Just don't bring that up, please."

"Thanks, Donna, I knew you'd understand. I've got about a half dozen plates. You want me to just text them to you?"

"No," she whispered. "That leaves a trail. Just read them to me, and I'll get back to you later. Everyone is in the office right now. I'll have to call you back once they go on break."

"Fine, appreciate the help," I said, then read off the license plate numbers from the night before.

"That's seven," she said as if to correct my earlier faulty description of a half dozen.

"Gee, you're right. That must be why college kids go for you."

She hung up.

"Now, who are you harassing?" Louie asked. He was standing in the kitchen doorway, wearing possibly the largest pair of Batman boxers I'd ever seen and scratching himself.

"Just my friend Donna down at the DMV. I had a couple of license plates I wanted to run."

"She must owe you big time," he said, shaking his head and then slowly shuffled toward the coffee pot as my phone rang.

"Wow, that was fast. Dev Haskell," I answered.

"Detective Manning, Haskell. My, but aren't we cheery this morning."

"I didn't know it was you, Manning."

"What? Now you don't care to speak with me?"

"No, I'm loving it. What can I do for you?"

"I just wanted to be the first to let you know that your car is available for pickup at the city impound lot."

"The impound lot?"

"Yes, I took the liberty of having it towed down there, thought it might be more convenient for you."

"Gee, thanks, I suppose there's a fee."

"*A* fee? Oh, no, there's several."

"What?"

"Let's see, a tow from your driveway to the crime lab, another tow down to the folks at impound…of course, three days and counting while it's been sitting down there."

"I could have picked up my car three days ago?"

"Gee, must have gotten lost on my desk. I've been really busy."

"Listen, Manning, this is nothing short of harassment. Hello? Hello?"

Louie looked at me and raised his eyebrows. "Another love message from that charmer, Manning?"

“Yeah. Hey, can you please put something on? I’m trying to get my morning off on the right foot. Then can you give me a ride down to the impound lot so I can get my car?”

“Give me five minutes,” Louie said.

It was closer to forty-five. Louie had dodged into the bathroom for a good half hour. When we finally arrived at the impound lot, he pulled over to the curb. “Hey, I can wait if you want, but I better not turn this thing off. I’m worried it won’t start up again.” With that, a cloud of exhaust seemed to get sucked into all four open windows, and we both began fanning the air.

“No, you go on. Appreciate the lift down here. I’ll see you back at the office.”

Fifty-four

I was seated at my desk, writing down the names and addresses from the license numbers as Donna read them off to me.

Louie was sleeping in his office chair with his feet resting on the picnic table.

"That should do it," Donna said when she'd finished.

"Thanks, Donna. As always, I appreciate it."

"Dev, I'm sorry if I was a little short earlier. It's just a rather delicate subject with me. Maybe we could work out some other arrangement if you wanted to get together sometime. We could discuss some options over a couple of drinks. I always thought it would be fun to get to know you better, much better."

"Actually, Donna, I'm kind of in enough trouble right now."

She hung up.

Louie started to come to at that point.

"I see you still have that unique effect on women."

"It's an acquired skill. Hey, these names mean anything to you?" I said, then handed him the list of names I'd just written down.

He took a moment to read through them then looked up at the ceiling deep in thought. "A couple of these I recognize. Heavy hitters. I'm guessing if you told me about the others, I'd say something like, 'Yeah, now I remember.' Lester Dalton, wasn't he one of those real estate developers who went tits up when the economy collapsed? And this other guy, O'Leary. If it's the same guy as I'm thinking, he was disbarred awhile back. Did some time for embezzlement of trust funds. I just didn't realize he was already out of prison."

"So this group of charmers makes up the get-together along with the D'Angelos after midnight last night. You remember, the brothers that haven't left their house for over a week now?"

"You got the address they were at?"

"It's at the bottom of that list. If you're thinking of checking county tax records, I already have. The place is in foreclosure, so there's a good possibility it is or at least should be, vacant."

"Remember the rumors I mentioned about the D'Angelos and a gambling operation? Ten to one, this is it," Louie said.

"Still doesn't get me any closer to Candi."

"Maybe it does, and we just can't see it. It might be worth a call to LaZelle on this."

"What, so they can go crashing in there and arrest everyone for playing some stupid card game? They'll goof it up, and I'll be no closer to finding Candi. I got a better idea."

"Do I want to hear this?" Louie winced.

"Probably not."

Fifty-five

The backyard of the foreclosed condo the D'Angelos had been in last night butted up against the River Bluff Golf Course. It was after midnight when I began to cut across the fairways to get to the place. It was the first time in a couple of months we'd had a cloudy sky. I misjudged my direction in the dark and ended up maybe a dozen lots to the east, but eventually, I found my way.

With the exception of different gas grills standing out on the patios, the backsides of these places all looked the same. Fortunately, the unit I was looking for was the last one at the far end, so I headed in that direction.

The place looked dark and quiet as I sat in the fairway rough for the next hour, brushing mosquitoes away. Mercifully, there was just enough of a breeze to keep all but the most vicious at bay. After some time, I began to think I may have drawn another blank when suddenly a thin sliver of light flashed on in an upstairs room. The shades or blinds had been drawn, but the light managed to escape just along the bottom edge of what looked like a bathroom window. The light was on for no more than two minutes before it went off.

I stayed there crouched in the rough for another fifteen minutes. The breeze had picked up, and I thought I might actually smell rain. Shortly after that, a distant rumble of thunder began to roll down the river valley. Off to the west, the occasional flash of lightning momentarily brightened the sky.

The temperature seemed to drop ten degrees just before large drops of rain began to fall. It was the first rain we'd had in almost two months. It figured this would be the night I was outside. I made my way across the backyard and up to the patio to see if I could hear anything. The rain began to come down a little harder as I approached. I crouched behind the patio hedge and waited for a few more minutes despite the rain splattering on the patio stones and the distant thunder. I thought I could hear a conversational hum punctuated by the occasional shrieking laugh or the odd raised voice.

It was pouring down now full force, and I was immediately soaked. I crept across the patio to see if I could make out what was going on. If I pressed myself against the sliding glass door, I could make out different voices and hear snippets of conversation. The overhang from the roof kept a good portion of the rain off me, although I was so wet at this point, I didn't think it made much difference.

The conversations were becoming clearer, and I moved up against the glass in an effort to hear.

"Oh, come on, I want to see. It's been months, for God's sake," a woman's voice said.

She sounded very near. I pressed my ear against the glass just as I felt a slight vibration, and then the entire door slid past me. I'd pushed myself up against the glass so hard that I fell onto my hands and knees as the thing slid sideways. I looked up from a puddle at a half dozen pairs of feet.

"Come on, people. Look, its gorgeous," some happy female voice said.

Then a not-so-happy voice shouted, "What the fuck?" and suddenly someone was pulling me back by the ankles just as I attempted to scramble away on all fours.

Another voice shouted, "It's the cops," and then there was an explosion against the back of my head, and I saw stars.

When I came to, I was lying on a carpeted floor, wrapped mummy-like with an orange electrical extension cord. The room seemed extremely dim as if it only had ten-watt bulbs in the sockets. Two big guys in white shirts and black tuxedo trousers were hurriedly folding up large tables and leaning them against a wall. Napkins, bits of food, some paper plates, and a couple of plastic drink glasses were scattered along a trail leading to the front door suggesting the crowd had left in a hurry. A roulette wheel leaned against another wall along with what looked like the top to a blackjack table. Some guy in a T-shirt suddenly hurried into the room, carrying a box of clinking bottles. He set the box on top of two others already stacked in a corner, then hustled back from whence he came.

I was aware of three or four sets of high heeled shoes hurrying down a staircase and out the front door. One of the women called over her shoulder, "You gotta make this right by me, Tommy," then squealed as she ran out into the downpour.

One of the white shirts glanced over and caught me looking around. "Oh, shit," he said. I watched helplessly as he picked up a folding table from against the wall, took a couple of running steps in my direction, and threw the thing on top of me.

I regained consciousness at some point, but I was still stuck under the table. There were voices coming from somewhere, male and female. My head was pounding too much to be able to make out anything that was being said. I thought the tone might have suggested an argument, but I wasn't sure, and to tell the truth, I hurt so much I just didn't care.

"He can finger everyone who was in the room," some guy growled as they seemed to come closer.

"But he won't," a woman responded.

"You don't know that. For Christ's sake, he'll ruin everything we've been working so hard to build."

"No, I won't have it. I won't let you."

"I'm sorry, honey, you got nothing to say about it."

"Don't do this, please."

"You kiddin'? We got no choice in the matter. You shoulda seen this coming. It's for your own damn good."

"No, let go of me. Let go, damn it." There was a sudden smacking sound, maybe a loud slap, and then a crash like something had been knocked over.

"I told you not to screw with this, but you didn't listen. This is what happens. Come on, we're taking him to the warehouse." A moment later, the table was lifted off me, and the D'Angelo brothers stood there with Tommy glaring down.

"Better watch him, Gino. He don't like Cookie Monster, and he wants to hurt him," Tommy said.

Gino's blank stare morphed into a snarl.

"Give me a half minute, then pick him up and drag his worthless ass out to the car," Tommy said. I heard the chirp of a car alarm a moment later. Gino picked me up effortlessly and hoisted me over his shoulder. As we went out the door, I glanced back into the room. Standing there, biting her lower lip with tears running down her face stood Candi.

She gave me a little wave good-bye.

"Candi, hey, Candi," I called and tried to kick myself free. It didn't work. Gino suddenly dumped me into the trunk of the car. Tommy shoved my legs inside and slammed down the lid. A moment later, the car started, and I could sense us speeding off.

Fifty-Six

I struggled for a while, trying to wiggle my way out from the extension cord wrapped around me without much luck. Despite the advertisements, I didn't find one thing roomy about the trunk space in this Mercedes. I was thinking my only hope would be they'd take a long drive, and I'd be able to eventually free myself when I suddenly felt the vehicle slow down.

We seemed to cautiously roll over some dips in the road, maybe a minute later we came to a complete stop. Someone got out of the car, and there was the sound of a garage door being opened. The car pulled ahead and stopped again a moment later, only this time the engine was shut off, and I heard the garage door noise again.

Suddenly Tommy's voice said, "Cookie Monster's going to be really proud of you, Gino." Then the trunk opened and both D'Angelos looked down their noses at me.

"Get him out of there, Gino, and put him on the bench," Tommy said.

Gino wrapped his big hands around the electrical cord and pulled me out like a sack of potatoes. During the ride, the cord had somehow shifted up toward my shoulders, but my arms were still hopelessly bound. He stood me up for a brief moment, then gave a grunt, hoisted me over his shoulder, and followed Tommy. I tried to kick a bit, which only made Gino reach behind his back and hit me a couple of times on the side of my head.

I had no idea where we were other than it looked like a large, empty brick warehouse. There were a series of windows about eight feet up from the cracked concrete floor. The windows appeared to be covered with a heavy-duty industrial screen. Most of the glass panes were cracked and broken. The parking lights on the Mercedes were the only source of illumination in the cavernous space.

"Throw his ass down there," Tommy said. Two steps later, I was slammed down so hard, it almost knocked the wind out of me.

Gino stepped back, twitching and scowling.

"You're gonna tell us a couple of things, and we'll get along just fine," Tommy said.

"I don't know anything," I pleaded.

"What did you do with all the cookies?" he said and smiled.

Gino nodded and then started to bob and weave, occasionally he threw a looping punch.

"What?"

"The cookies you took. What'd you do with them?" Tommy laughed.

I suddenly caught on. "Cookie Monster said I should save them for…for Gino."

This stopped Gino for a moment. Tommy looked over at him and said, "I think we're gonna need the helper. Better get it."

Gino drifted out of the pool of light and into the darkness.

"You a cop?"

"No, I'm not a cop. Look, I won't say a word to anyone, honest. I don't care what the hell you're doing. Really, I don't. This is all just one terrible misunderstanding."

"Yeah, well, we're going to begin understanding everything better in just a minute. Why the hell have you been following us? What the hell were you doing at the games tonight?"

"I was looking for Candi. I was worried something happened to her."

"Candi? I don't think you're her style, asshole. What are you really up to?"

"That's it. I was afraid something happened to her. I wanted to make sure she was okay, that's all."

"I don't think so," Tommy said. Gino suddenly bobbed back out of the darkness carrying a car battery and a set of jumper cables.

"Hey, you guys aren't gonna need that. I'll tell you anything you want to know. Please, believe me."

"We're gonna find out soon enough." Tommy chuckled. He took the cables from Gino once he'd set the battery on the dusty concrete floor. The battery was grayed around the edges from the sulfuric acid that had leaked out over time. Gino stepped back and wiped his hands across his T-shirt.

"I'm gonna ask you again. You with the cops?" Tommy said. He bent over and clipped the red-handled brass clamp onto the positive pole of the car battery.

"No. No, I'm not, Mr. D'Angelo. Really, I'm not," I pleaded.

"Like I said, pal, we're gonna find out pretty damn quick." He laughed and clipped the black-handled clamp to the negative post.

"Please, please, don't. I just didn't want to get fingered for Dudley Rockett's murder, or that hit and run, that's all. And then Candi disappeared and…"

"And you grabbed Swindle for yourself," Tommy shouted and then slapped the two clamps together, causing them to arc viciously.

"Oh, God, don't. I didn't take Swindle, honest. I'll tell you anything you want—"

"That's just what Rockett said." Tommy laughed, then slapped the clamps together a couple of times, causing them to arc and scare the living daylights out of me.

I slid further down the bench to get away.

"This is gonna hurt you a lot more than me. Don't let him get away, Gino. Hit him if he tries." Tommy chuckled.

Gino took two steps toward me and went into a fighter's stance, rolling his fists back and forth, smiling an idiotic grin.

Tommy laughed, then slapped the clamps together a couple more times, making them crackle and spark.

I tried to slide away on the bench, but Gino stepped in and clubbed me hard on the back of the head with a heavy left hand.

I suddenly drew my right leg up and kicked him as hard as I could. I caught him just at the knee, then leaped off the bench and jumped over him as he crumpled to the ground.

"God damn it. Come here, you," Tommy yelled. He grabbed for me with both hands, dropping the jumper cables on Gino in the process.

Gino gave a high pitched scream as the cables arced. I hobbled off into the darkness. I had no idea where I was going other than away from those two. I heard footsteps behind me, so I picked up speed and kept going until I became aware of a wall looming in front of me. I took a sharp turn to the left and didn't hear anyone following.

A moment later, I heard a car door slam, and the Mercedes fired up. The tires screeched as the car accelerated and circled toward me. My arms were still wrapped tightly in the coil of the orange electrical cord. I took off, running parallel with the brick wall toward the front of the building. The car raced toward me, scraping against the wall in the process. I faked a couple of steps to the left then jumped back against the wall just as the Mercedes shot past me. The side mirror clipped the coil wrapped around me, knocking me down to the concrete floor. I looked up as the brake lights flashed and the car screeched to a stop.

I was up and running across the middle of the floor, back toward the bench as the Mercedes shot back in reverse and slammed into the brick wall. I ran toward Gino, sitting on the floor in front of the bench. His knee was bent at an odd right angle, although he didn't seem to be in any pain.

Tommy floored the Mercedes in my direction then screeched to a stop just a foot or two in front of Gino. I faced him on the other side of the bench and rocked back and forth, dodging left and right. He glared at me from behind the wheel, then backed up and made a large loop to come behind the bench.

I took off into the darkness and headed for the garage door, thinking maybe I could somehow raise the thing and roll under it to get out of the building. I made it to the door just as the headlights caught me in their glare. There was maybe just an inch or two of space at the bottom of the fiberglass door. Just barely large enough to let me slip my foot underneath and try to raise the thing.

As I began to raise the door with my foot, I heard the Mercedes pick up speed. I knew I wasn't going to make it and tumbled to the side just as Tommy sailed past me and through the garage door.

There were flashing lights outside, three sets with a fourth coming across a distant parking lot. Squad cars, St. Paul's finest. One of them threw a spotlight on the

Mercedes as it skidded to a stop. Tommy backed up and attempted an end-run off to the side. The squad car coming across the parking lot flicked on a spotlight and cut him off. Tommy jumped out of his car and ran half a dozen steps before a voice on the loudspeaker shouted, "Stop. Stay where you are. Keep your hands where we can see them."

He took a few more steps, then stopped, turned to face the spotlight, and said, "I caught this guy breaking into the warehouse. Thank goodness you got here. He assaulted me and my handicapped brother when we tried to stop him."

I was kneeling on the warehouse floor where the garage door used to be. I was still wrapped up with the extension cord. Gino was somewhere behind me in the dark, singing the theme to Sesame Street.

Fifty-seven

Aaron and Manning were both seated on neon-pink, hard plastic chairs that had been dragged from the hallway into my hospital room. Louie sat in the corner, sinking into the cushioned visitor's chair.

"The nine-one-one call came through on a phone registered to Swindle Lawless," Aaron explained.

"We've had her under lock and key in the psyche ward ever since she was released from Detox," Manning added.

"So, what are you saying? That Swindle didn't place the call?"

"I don't see how she could," Aaron said.

"And the gambling club or whatever the hell was going on there?" I asked.

"Based on the list your attorney gave us—" Aaron shot a glance at Louie, who smiled politely. "The property was one of a number in foreclosure. At one time they all belonged to Lester Dalton."

"The developer?"

"Yeah, they'd reverted back to the bank some time ago, but he still had access. You know how the banks are," Aaron said.

I nodded.

"We've discovered evidence that suggests they worked Rockett over at that warehouse location and then transported him to the address where he was found. They drowned the poor bastard in the bathtub just to finish him off. Another Lester Dalton place, by the way."

"So how come they got away with this stuff? You kept telling me they were monitored, or at least Gino was. You guys said they never left the house."

"Well, that's pretty much the case," Manning said, looking more than a little uneasy.

"Pretty much the case?" I said and looked at Louie.

"Go ahead, Detective, be my guest. Enlighten my client," Louie said.

"Well, you see, it seems that Mr. D'Angelo had lost a part of his leg, and we seem to have inadvertently attached the monitor around his prosthesis."

The room was quiet for a long moment.

"You mean to tell me you guys put the monitor on Gino's fake leg?" I spoke slowly and very deliberately.

"It would appear that was the case," Manning said, not looking directly at me. His bald head was shifting from pink to a deep crimson.

"So as long as the leg was left in the house, you didn't know the difference, that right? He probably just strapped on a spare wooden peg he had lying around, went out, and painted the town, right?

"Well, that might be a little far fetched."

"I'm not so sure. Really great job, Detective. Very well done. Can't tell you how safe that makes me feel. And then I end up being accused of murder because you guys can't figure out the difference. You gotta be kidding me. My life has been hell. I almost get killed, I…"

"You weren't officially charged," Aaron said.

"Thanks for that," I replied.

"Yeah, well, it's all coming together. Look, you might as well hear it from me," Aaron said. "Your gal Candi…seems she and your buddy Joey Cazzo might have had a thing for one another."

"You're kidding, Cazzo? How long have they been an item?" I asked.

"Oh, I'd say up until about early this morning when Tommy D'Angelo fingered Cazzo for the hit and run on Ruggles. Apparently, the guy called Candi a name or something. Cazzo took offense, and they used Swindle's car to run Ruggles down."

"Cazzo ran the guy down in Swindle's car?" I asked.

"No, it was most likely Gino D'Angelo driving, not that he's able to remember," Manning said.

"Small world, isn't it? You meet someone at a concert, and it just goes downhill from there. Look, Dev, at least we're beginning to get things all cleared up. We'll get two murders off the books, and we broke up this gambling ring. You should probably rest up." Aaron smiled and stood.

"No hard feelings then, Haskell?" Manning said and extended his hand.

"Get the hell out of here," I said.

Aaron and Manning left. Louie hung around for a bit until I drifted off to sleep. I woke up when someone gave me a kiss and slid her hand under the bedcover. My first thought was the nurses here were really into full service. I blinked my eyes open.

"Did I wake you, bad boy?" Candi whispered.

"Candi. Am I dreaming?"

"No, it's really me. Miss me, Baby?"

"I saw you at that house. What in the hell is going on? They almost killed me last night," I said.

"But you're okay, aren't you?"

"Well, yeah. I mean, I'll live, but where have you been? Why did you disappear?"

"I've been in Las Vegas, Dev. I just needed some time off. I came back this morning as soon as I heard."

"This morning? I saw you last night when they dragged me out of there. They were going to kill me, Candi. Did you know that? They were going to kill me, damn it, and all you did was wave good-bye."

"But they didn't, did they?"

"Jesus Christ, do you know what almost happened? They were gonna shock me. That God damned maniac Tommy and his lunatic brother tried to run me down. I'm not kidding they tried to kill me."

"But they didn't, Dev. The police got there just in time and stopped them, didn't they? And now you're safe."

"You and Joey Cazzo, you were playing me."

"Dev, where did you ever get that idea?"

"Where? Hell, the cops told me. Plus, I saw his clothes in your place…the sport coats, the golf shirts—It was you and Cazzo all along, wasn't it?" I said, suddenly figuring things out.

"You're sounding crazy, baby."

"Besides, Tommy D'Angelo fingered Cazzo on the hit and run," I gambled.

"That Ruggles bastard called me fat," she shot back.

"I knew it."

"What are you talking about?" she said, suddenly sounding nervous.

"You and Cazzo, you took those photos when you drugged me. You two took those photos of Swindle, planted that phone on Rockett. You were in on it, Candi. You set me up. You drugged me for Christ's sake. They were gonna kill me, Candi."

"You seemed to enjoy yourself. I didn't hear any complaints from you at the time. Anyway, you can forget all that. It's all in the past." She smiled, then bent over and kissed me.

"Candi, damn it, that jerk, Joey Cazzo?"

"Don't worry about him," she said, then leaned down very close, nibbled my ear, and whispered, "Besides, he's out of the picture now, Dev. He's gone forever."

"Candi," I said and sat up in the bed. "You can't do this."

"Oh, really? Gee, Dev, sorry, but it's already done, and I've been out in Vegas for a few days." She laughed. "See, check it out. I've even got airline tickets and credit card receipts from the Bellagio." She laughed, then reached into her purse and pulled out a couple of airline boarding cards and what looked like a bunch of credit card receipts.

"That's all fake, and you know it. You might fool the cops, but I know. It's all bullshit. You just sent someone out there using your name."

"Well, sometimes a girl's just got to do certain things to get ahead."

I shook my head but couldn't think of anything to say.

She smiled, shrugged, and looked at me for a long moment. "Well, what do you have to say?"

After a while, I turned and stared out the window. "They were gonna kill me, Candi," I mumbled.

I heard her exhale heavily, then after a bit, she said, "Last chance, bad boy."

I continued to stare out of the window.

"Okay, suit yourself," she said, then picked up her purse and took a couple of steps toward the door before she turned. "Oh, something for you," she said. There was an edge to her voice I'd never heard before. She reached into her purse and pulled out an iPhone housed in a sequined leopard skin case. She tossed it onto my bed, then stormed out of the room without saying another word.

Fifty-eight

We were standing in a lobby on the fourth floor of the police department, just outside homicide. “Where did you say you got this?” Manning asked me.

“I was on my way to work, I opened the front door, and there it was. I thought I should drop it off down here,” I said.

“Someone just left an iPhone on your doorstep?” he said, turning the phone over and examining the sleazy leopard skin case.

“I guess. I think it might be registered to Swindle.”

“How would you know that?”

“Just a guess. I saw her use it once. Kind of hard to forget that sequined case the thing is in.”

“So why bring it to us?” he asked.

“Just thought it might be pertinent to one of your investigations. Besides, don’t you guys deal in lost stuff? You know, when you’re not out chasing bad guys.”

He nodded but didn’t say anything.

“See you around, Detective. I’ve gotta get to work,” I said then walked back down the hall to the elevators.

Fifty-nine

I was sitting on my front porch, thinking about Candi, watching the world go by and sipping another beer. I was worried about her, wondering if I'd been too harsh and hoping she was okay. I sort of came out of my cloud when a skateboarder skidded across my front lawn on her hands and knees.

"Dev, is that you?" she said, getting back up.

I stared at the blonde hair, the bikini top, the tight shorts, and the skateboard under her arm. Her hair was pulled tightly into a ponytail. She'd had her navel pierced since the last time I'd seen her, but it was still surrounded by that sunburst tattoo. She looked reasonably together. It took me a moment before it all clicked.

"Swindle, wow! You look great. How are you doing?"

"Oh, fine, just fine. Been sorta straight for a while, kind of," she said and smiled.

A kid maybe twenty years her junior suddenly skateboarded up alongside her and came to a quick stop, flipping the skateboard up into his hand.

"Oh, Dev, this is Marcus. We met in treatment. Marcus, this is Dev. I knew him in my other life," Swindle said.

Marcus looked me up and down, turned to Swindle, and said, "New friends, new contacts. We put everything else behind us, my precious."

"'Spose you're right, as always." She shrugged. "Anyway, good to see you, Dev."

"Yeah, same here, Swindle. Like I said, you look great. Hey, you ever see Candi?"

"Not really. Umm, you know, new friends, new contacts."

"Put everything else behind us," I joined in. "Yeah, I just wondered where she was working now, that's all."

"Working now? Are you kidding? She got all sorts of real estate, and now she owns the Tutti Frutti Club. I can't believe you didn't hear about it. It was in all the papers. Her two uncles and that fiancée of hers got life sentences."

"Fiancée? Uncles?"

"Come on, put everything else behind us," Marcus said, then pushed off on his skateboard and headed down the street.

"Gotta go, Dev. I'll probably see you around," Swindle called, and rolled away.

The End

If you enjoyed **Tutti Frutti** please tell 2-300 of your closest friends. Since I'm indie published a review from you really, really helps even if it's just a sentence or two. Many thanks,

Mike

Don't miss the sample of **Last Shot** on the next page.

Sneak Peek

Last Shot

Second Edition

MIKE FARICY

One

Annie was a petite blonde with large brown eyes, who stood barely an inch over five feet. We'd casually linked up from time to time over the past couple of months. Up until now, all of our meetings had been spur of the moment, meaning she called, and I suggested maybe she would like to come right over and 'chat.'

Tonight's 'chat' was different. For the first time, she invited me over to her place. We feasted on undercooked spaghetti with little cut up bits of hot dog floundering in a runny ketchup sauce. Apparently, the kitchen wasn't her strong suit, so the bottles of wine I showed up with helped us survive her lack of gourmet skills.

It was drizzling softly outside when we finally took a break. Annie was lying next to me with one of her gorgeous shapely legs draped over mine. She was tracing four-letter words and triple-X suggestions across my chest with her fingertip, giggling. We'd been frolicking up in her candlelit bedroom for a couple of hours, a room I'd never been in before. During our break, I was beginning to check the place out.

The walls were painted a dinged-up off-white. A large oak double-chest of drawers with a matching mirror that covered most of the wall was wedged in next to the door. About four dozen Mardi Gras-style beaded necklaces hung from either side of the mirror.

A smaller dresser, once painted olive drab now chipped and scratched, stood at the end of the queen-size bed. A flatscreen TV sat on top of the dresser and half-covered one of the two-bedroom windows. It all made for tight quarters, and I'd had to turn sideways just to squeeze around the end of her bed.

Six-foot mirrors on the bi-fold closet doors reflected our image as we lay in bed. Next to the closet, the clear imprint of a heavy-treaded boot, about ten sizes larger than Annie's demure little feet was stamped on the wall.

"Did you play a lot of sports in school?" I asked.

"No, not at all, I was a pretty geeky kid. About the only thing I played was the clarinet in the school band, and I didn't do that very well."

"Then where'd you get all the trophies? There must be a couple dozen up here, looks like you're into ballet or dance or something. What about all those medals and ribbons in the two cases on the wall? Are they from your school band?"

"All that junk belongs to Lydell."

"Lydell?"

"He was my boyfriend. Well, until I broke up with him."

"And he left all this stuff here?"

"Well, I only sent him the text last night."

"The text?" I asked and rolled over to face her.

"Yeah, telling him we were through. I really didn't feel like talking with him. He gets so dramatic, and he's kinda got a temper."

"You didn't tell him in person?" I was getting a warning sign flashing inside my thick skull.

"How could I, Dev? He's out of town," she said, suddenly sitting up and looking down on me.

"Out of town? You mean just across the river in Minneapolis or like way far away out of town?" I sat up to face her.

"Relax, he's in Chicago," she said, bouncing her surgically enhanced chest from side to side.

I completely forgot what I was going to ask next.

"He's such a big baby."

"Chicago?"

"Yeah, that stupid UFC."

"UFC . . . is that where he goes to school?"

"No, dopey," she said and pushed me down. She straddled me and began to lightly run her nails down my stomach, smiling in a leering way. "It's his crazy obsession, baby, that idiotic Ultimate Fight Club. God, I'm so sick of it. He trains all day long, lifting his big, dumb weights and drinking all those smelly old protein drinks. Five days a week, he spends at least an hour in a cage sparring with some other obsessed animal."

"Sparring in a cage?"

"Yeah, he—" Her iPhone rang at that moment, and she reached over to grab it off the top of the double chest of drawers. "Oh, God, can you believe it? Go figure!"

"What is it?" I asked.

"Hello, Lydell?"

I attempted to sit up, but she pushed me down again. "Shhh-hhh," she said, signaling with her index finger to be quiet.

"So, you got my text message?"

I could feel my heart beginning to pound, but then again, he was in Chicago.

"No, we've talked about all this before. No, I don't care. This time I really mean it."

I wasn't sure she should be sitting on top of me during this conversation.

"What?" she said. "You did? When?"

Whatever it was, Lydell had her attention. I was guessing a tattoo with 'Annie' emblazoned across his heart.

"No, Lydell, this time I'm not kidding," she said, sounding like she really wasn't.

I was thinking maybe some of the passion and romance in the air from just a moment ago was beginning to dissipate.

"Fine, go ahead! So what? Oh, really? Is that supposed to be a threat, Lydell?"

Oh-oh.

"I don't care if you are parked out front. Besides, this just isn't a very good time for me."

Out front?

"Well, you should have called me first."

Not what I wanted to hear.

"Don't you talk to me like that, and it's really none of your business."

Alarm bells were sounding in my head.

"Well, just go ahead and try. See if I care. Anyway, I had the locks changed."

Not good.

"Don't you dare! You kick that door in, and you're going to pay for it. I'm warning you, Mister."

I took that last line as my walking papers. I rolled out from underneath Annie just as a loud boom sounded downstairs.

"God, I just hate it when he goes crazy like this. He gets so worked up he's liable to do anything. You probably should leave, Dev," she said, then slid off the bed and tossed her phone onto the pillow.

I heard wood splintering in the door frame downstairs.

"Oh-oh, might be better if you just went out the window." She made it sound like it wasn't the first time someone had fled by that route

"Annie, damn it," a voice roared from downstairs.

"Better hurry," she half-whispered, then motioned me away with her hands before she peeked into the hallway.

I raised the window and stared into the wet night. God, it was at least a story and a half drop. There was some large bush spreading out right below the window. A light flashed on in the house next door, and I could see a little high school girl filling a glass of water at the kitchen sink.

"Annie, where the hell are you?" Lydell roared. It sounded like he was stomping through the dining room, making his way into the kitchen.

"You gonna be okay?" I asked.

"Don't worry. He does this every once-in-a-while. Soon as he sees me with my clothes off, he'll calm down and get all apologetic, but you better go," she whispered and nodded toward the open window.

"Annie," he screamed as he stomped back into the dining room.

I figured a 911 call wouldn't get the police here fast enough. What the hell, just a story and a half. I was out the window, hanging from the sill, dropping. Ouch! Snap, crackle, and pop! I landed on my feet and tried to do the crouch, tuck, and roll just like I'd learned in the Army, but I'd never done it naked before, and then there was that damn bush. I heard something break as I tumbled into the mud. Fortunately, it was a branch on the bush. I didn't care to contemplate a misplaced limb.

I'd barely landed when my jeans and T-shirt flew out the window. One of my shoes sailed out next. Then the other, hastily tossed, landed on the roof of the back porch next door.

The high-school girl at the kitchen sink stared at me wide-eyed as I picked up my T-shirt. She looked up toward the ceiling when my shoe thumped across her roof, but I really couldn't worry about that just now. I was more concerned about that Ultimate Fight Cluber, Lydell, flying out the window after me. I couldn't find my boxers and didn't have the luxury of time to search. I pulled my T-shirt on over the mud and scratches then quickly stepped into my jeans, zipping them up on the run.

I only had one shoe. Fortunately, my wallet and car keys were still in my jeans. I limped across the backyard and out to the alley so I could circle the block. The high school girl had moved from the kitchen window to her backdoor and watched me as I faded from view under the alley light.

Luckily, I had parked across the street and down a couple of doors. A bright red pick-up truck had skidded to a stop after barreling fifteen feet through the hedge into Annie's front yard. The thing had dual rear wheels and an Ultimate Fight Club bumper sticker that said 'Go Ahead - Take Your Best Shot.' The driver's door was still open with some country chorus blaring 'Death before Dishonor.' Pretty safe guess the vehicle belonged to recently returned Lydell.

As I drove past, I could see the back of a broad-shouldered muscular guy with a shaved head standing in Annie's front entry. His head looked like a shiny globe and appeared to be hanging in abject surrender on his muscle-bound body. He was nodding slightly, and it looked like he had already been reduced to the apologetic mode. I could just see Annie from the knees down, standing halfway up the stairs. Hopefully, she'd make him sleep on the floor against her ruined front door.

I drove home scratched, muddied, but still alive.

TWO

Pauley Kopff was a ninth-grade dropout, a doper, a failed petty criminal, and, in general, a lifelong disappointment to anyone who had the misfortune to come in contact with him. Even worse, he still owed me close to two hundred bucks for some investigative work I'd done at his behest a while back. Like all things where Pauley was involved, someone got stiffed. In this case, me. I figured two hundred bucks wasn't worth the trouble of dealing with Pauley again.

Unbeknownst to me, he was currently working at Karla's Karwash. Fortunately, I'd seen him first and had successfully hidden in a retail aisle amidst packages of naked-girl air-fresheners and devil's-head gearshift knobs until I had to step up to the register and pay for my carwash.

Pauley stood no more than five-foot-six if you included his ridiculous gel-spiked hair. He held the door as I walked outside to my car. He somehow seemed to always have a wiseass look pasted across his face, and I felt the immediate urge to hit him, hard.

"Thank you for getting cleaned up at Karla's, please … Hey, Dev Haskell, right? Is that really you? Didn't recognize you with all those scratches. Did someone change her mind?" he said, then laughed just a little too loudly. "Get it? Change her . . ."

There were too many witnesses around for what I had in mind, so I decided to ignore his comment.

"Hi there, Pauley. When did you get out?"

"Two months and twenty-six days ago. I only had to pull two years on a four-to-six. Good behavior," he bragged as if it was somehow an over-the-top lifetime accomplishment.

"Congratulations, Pauley. I hope things continue to work out for you," I said, still on the move, trying desperately to put more distance between us.

"Got another four days, six hours and thirty-nine minutes and I'm out of that half-way house. But, who's counting?" He chuckled after me.

I figured the folks at the half-way house were counting the seconds and crossing the days off their calendars. The entire staff probably had a party lined up to celebrate Pauley's imminent departure.

"Good for you. Sounds like things are getting back on track. Keep up the good work, Pauley," I said, all the while, hurrying toward my car. I slid behind the wheel and tried to pull the door closed.

A woman stepped between the car door and me. She had shoulder-length auburn hair pulled back in a ponytail. She pretended to wipe the doorframe dry then caught me trying to look down her T-shirt. There was a gold chain around her neck, but it had slipped inside her

T-shirt and gotten lost somewhere in that healthy cleavage, so I couldn't see what lucky medallion dangled on the end.

She stared up at me with brown eyes before she whispered, "I could really use your help, Mr. Haskell."

"Do I know you?"

She visibly blushed, then glanced around quickly to see if anyone else was listening.

"No." She shook her head. "But Karla told me about you. She's a friend of mine. I heard Pauley say your name. Will you give me a call, please? Promise?" She handed me a card that advertised a dollar off my next carwash. Her name and number were hastily penned across the back.

"Gee a dollar off…how can I refuse?"

"Promise?"

"You're Desi?" I asked, reading the name scrawled across the back of the card.

A car honked behind me. Pauley was behind the wheel, slowly rolling forward with the driver's door open. He sprayed glass cleaner on the inside of the windshield then honked the horn again.

"I'm finished here at three," she said softly, then stepped away and closed my door.

"I'll give you a call," I said, nodded and checked her out in my sideview mirror as I drove off.

I left a message on Desi's phone around dinner time.

I'd fallen asleep later that night on the couch watching the Twins lose. I had no idea what time it was or who was on the other end of the phone when it rang.

"Hi, Mr. Haskell, I hope I'm not calling too late," the voice said after my hello.

"No, not a problem. I was just going over some paperwork here. How are things on your end?" I asked, fishing for some clue, trying to determine who in the hell I was talking to.

"Fine, I guess, as long as you don't go into any real detail."

"Okay, I won't. What else is cooking?"

"Well, Mr. Haskell I…"

"Please call me Dev, okay?"

"Okay, Dev. Look, I wondered if we could get together and talk about my, ahhh situation. Karla said you were pretty good."

Got it, Desi from the car wash.

"Pretty good? That covers a lot of sins." I chuckled.

"I'd like to meet so I could maybe get your opinion," she said, ignoring my attempt at humor then added, "Some public place." Apparently, Karla had told her about me, and she was playing it safe.

Today was the seventh or eighth, and other than Jameson night next Thursday at The Spot bar, I had an open calendar for the rest of the month, so I asked, "What's your week look like?"

"I'm working from noon till seven at night for Karla, and I picked up a bartending gig at Nasty's on the weekend, nine ‘til close. Other than that, I’m pretty much free.”

“You know Nina’s?”

“That coffee place?”

“Yeah. Right, I could make some calls and reschedule things to meet you, say tomorrow morning? Does that work?”

“You sure? I mean, I don’t want to cause any problems. I’m guessing you’re really busy.”

“I think I can move some things around. Let me get to a couple of people. I don’t anticipate any difficulty. I’ll see you at Nina’s, nine-thirty tomorrow morning.”

“Thank you, Mr., I mean, Dev. I’ll see you there.”

Three

I walked into Nina's ten minutes early. Desi was already seated at a far table and gave me a wave. Her auburn hair was like a flashing beacon in a sea of 'not-quite-awake' folks surgically attached to their coffee. As I approached, seeing her away from the noise and blur of the car wash, I noticed she had a figure that garnered a double-take.

"Hey, I guess the early bird gets the worm. Been here long?"

"Only a minute or two. I just sat down," she said.

If she'd just sat down, she must have drunk her large coffee standing up. Her mug was empty. She was dressed in blue jeans and a v-neck T-shirt. The T-shirt had sharply creased sleeves and looked to have been ironed. A Claddagh dangled from the gold chain around her lovely neck; hands holding a heart with a crown, the Irish symbol for friendship, love and loyalty.

"I'm gonna get a coffee. You want another or something to eat? I was actually thinking of ordering some breakfast."

"A coffee would be great. Just black, nothing else for me," she said.

There was something in her look. I'd been in these situations before and maybe picked up on her starving eyes. If we were dating, she would have wanted just 'one little bite' of my dessert then inhaled the entire thing. I got two coffees, ordered two omelets and a caramel roll.

"Thanks for the coffee," she said as I sat down. "Wow, that looks really good." She nodded toward my caramel roll.

Oh-oh.

"I hope you don't mind. I took the liberty of ordering you an omelet. I didn't want to be my usually piggy self and eat in front of you. Here, you gotta try half of this. They're really good," I said, cutting the caramel roll in half.

"Oh, no, I really couldn't," she said at the same time she grabbed the larger half.

"Go ahead . . . the omelets should be out in just a couple of minutes."

"You sure you don't mind?" she said, then crammed a good portion of the caramel roll into her mouth, not waiting for my answer.

"So, you mentioned a situation. How can I help?"

Desi quickly chewed, then swallowed and glanced longingly at her remaining portion before looking up at me.

"Well, see, I didn't always wash cars and tend bar at a strip joint."

I shook my head and gave a little shrug suggesting it wasn't important where she worked or what she did.

"No, really, I was somebody. I went to school and even made the Dean's List in grad school. I was an architect here in town. I was making something of myself."

"An architect?" I didn't mean to sound so surprised.

"Yeah." She nodded then shoved the rest of the caramel roll into her mouth.

"Why aren't you working as an architect now?"

"Have you read the papers? You remember that little thing called the great recession? No one was building anything for about five years, let alone looking for someone to do design work."

"So, you went from being an architect to washing cars?" That sounded pretty drastic, and I wasn't quite following.

"Not quite that direct a route, but then that's what I wanted to talk to you about. Karla said you were someone who would understand."

"You two friends?"

"We were friends in high school but drifted apart when I went off to college and then grad school. We were out of touch for years, then when I hit rock bottom, Karla was one of the few who didn't turn their back on me."

Two large omelets arrived. Desi held back from immediately stuffing hers into her mouth. "God, this looks absolutely fabulous, but I'll never be able to finish it all," she said.

"Well, do your best. They're even better than they look. Dig in. So you were telling me about learning the car wash business from the ground floor up."

She smiled a sad smile, shoveled a forkful of omelet into her mouth and chewed for a moment.

"I graduated from Clemson and got hired by a firm in town, Touchier and Touchier."

I nodded, pretending I was familiar with the firm.

"You know them? Most people don't, but then again, I suppose in your line of work you would."

"Give me the short version," I said.

"Well, as you know, we were into the security thing, financial institutions, a couple of high-security detention facilities, the occasional federal building."

I nodded knowingly, not having the slightest idea what she was talking about.

"Anyway, that's where I met Gas. He was one of the senior partners."

"Gas?"

"Gaston Driscoll," she said off-handedly like the name needed no explanation.

"That rings a bell, but I can't tell you why."

"Probably because I was charged, tried and convicted, and that bastard got off without so much as a slap on the wrist."

I suddenly got it. "Does this have something to do with the security system at the Federal Reserve Bank?"

"That was part of it, along with the security system at the Federal facility down in Rochester."

"Minnesota?"

She nodded and shoveled another bite of omelet into her mouth.

"Oh, yeah, there was an escape or something. That sound right?" I said.

She nodded, followed with another forkful, then said, "Yeah, literally a genius. The media called him Little Jimmy Fennell. He was some kind of savant, only about four-foot-three. I don't know what the politically correct term is, height-challenged, or something. Anyway, he'd been transferred to the Federal Medical Center in Rochester for health reasons."

She stuffed another forkful of omelet, chewed a moment, thinking and then swallowed.

"I could say he escaped. Actually, that's the official story, but the truth is he just walked away from the Federal Medical Center one day. No one thought him capable of ever getting out of his wheel chair. Apparently, he'd been successfully fooling everyone for a couple months. Then one day, he just got up and walked out the door wearing an orange jumpsuit. I guess there was a car waiting for him."

It was ringing a bell. The story was like something out of a bad movie.

"Yeah, I remember this. Someone ends up with the security plans to the Federal Reserve Bank, right? They bypass security with that Little Jimmy guy's help, make a big haul, but didn't something strange happen to this Little Jimmy character?"

"Yeah, he's found on the top steps of the Cathedral, prostrate and dead. It was around the time of that book, The Da Vinci Code, and people went crazy thinking there was some message because of the way he was laid out. I think in reality, he was just a guy who'd eaten one too many White Castle's and happened to be walking past the Cathedral when he suffered a major heart attack."

"But the money was never recovered, and it was a lot of money," I said, remembering.

"Millions," Desi said, then scraped up the last bit of omelet from her plate and looked longingly at the remaining portion of my caramel roll.

"Go for it," I nodded.

"Thanks," she said, quickly stuffing it into her mouth. "Anyway, right. In fact, if not for his association with bank security systems, there was a good chance no one would have even linked Little Jimmy to the robbery."

"But didn't they find money on him?"

"Yeah, nine crisp one hundred dollar bills with consecutive serial numbers. Poor little fool had them hidden in his sock. They suspect he probably passed one at the White Castle, but they never found it."

"And your involvement? How did you know this guy?"

"I didn't know him at all. I just read about him in the paper. My involvement? I can sum it up in two words, Gaston Driscoll. We had a little thing going, at least, that's what I thought. Turned out, he was just using me as a delivery girl. Well, and his mistress."

"Was this a one-time get-together over too many drinks, or was it more of a relationship?"

"It was a relationship, definitely a relationship," she said, then seemed to reconsider. "At least, that's what I thought at the time."

I was treading carefully. More than one guy I knew didn't realize he was in a relationship after an alcohol-fueled wrestling match in the backseat of a car.

"How long did the relationship last?"

"Until the day he had me fired. He had me escorted out of the building by a woman from HR who seemed to be about as thrilled with the situation as I was. Jesus, we were both in shock and tears."

I just nodded.

"Gas and I had been together for maybe ten months if that's your question. He told me he was making plans to divorce his wife. He told me he'd been trapped in a loveless marriage for years, and I was like an open window that let the sunshine in. Of course, I wasn't adding two and two. Jesus, they still lived together. They were actually on vacation in Florida when he had me fired."

"Did he ever try to contact you?"

"Since the day he had me fired, I haven't heard so much as a peep from that creep."

"Can you prove any of this?"

"The mistress part?" she asked and then brushed a strand of hair off her pretty face. "You mean, do I have love letters or the home videos he took of us making love? A book of photos from our beach trip? No. He bought me gifts, lingerie, a lot of lingerie. He gave me a set of pearls one time. He surprised me with diamond earrings on Valentine's Day. He promised to take me to Ireland, where my grandparents were from. But no, nothing I can document."

I nodded and continued to listen. Desi was looking at me, but I didn't think she could see me. She was remembering candlelight dinners and that crazy, wonderful head-over-heels infatuation that came with falling in love. The fact that you just couldn't believe your incredible good fortune at finding the world's most wonderfully perfect partner, that was usually just before everything went to hell in a hand-basket.

"Funny, my grandparents came from a little village in County Sligo, Ireland. Turns out his family came from the same area, in fact, he owns a house over there. Well, at least that's what he told me. He pointed it out to me on the map one time. Course, stupid gullible old me, I thought it might be some celestial sign like we were made for one another." She was looking through me seeing something else, something not actually there. Her lips formed a slight smile, yet somehow she looked sad. Then she blinked and seemed to come back to the here and now.

"When the bank foreclosed on my home, I still had his favorite wines laid out in my pantry. The CDs he liked were still in my living room. Oh, and a giant jar of chocolate topping was in the drawer next to my bed," she said but didn't elaborate.

"The map of Ireland was spread out on the dining room table with my grandparent's village circled and a red heart I'd drawn around the town his family came from. He told me we were going to travel there once his divorce was final, not that he ever filed for divorce. It was going to be just the two of us loving it up in Ireland for a couple of weeks. Maybe we'd begin to decorate the house he owned. You know, make it our own little private vacation spot. Jesus Christ, sorry." She sniffled then blinked back her tears.

"Anything you can document?" I asked, moving on.

"He's got a tattoo of the Ace of Spades on his ass. I used to think that was really cute."

"He's a poker player?"

"Not really. It was from when he was in Vietnam. I guess they used to leave an Ace of Spades on enemy bodies. At least that's what he told me. Anyway, that's about the only private info I have on him. He's got a white scar on his chin…shrapnel he said, except he lied about everything else, so I can't be sure. I didn't realize it at the time, but he was pretty cautious. I've come to understand I probably wasn't his first love scam and certainly not his last. I was the latest stupid head-in-the-clouds girl falling for a rich, sexy older guy. I just think I'm the only one who ended up going to jail because of it."

She said this very matter of fact, with no emotion, like she'd had plenty of time to think about it. Time served, I guessed.

"And you mentioned you were the delivery girl?"

"In layman's terms, the plans for secure federal facilities are kept under lock and key. Gas basically prepped me so I could override the firm's security using his access code, copy the plans, deliver them to his contact…oh, and then take the fall. I lost my job, my home, everything I'd ever worked for. I was charged, tried, convicted, and did six years of a ten-year sentence in a woman's facility. I've got nine years and two months left to go on probation."

"Nine years and two months," I said, doing the math and thinking that rounded up to an even decade.

Desi nodded. "Nine years of going in once a month and peeing in a cup. Nine years of reporting every month to a probation officer. Nine years of idiotic interviews and stupid questions about why I'm washing cars and tending bar in a strip club. You tell me, Dev. Would you hire an ex-con to help design your hundred-million-dollar secure facility?"

"So, what would you like me to do?"

"I suppose I couldn't ask you to kill him." She laughed, but I had the sense she was only half kidding. "I want you to get the goods on Gaston Driscoll. I want him to be charged. I want him to go down like I did. That creep laughed all the way to the Federal Reserve Bank, or from it. He set me up, and I want him to feel what I have to feel, lose what I've lost. He took everything from me, Dev. My folks died thinking I was a criminal. I've lost everything," she spat out this last bit in a harsh whisper, verging on tears that caused a couple of nearby heads to turn. Her eyes had watered again, and she attempted to blink them clear.

"You want revenge," I said.

"You're damn right, I want revenge," she hissed the words out.

"Desi, you seem like a nice woman. But I'm not in the revenge business. Besides, just looking at it from my end, it's quite possible I could spend a lot of time and energy on this and not come up with a damn thing. You could be talking thousands here, tens of thousands of dollars in fees, and absolutely nothing to show for it."

She glanced around to make sure she wouldn't be overheard then softly whispered, "Karla mentioned you might be amenable to me working off the debt," she said, and gave a little shrug.

I immediately thought, 'Thanks for keeping our secret, Karla.'

"Look, Desi, not that I don't find you attractive. You're very attractive as a matter of fact. But like I said, I think an investigation of this sort could go on for quite some time. And to be—"

"I don't care how long it would take. And I could figure something out to get you the money if that's the problem," she interrupted.

"Actually, it's not the money. To be honest, this is out of my league. If you need to find out if this Driscoll guy is stealing cars, into insurance fraud, or taking bets on the Super Bowl, I'm maybe your guy. But the level you're suggesting, I don't really swim in those waters."

"But if you don't take this, there's really no one else I can ask. You were my last shot. I don't know, but I just have a feeling."

"A feeling?"

"Relax, it's nothing," she said, shaking her head while pushing back her chair. "I'm sorry to take up your time. Look, what do I owe you for breakfast?" she said, reaching for her purse.

"How about you work it off sometime?" I joked.

She looked up at me and stared for a long moment. "Actually, I would have liked that. Well, thanks for listening." She stood up, draped her purse over her shoulder and put her hand out to shake. "I better get to work. A lot of people probably need their cars washed. Thanks for listening, Dev."

I shook her hand, then watched her walk out the door and disappear around the corner.

To be continued...

Don't miss **Last Shot**

Dev decides the best thing he can do is turn down Desi Quinn's request for help. He's not the guy to get involved in a long term investigation that's guaranteed to cost Desi a small fortune and offers little promise of a result. That's before events take a turn for the worst and now Dev has a debt to pay. Click on the link below to learn what happens.

Books by Mike Faricy

Crime Fiction Firsts

A boxset of the first four books in four crime fiction series:

Russian Roulette; Dev Haskell series
Welcome; Jack Dillon Dublin Tales series
Corridor Man; Corridor Man series
Reduced Ransom! Hot Shot series

The following titles comprise the Dev Haskell series:

Russian Roulette: Case 1
Mr. Swirlee: Case 2
Bite Me: Case 3
Bombshell: Case 4
Tutti Frutti: Case 5
Last Shot: Case 6
Ting-A-Ling: Case 7
Crickett: Case 8
Bulldog: Case 9
Double Trouble: Case 10
Yellow Ribbon: Case 11
Dog Gone: Case 12
Scam Man: Case 13
Foiled: Case 14
What Happens in Vegas… Case 15
Art Hound: Case 16
The Office: Case 17

Star Struck: Case 18
International Incident: Case 19
Guest From Hell: Case 20
Art Attack: Case 21
Mystery Man: Case 22
Bow-Wow Rescue: Case 23
Cold Case: Case 24
Cash Up Front: Case 25
Dream House: Case 26
Alley Katz: Case 27
The Big Gamble: Case 28
Bad to the Bone: Case 29
Silencio!: Case 30
Surprise, Surprise: Case 31
Hit & Run: Case 32
Suspect Santa: Case 33
P.I. Apprentice: Case 34

The following titles are Dev Haskell novellas:
Dollhouse
The Dance
Pixie
Fore!

Twinkle Toes
(*a Dev Haskell short story*)

The following are Dev Haskell Boxsets:
Dev Haskell Boxset 1-3

Dev Haskell Boxset 4-6
Dev Haskell Boxset 7-9
Dev Haskell Boxset 10-12
Dev Haskell Boxset 13-15
Dev Haskell Boxset 16-18
Dev Haskell Boxset 19-21
Dev Haskell Boxset 22-24
Dev Haskell Boxset 25-27
Dev Haskell Boxset 28-30
Dev Haskell Boxset 1-7
Dev Haskell Boxset 8-14
Dev Haskell Boxset 15-19
Dev Haskell Boxset 20-24
Dev Haskell Boxset 25-29

The following titles comprise the Jack Dillon Dublin Tales series:

Welcome
Jack Dillon Dublin Tale 1
Sweet Dreams
Jack Dillon Dublin Tale 2
Mirror Mirror
Jack Dillon Dublin Tale 3
Silver Bullet
Jack Dillon Dublin Tale 4
Fair City Blues
Jack Dillon Dublin Tale 5
Spade Work
Jack Dillon Dublin Tale 6

Madeline Missing
Jack Dillon Dublin Tale 7
Mistaken Identity
Jack Dillon Dublin Tale 8
Picture Perfect
Jack Dillon Dublin Tale 9
Dublin Moon
Jack Dillon Dublin Tale 10
Mystery Woman
Jack Dillon Dublin Tale 11
Second Chance
Jack Dillon Dublin Tale 12
Payback Brother
Jack Dillon Dublin Tale 13
The Heist
Jack Dillon Dublin Tale 14
Jewels To Kill For
Jack Dillon Dublin Tale 15
Retirement Scheme
Jack Dillon Dublin Tale 16

Jack Dillon Dublin Tales Boxsets:

Jack Dillon Dublin Tales 1-3
Jack Dillon Dublin Tales 4-6
Jack Dillon Dublin Tales 1-5
Jack Dillon Dublin Tales 1-7
Jack Dillon Dublin Tales 6-10

The following titles comprise the Hotshot series;

Reduced Ransom! Second Edition
Finders Keepers! Second Edition
Bankers Hours Second Edition
Chow Down Second Edition
Moonlight Dance Academy Second Edition

Irish Dukes (Fight Card Series)
written under the pseudonym Jack Tunney

The following titles comprise the Corridor Man series:

Corridor Man
Corridor Man 2: Opportunity knocks
Corridor Man 3: The Dungeon
Corridor Man 4: Dead End
Corridor Man 5: Finger
Corridor Man 6: Exit Strategy
Corridor Man 7: Trunk Music
Corridor Man 8: Birthday Boy
Corridor Man 9: Boss Man
Corridor Man 10: Bye Bye Bobby

Corridor Man novellas:

Corridor Man: Valentine
Corridor Man: Auditor
Corridor Man: Howling
Corridor Man: Spa Day

The following are Corridor Man Boxsets:

Corridor Man Boxset 1-3

Corridor Man Boxset 1-5

Corridor Man Boxset 6-9

All books are available on Amazon.com

Thank you!

Contact the author:

- Email: mikefaricyauthor@gmail.com
- Twitter: @Mikefaricybooks
- Facebook: Mike Faricy Author
- Website: http://www.mikefaricybooks.com

Published by

MJF Publishing

Printed in the USA
CPSIA information can be obtained
at www.ICGtesting.com
LVHW011328051023
760085LV00063B/1679